Storm Swept

JOAN DRUETT

Old Salt Press

STORM SWEPT
Published by
Old Salt Press
Jersey City, NJ, USA

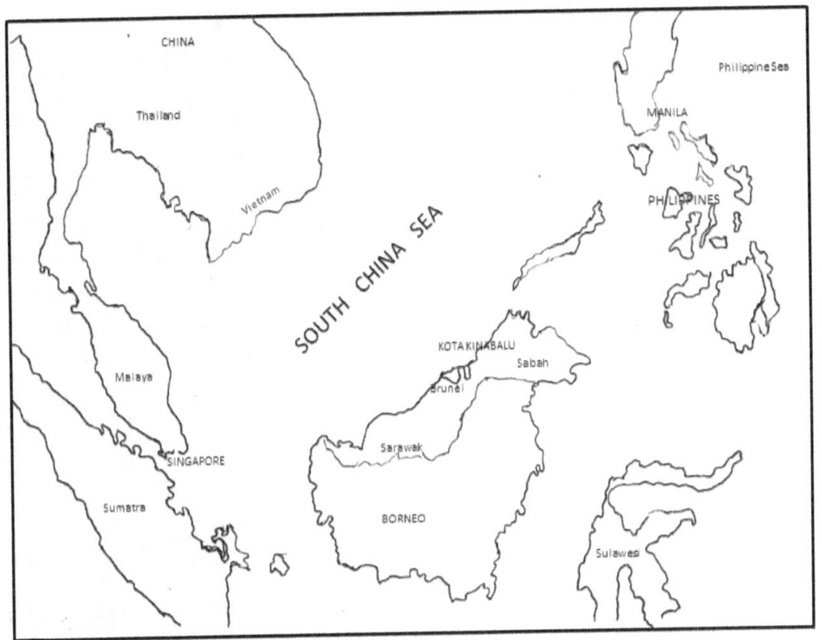

South China Sea

Prologue

The man in the wheelchair sat by the window. It was hot in the sun, but he liked the view. If he had to be stuck in Mexico for the rest of his miserable life, he may as well enjoy whatever he could. Or so he grimly thought. The heat was good, too. It might make him sweat, but it helped with the constant grinding pain in his back.

Outside, there was a street — the only paved street in this tiny village, as he knew all too well — and on the other side stood a couple of old-fashioned adobe buildings. One was a family-run restaurant and lodging house, and the other had serapes and pottery for sale, along with other local craft. As was customary, the boundaries of the individual yards were marked with low walls. The walls, like the buildings, were whitewashed, and painted with colorful designs of fishes, boats, flowers.

And lots of whales. It was part of the attraction for tourists. Between the buildings the view stretched through a few palms to the beach, where white-fringed blue water lapped gently on the black sand. Another attraction for tourists — not that there were many, this time of the year. Come the northern winter, the place would be crammed, even though the sand was black.

He turned his wheelchair to check the line in the waiting room. He fervently hoped he was next to see the doctor, as today his back was very bad. Everyone here, though, was in some sort of pain. He could smell their nervous sweat, the residue of sleepless, pain-wracked nights, along with the ever-present stink of rotten fish guts, which floated down the bay from the factory further up the coast. But it was worth the heat and the summer stench to be in Puerto San Alvaro. Dr Dominguez was amazing. His medications helped a lot, but the touch of his massaging hands was magical.

Back in the United States, as the man in the wheelchair was acutely aware, he would have run out of money long ago. But because the car crash had happened in this country, the insurance pay-out for the wipe-out of the Porsche had not just covered the fees for Dr. Dominguez, but had paid for his little house up-street. And the weekly wage to the woman who was his carer. Thank God that the crash, if it had to happen at all, had been in Mexico, and not in Washington, D.C..

There was a glossy magazine on his lap. The nurse had given it to him when he arrived, but he had not felt enough interest to turn the pages. It was a women's magazine, all about décor, and fashion, and makeup. It belonged to his distant past, and had never been his kind of reading, anyway. And, though it was an American periodical, it was the Spanish edition, and while his spoken Spanish was reasonable, he found reading the language difficult. So why bother?

The nurse came in and, like everyone else, Brooke looked up hopefully. But the name she called out was not his. So he opened the magazine, just for something to do, flipping the pages at random. Then he froze, riveted. The full-page photo was of a society hostess in Manhattan, New York, a woman in her late forties, tall, very slender, with platinum hair.

His ex-wife, Helen. *My God*, he thought, she looked just a handful of years older than the night he'd first met her, almost exactly twenty-six years ago. The intervening time had treated her very kindly indeed. Her silver-gold hair was now short, but the cameo-like face was as smooth; she was just as elegant. He was only a couple of years older than Helen, but the contrast to what he saw in the mirror when he shaved each morning was grueling.

Pierce Brooke shut his eyes, dragged into the distant past. When he had first met her, her name had been Helen Howland. Her eyes, face, body, had drawn him like a magnet, utterly compelling. And she had felt the same about him; the instant he had touched her, he had felt the same shock of awareness in her. They had abandoned the cocktail party without caring about their reputations, rushed to his hotel room, and fallen onto his bed in a hot, gasping tangle. As he ruminated sardonically now, it had been lust at first sight.

Within days they had been married, and for a little while, it had been great, really great. The first month had been an amazing blur of sexual delight. But then work had called. Brooke had been a business mediator, setting up lucrative deals between foreign potentates and politicians. Which meant that he had to be away from the Washington apartment a lot, flying to the Middle East and Europe to broker deals, connecting high-flying businessmen with sheiks, sultans, cabinet ministers and princes.

Helen had accompanied him the first time, but had proved to be an unwelcome distraction. With growing horror, and then anger, he realized that other men lusted after her, just as he had himself. By some female magic, she managed to combine cool elegance with sex appeal, a melding of come-hitherness and remoteness that fascinated the clients. He remembered how their eyes had followed her; their avid expressions, and how important discussions had petered out when she was in the room.

After that he had flatly refused to take her along. Helen had protested at the time, particularly as he had refused to give a reason, thinking it obvious to even an idiot. But why should he have taken her, anyway? She was a married woman, and supposed to be at home. If she'd gotten pregnant, it might have been different. But nothing had happened. Probably because she had taken precautions without bothering to tell him.

The bitterness was sour inside him. Instead of fulfilling her proper role as wife and mother Helen had started up her own business, teaching deportment and Washington etiquette to the wives of newly elected politicians. And so, despite the unfailing sexual connection, he and his wife had finished up with separate lives.

He might have been indiscreet with his various flings, but he was a man, wasn't he? When a woman was beautiful, making love to her was just a compliment. Especially when in a foreign country. And, dear God, ever since that car crash sex had been a distant memory. But before the crash there had been that last, fatal affair with a French actress. Photographs had been taken by someone undercover — by someone who had been hired by one of his clients! Harold Pederson, the shipping tycoon.

Brooke had been brokering deals for Pederson, mostly in Geneva, and partly in Washington. Because of his rule that Helen was not to be involved in his business affairs, she should never have met the wife-stealing bastard. But there been an accidental encounter at a Washington banquet, and Brooke had been forced to introduce them.

He remembered how Pederson's small blue eyes had focused on Helen, studying her minutely; he remembered how Pederson had held her hand for too long, staring down at her all the time. It was as if he were sizing her up for a job — the job of wife and hostess — but, back then, Brooke had not had the slightest idea that this was the moment that the magnate became determined to make her his own.

For God's sake, it should not have happened! Pederson was not just big and ugly, but he was twenty years older than Helen. He should not have had a hope of making a conquest. And it certainly would have been different if Brooke hadn't been away in Egypt, France, Switzerland — Geneva, oh God, Geneva ...

Pederson had seized the time to entertain and woo Helen — and then, when he saw she was on the verge of succumbing, he had made sure of it by sending the telltale photographs to *her*, and posting the divorce papers to *him*.

The documents had been waiting at Brooke's London apartment when he had got back from Geneva. Stuck under the door by a lazy lawyer's clerk — along with Pederson's check for one hundred thousand dollars. Like buying a wife — Brooke's lawful wedded wife! Nothing less than a pay-off and a bribe.

Pierce Brooke remembered the hot rage that had burned throughout the flight from Heathrow to Washington. *My God*, he thought again, his eyes tight shut. When the cab had dropped him at the apartment he had hammered on the door, too furious to find his key, and Helen had opened it. It was the middle of the night, and she was wearing a flimsy nightgown — waiting and ready for Pederson, of course. The burning fury had been with him as he grasped her shoulders — and the old lust had taken over.

As always, it was mutual. But when the frantic coupling was finished, Helen had blinked, and shaken her head as if she were coming to her senses. Her face white, she had grimaced with obvious and mortifying disgust that her body had betrayed her. Coldly, she had shown him the photographs, then told him to get out of her life.

Brooke remembered how he had stormed out, slamming the door behind him. After cashing the check he had flown to Mexico City in a fury, signed and mailed the divorce papers, bought the Porsche on a whim, taken it for a drive, and failed to take a corner. He had been paying for that ever since, in agony and penury. Helen had married the shipping tycoon, and he had never seen her again.

Until now.

Pierce Brooke opened his eyes and stared at the magazine. The page was in full color. Platinum hair, fawn silk suit, vividly outlined smile. She looked so ... gracious. He turned another page. There was another picture, this time of Helen with a girl. They were walking away from the photographer, holding hands, and were looking at the camera from over their shoulders, each with exactly the same smile. Their figures were very similar, too, tall and slim, though the hair color was very different. And their vivacious expressions were identical.

Helen's daughter? He was suddenly sure of it, though the girl was brunette where Helen was fair. If Helen had done the decent thing, and permitted herself to get pregnant, this girl could have been his daughter. The thought, again, was bitter.

But Harold Pederson was of Swedish stock, fair and ruddy. Brooke remembered him so very well. This girl could not be Pederson bred. The realization hit him like a physical blow — and at the same instant he was struck by a sense of recognition. His mother! — the girl was almost the image of his mother when young. *Dear God*, he thought. *I have a daughter. And Helen owes me for all these terrible years.*

For once his tortured back was forgotten. Pierce Brooke wheeled out of the clinic, intent on getting home to his computer.

One

The phone rang. Jerry Giacomo said, "Yup?"

Harold Pederson barked, "I need to talk to you. Now."

"What's so urgent?"

"Pirate problems."

What? Jerry's eyebrows shot up into his hair. Then he sighed. Up until this moment he had been enjoying himself, drinking beer in the company of two of the most beautiful girls in New York City. They were on the open balcony of a bar that was sixty-four floors up. A long, long way down, the traffic and the people looked like rushing ants. It was weird, being so high and yet out in the open, but until the phone had rung Jerry had been feeling marvelously content.

He said grumpily into the phone, "What kind of pirates?"

"How many kinds are there? Pirates who try to seize ships, of course."

Well, Pederson was a shipping tycoon, so that figured. Jerry sighed again. "Harold, where are you?"

"Manhattan."

"Wa-al, ain't that a coincidence."

"This is a job," the shipping magnate said, unmoved by the sarcasm.

"I don't hunt pirates." Though, when Jerry thought back to the years he had spent with the British Army, he had come pretty close at times.

"This is more like anti-pirate action."

"Insurance?"

"Armed guards. That kind of thing."

Jerry burst into a roar of laughter, which turned heads all around. "I am seventy-two years old, sir! And I do not carry a gun!"

Suddenly aware that the entire bar had silenced, he lowered his voice as he repeated, "I never carry, sir."

"This is more in the nature of security management. Come down to the restaurant, and we'll talk about it."

So Pederson had tracked his precise whereabouts. Jerry grimaced. "I have the girls with me."

"Then bring them."

And the connection was cut without another word. Which, as Jerry ruminated, was exactly Pederson's style. He stood up, a muscular, very fit man who looked shorter than he was because of his broad build. As contrary as ever, he was casually dressed in plaid shirt and well-worn jeans. His gray moustache drooped, and his gray hair was gathered in a ponytail. As the girls occasionally remarked, he looked like a superannuated country singer.

"We're summoned," he said to the girls. "Drink up. Harold is downstairs and wants our company at lunch. He feels a pressing need to talk to us."

"Oh good, I'm hungry," said Kate Giacomo, standing up, and Maggie Bacchante joined her with alacrity.

To Jerry's amusement, the expressions on their faces were identical. Kate was a half-head taller than Maggie, but otherwise they were startlingly alike, in mannerisms as well as appearance. Both girls were olive-skinned, and had large, dark eyes fringed with naturally black lashes. They often wore each other's clothes, and they always went to the same hairdresser, so that their glossy dark hair was streaked with the same shade of caramel. Tonight, they were both wearing a dress that Maggie had designed.

Both, thought Jerry, looked stupendous.

"What are we going to talk about?" asked one.

"Pirates."

"Wow," said the other.

The restaurant was crowded, but the maître'd ushered them to a private alcove where Harold Pederson was already seated. He had a glass of what looked like Scotch whisky.

As soon as he saw the girls, he stood up, taking their hands and kissing them on both cheeks. Jerry, watching from a short distance, wondered which of them the shipping tycoon preferred. At one time, Pederson had had the weird idea that he could claim one or the other as his biological daughter, but since recognizing the truth — that they both belonged to the sprawling Bacchante family — he had been merely avuncular. Which, as Jerry thought, was great.

Harold Pederson looked remarkably well, considering his age — which Jerry knew was not far off seventy — and the fact that the Justice Department was after him for money-laundering. And also considering that there was a problem with pirates, or so it seemed. The shipping magnate looked more than ever like the rough, ruddy-faced Swede he was reputed to be. The bristling eyebrows were still mostly yellow, as were the curls clustered on his large head. He stood tall, was still big-chested, and his handshake was brisk and strong.

They sat down. Maggie sat at Pederson's elbow, where he always liked her to be, and Jerry and Kate sat opposite. It began politely. After their orders for drinks had been taken, Kate asked warmly after Pederson's wife, and received an approving nod in return. Helen was presiding at a meeting of the board of one of her favorite charities, a foundation for the support of children with communication difficulties.

"But she will be there on Friday." On Friday Helen Pederson, who sponsored both Maggie and Kate, was hosting a launch for Kate's new book. "Unfortunately," Harold added, "I will not be present." Which was nothing less than expected. The Pederson shipping empire spanned the world.

Then the conversation got down to earth as he explained his latest problem. One of his small discovery cruise-ships had been attacked by pirates. There were five of these vessels, variously named *Wind Swept, Wave Swept, Sun Swept, Star Swept* and *Storm Swept*, all of which were peculiar names for top-class cruise-ships, or so Jerry privately thought. They must have been appealing enough to the well-heeled public, though, as the Pederson cruise line had done very well. The ship that had been attacked was *Storm Swept*, which Jerry thought was rather appropriate, considering the name.

He said, "Where is the ship now?"

"Back at my base in Singapore, with some damage being fixed up."

"You paid the ransom?"

"There wasn't one. The ship wasn't seized. The attack failed."

The drinks came as they all stared at Harold. Finally, Kate said, "What happened?"

"The passengers fought the pirates off."

Both girls were wide-eyed. Maggie repeated, "The *passengers*?"

"You heard me. The guests saved the ship." Pederson's expression was sour.

Jerry said, "How many passengers were there?"

"The ships are all rated for 120 passengers, maximum. *Storm Swept* was carrying one hundred and five at the time."

Kate guessed, "This was not a seniors cruise."

"On the contrary, quite a few of the passengers were pensioners."

Maggie dimpled. "I bet the old ladies were the worst."

This earned her a reproving stare from under the bristling eyebrows. As Jerry had often noticed, Harold Pederson had no sense of humor. Unabashed, Maggie urged, "Tell us more."

The magnate shrugged. "Does it matter?"

"Yes!"

Jerry said, "Where exactly did this happen?"

"Off the northern coast of Borneo, on the way to exploring one of the estuaries."

They were interrupted by the waiter, who arrived to take their orders. The girls were uncharacteristically casual about choosing, merely saying, "Fish," and then they all watched Pederson expectantly as he pondered through the menu. Then, at last, he made up his mind, and the waiter went away.

"What the hell was *Storm Swept* doing off Borneo?"

"You should read up more about Pederson Cruises," the owner said acidly. "That is what we specialize in — small-ship expedition cruises out of Singapore, focusing on south-east Asia and the western Pacific. The ships can navigate quite shallow waters, and so going up rivers is relatively easy. We have been featured several times in *National Geographic,* and on television, too. Wildlife photographers love us."

"I see," said Jerry, who was mentally visualizing rubber boats, treks in headhunter-haunted tropical jungles, wading through monsoon rains, and visits to primitive villages. He supposed it had an appeal for the young and adventurous — but seniors?

He said, "And what time was the attack?"

"Cocktail hour. Most of the guests were in the lounge — there was a classical string quartet playing. But a few were at the stern of the promenade deck, watching the sunset."

Hoping to glimpse the famous green flash as the sun dived below the tropical horizon, Jerry guessed. "And?"

"One of the women happened to lean over the rail, and saw a boat right under the stern."

"A local boat? A *prahu*, perhaps?"

"A big outrigger, with an outboard motor, but it had arrived in silence. The crew had paddled up close, and thrown up a rope."

Jerry frowned. Tossing a rope up from under the stern and hoping it would catch fast was quite a feat. Had there been cooperation from one of the crew on board? It was a distinct possibility.

"There were five in the outrigger, all armed with AK-47 guns, and another one climbing the rope. He also had a rifle, but it was slung over his shoulder. He was halfway up when the passengers saw him. They threw down tables and deckchairs, and knocked him off. He fell into the water, which confused the pirates for a moment. When they had recovered the one who had fallen, they started firing their rifles, but meantime a passenger had detached the rope and thrown it away, while the others chucked down more furniture, which put the pirates off their aim. Then the captain arrived. He produced a hand gun and fired back, and the pirates retreated. Dark fell, and they were seen no more."

Good lord, thought Jerry. It sounded like a bad movie.

He said, "Where was the captain before all this?"

Pederson said grimly, "In the bar."

"And no one on the bridge had checked the radar?"

"Naturally, the captain has been fired, along with the officer who was supposed to be on watch. Though," Pederson added, with some reluctance, "the captain did keep his wits about him when his phone rang. The caller claimed to be a Malaysian maritime official. A report had come in that *Storm Swept* was in trouble, he said, and so it was necessary for the captain to give them his precise location, so that all assistance could be rendered. The captain had the sense to realize it was a fake call, and called for full speed ahead. They arrived safely in Singapore a couple of days later."

"So, all in all, it was a good outcome," observed Jerry.

"Except for the publicity."

"Ah."

"Yes."

"I would have thought it would be a good advertisement for an adventurous cruise," mused Maggie, which earned her another bristling look.

"So that is why you want to establish some kind of anti-pirate program," observed Jerry. "One that you will publicize to the hilt."

"Exactly. And you are the man I want to set it up."

"Why me, for God's sake?"

"You have a reputation for being tough in a tough situation. You are well known. Your name is famous in the right circles."

They were interrupted again. A youngish man approached the table, looked at them all, and then addressed Kate. He said, "Excuse me, but aren't you Kate Kelly?"

Kate paused. "I write under that name."

Fishing out a business card, he said, "I write for *Balustrade Magazine*, and would very much like to interview you about your latest book. Being launched this Friday, isn't that right?"

They all looked at him. He had a smooth, cleanshaven face,

and short brown hair that was gelled into spikes. His suit was pearl gray, and his shirt was pink, while his tie was indigo blue.

"Yes, that is right," Kate allowed.

"My name is Graham Waters. I am booked in here — in this hotel — but unfortunately will not be here on Friday. I am staying in New York for just one night, and am flying out in the afternoon. Would it be possible to interview you for one hour in the morning?"

"It would have to be early. I have a very full day."

"But of course. Breakfast at eight?"

"Seven-thirty would be better."

"In my room, then. I'll have breakfast sent up. There will be a photographer," he added.

Kate opened her mouth, but Jerry interrupted. "Just one moment," he said, and plucked up the business card.

Hauling out his phone, he tapped out the number, and waited. According to his calculations, it was suppertime in London, so he might be out of luck, but he was rewarded when a crystal clear British voice came onto the line, announcing itself as *Balustrade Magazine*, and asking how it could assist. Jerry stated the man's name, listened, and nodded.

Kate took out a pen and wrote the room number and time on the back of the card. The journalist gave them all a wide smile that showed off his pink gums, and executed an odd little bow. Then he was gone.

She turned to Jerry and said, "Was that call necessary?"

"Yes," said Jerry.

"Yes," said Pederson.

"But he didn't look like a pirate."

"And I *loved* his color coordination," said Maggie.

Two

When Kate arrived in the lobby of the hotel next morning, Jerry lounged up beside her.

"Thought you could do with some company," he said.

"Jerry, I am twenty-two years old!"

"So you are," he agreed, and guffawed. "And you don't think that doesn't seem awful young to me?"

Waters opened the door with a wide, gummy smile that slipped so obviously when he saw Jerry with her that Kate felt her first doubts. The journalist was wearing the same pearl gray suit that Maggie had admired, but today his shirt was mauve, and his tie was dark green. Kate wondered what Maggie would have thought of the new combination.

The room inside was the lounge part of a suite, with two unmade beds visible through an open door. Another man stood up from a settee as they walked in. He was dressed all in black: black jeans and a black open-necked shirt; a weedy looking character with lank hair and spotty skin. Without waiting for introductions to be made, he produced a release form, which he asked Kate to sign, saying, "I will be making a video of the interview, as well as taking photos."

Kate hesitated, but Jerry said nothing, and she remembered that *Balustrade* was a long-established and respectable magazine.

So she scribbled a signature, and they all sat down.

There was a tap on the door, and breakfast was wheeled in. The coffee smelled good and strong, and there were crusty bread rolls, damson preserve, butter and French brie. The journalist tipped the waiter and then played host, pouring coffee while Kate and Jerry helped themselves to bread, jam and cheese. The photographer took nothing to eat or drink, snapping with his camera instead.

Then they were all settled. "Your first book was a big hit," Waters began. "*The Man who Played with Fire.* What gave you the idea of writing a novel about a man who puts out oil well fires?"

"He did." Kate nodded at Jerry. "That's what he does. He's famous."

The camera shifted to Jerry's face, and for the first time Kate realized that it was now in video mode. Instead of clicking, it was silent.

The journalist studied Jerry with interest. "Giacomo is an Italian name. You were born and brought up in Italy?"

"No."

Waters said nothing, simply waiting for more, and finally Jerry shrugged and began to talk, while the journalist prompted him with the occasional question. Kate listened with fascination as her adoptive father skimmed over the surface of his life, revealing parts of his past she hadn't known before.

His upbringing had been much rougher and harder than she had realized. Jerry's father had been an Italian itinerant farmworker, laboring on an English farm when Jerry was born. His mother had died when he was twelve, and four years later he had left school to enlist in the British Army.

Waters made notes, and then looked up and said, "Wasn't the army popularly thought of as the cop-out for losers?"

Jerry snapped, "That's an insult, and a belief held by far too many people. The country — the world — is served by many fine men and women in uniform. And what do they get for it? Certainly not cheers and thrown flowers, wars being so unpopular now. I fought in the Middle East, you know — though how could anyone expect troops that had been trained on a Salisbury plain to function in the desert is still beyond me."

"Yet you left the army?"

"Yes."

"You were not enchanted with army life?"

"Enchanted? That's a strange word, but you are right, maybe I was enchanted, at first. The rank and file are fine, despite a few bad eggs. But then, because I was good at it, I rose in the ranks, only to find that too many officers were more interested in class ritual and military etiquette than in real fighting."

"So that is when you left the army?"

"Unfortunately, no, as I still had ideals. But, my God, I should have gone right then. The backroom boys had found out that I was good at languages, so I was shifted to intelligence. It sounded promising, but then I found I was assigned to the basement stuff. That, quite frankly, made me sick. It was all part of what they called 'counter-insurgency' — which was just a fancy name for suppressing domestic resistance to military occupation. So I sat there through interrogations, interpreting questions and the replies. Though I was only the translator, it was plain to me that the interviewees — if you can call them that — either had false information they wanted to plant, or were so terrified they would say anything to make the cross-examination stop. Whatever information they gave up was so suspect that I queried it constantly in my reports, but the high hats fell for it, lock, stock and barrel, just because it fitted their agenda."

"Agenda?"

"This was the British Army, remember — ultimately controlled by politicians who were in thrall to America. At the top, there was no accountability. Generals and brigadiers with records of appalling failures were rewarded with medals."

The journalist pounced. "In thrall to America?"

"Blame the politicians, who were definitely in thrall. It is one thing to have your military stationed all around the world in order to support your own interests — and I am talking about the South China Sea and the Western Pacific, in particular. But it is something else when it is done at the behest of another power."

Waters said nothing, head down, scribbling hard. Jerry was staring at him, his expression angry, though Kate thought his eyes were very distant, as though he were in another place and another time.

He said, "So I applied for something on the front line, and they made me a commander of an élite unit — in an era when the British were trying desperately to prove that they as good at war as the Americans. There were terrible crimes committed against the locals — not by my unit, but witnessed by me. The perpetrators were court-martialed — and I was often a prosecution witness — but even if they were imprisoned, they walked out within months, and next thing I saw them as guests on morning television. Dear God," he said. "Is it any surprise that I gave up and left the army for something more useful?"

"And that was?"

"Fighting oil well fires — as described in Kate's book."

"And he is now recognized as the best in the world at it," said Kate.

Without bothering to look at her, Waters said to Jerry, "Surely a dangerous choice of career?"

"It just happened." Jerry shrugged. "My years on the front line got me addicted to adrenalin, I guess. On my last deployment I was in charge of a squad in the Middle East — where there are a lot of oil wells, you know. One day we were seconded to help with a big fire in Kuwait, and I found an aptitude for it. There is immense satisfaction in putting out a big bastard. And from then on it was easy to make my way into the industry. There are not many applicants for the job, you know, and there were very seasoned men who were eager to pass on their tricks."

"So, how do you go about putting out an oil well fire?"

"Just like killing a human," he said blandly. "You starve it of oxygen."

Kate grinned to herself. It was Jerry's favorite joke, and it was always a treat to watch the audience wince.

"You've spent a lot of time in Saudi Arabia?"

"And all of the Gulf States. And Indonesia. And Malaysia. And South America. And Cebu."

"Cebu?"

"In the Philippines."

"I didn't know they had oil."

"The industry is in its infancy there. When it finally takes off, it will make the South China Sea even more interesting than it is now."

"Interesting?"

"Politically. Don't you watch the news?"

Instead of answering, Waters said, "What was it like in the Middle East?"

"Sand, lots of sand. Buildings low down because of sand storms. Ordinary people lying low, too, because of all kinds of storms, political and weather. Long, long roads heading for the horizon, making you wonder who the hell laid the tarmac and when and why, and strings of camels emerging from the mirage that is blurring the end. Really old trucks, all overloaded. Dotted along the way, ordinary people trying to live ordinary lives in dusty little villages. Warm yoghurt made out of goat's milk in little clay cups for breakfast, with honey trickled on the top if you are lucky. And a piece of flat bread, too. Tea, wonderful tea, in tiny hourglass-shaped glasses, that you drink through a cube of sugar, if you are lucky. Coffee so thick you can chew it. Minced lamb with pinenuts is a feast, eaten with more flat bread. Wonderful ordinary people, more honest than Westerners would believe, trying to live good lives. Unbelievably rich and decadent people at the top, living luxury-filled days and nights, who do not care about the rest. What else do you want to know?"

Instead of trying to respond, Waters shifted his stare to Kate. "You have an interesting relationship with Mr. Giacomo. You have shared any of these experiences?"

She wasn't sure that she liked his tone, and saw Jerry's eyes narrow. "I don't know what you mean by *interesting*. Jerry is my father."

The journalist's eyes widened. He looked from one to the other, and then said, "Surely you mean *grand*father?"

"Come off it," Jerry snapped. "I adopted her at the age of five, if you really want to know."

He had done it as a joke, to foil the *famiglia* Bacchante. She was an orphan that they were bringing up alongside their own little Maggie. They adored Kate just as much as he did, but he had never regretted the whim to claim Kate as his daughter.

"Very nice," said Waters, and grinned. "She must have been a sweet little girl. Very pretty. Cuddlesome." Kate did not like his suggestive smile. She stood up, set to leave, and he waved her down. "Please," he said. The smile had vanished.

She sat. He said, "So why Kate *Kelly*?"

"Kelly was my mother's name — the name she called herself. She was a dancer, and it was her stage name. And I write under that name as a memorial to her. Legally, I am Kate Giacomo, the adopted daughter of Jerry Giacomo."

"Your mother gave her surname as Kelly? So, what was her Christian name?"

"It was a complete name. As I said, she performed under that name."

"So what was her *real* name?"

Kate said impatiently, "Debbie Parkin. Why? Does it matter?"

"So who was your father? What was his name?"

Kate shook her head. "I don't know."

"But surely you know who it was," he said to Jerry.

"I know nothing, and had nothing to do with it. Kelly was my girlfriend," said Jerry. "My partner for four great months. I picked her up in London, and we had a great holiday in New Zealand. Drove around, explored, admired the scenery, ate, drank, slept in nice hotels. She was a very beautiful young woman. I was fifty and she was — what? — nineteen? But we were great together, all the same."

"Sounds wonderful."

"It was. Except for the hurricane." Jerry paused in contemplation for a moment, then went on, "But I am not Kate's father. Kelly was pregnant when I met her, and she never told me who got her into that fix, probably because I would have hunted him down and beaten the daylights out of him. As it was, I was simply the man who took her on a really nice vacation. Best time of her short life. And, because of that, I happened to be present when the baby was born."

"And she — this Kelly — she gave the baby to you? Even

though she must have known the name of her baby's father, she gave the baby to you — her partner on a holiday?"

"It wasn't like that," Kate protested. "What you are insinuating is just horrible, and it was not like that! She was a much better person than you make her out to be. I was born at the height of a terrible storm, at the same time and in the same place as Maggie — Maggie Bacchante — my foster twin. That was the hurricane Jerry mentioned, which tore the town apart, including the little hospital. The day I was born, my mother — Kelly — was moved to a house for intensive nursing, as it was safer there during the chaos, and she was very ill. After the storm had moved on Jerry looked for her, but she wasn't there."

"She had gone?"

"Yes. It should have left Jerry in a terrible bind, and it's a testament to his kindness and his sense of responsibility that he did not abandon me on the spot. A newborn baby! He certainly could not have been blamed. But the Bacchante family gathered me up when they came for Maggie, and Maggie's mother cared for me as Maggie's twin. And Jerry came with me. Because of their big hearts we are both members of the *famiglia* Bacchante."

"And where, exactly, were you born?"

Kate frowned, puzzled. "Homerville, on the east coast of the North Island of New Zealand, a very long way from here. Why? Is it important?"

"No, of course not."

But the journalist was scribbling hard. The photographer, still hidden behind his camera, said nothing.

Waters looked up. "And the Bacchantes are Italian?"

"Originally, yes. The patriarch of the dynasty sailed to New Zealand four generations ago, and worked hard until he had saved enough to buy some land. Then he — Andreas Bacchante

— founded Bacchante wines. Haven't you heard of them? Surely you must know the name! Their wines win prizes all over the world."

She paused, but Waters said nothing, scribbling instead of looking at her. Feeling impatient, she said, "Most of the extended family live on the main vineyard, in a huge stone mansion next to the press house. Some work at the satellite vineyard, a hundred miles or so south, near Homerville. Others, like Jerry and Maggie and me, have jobs elsewhere. But we all do our bit at the winery."

"Though you live in New York."

"My twin sister — my *foster* sister, Maggie — lives here. She is a dress designer, you know, with Bellissimo, and it is convenient for me to be here. I was lucky enough with royalties from *The Man who Played with Fire* to be able to buy a little Manhattan apartment. But when it is harvest time, we both fly home. And so does Jerry. And so does Skye. And we harvest the grapes, and work in the press house, and have a big party."

"This Skye is another father?" Waters' voice was smoothly insinuating again, and Kate was getting even more angry.

"He is another member of the Bacchante family!" she snapped. "And it was *his* father who inspired my new book."

"*The Barrel Carver.*"

"Yes!" she exclaimed. "The new book! Isn't that what we are supposed to be talking about?"

The journalist lifted his brows. He looked at his notes, and then at her again. "My apologies. I was distracted. Please tell me about it."

"Skye's father was Peter Hamilton, who became Michelangelo the barrel carver, and that is the background of my novel."

"Do tell me more."

For the first time, she thought, Waters sounded like a regular interviewer, instead of some kind of combatant. She settled down, starting to relax, shedding her anger.

"It's part of the history of Bacchante wines — it happened a long time before I was born, you understand, but it is such a great story that it begged to be turned into the heart of a novel. Peter Hamilton was a frustrated artist. He had given up his career as a promising sculptor to support his wife, who was a noted watercolorist. Then she died, and soon after that he lost his job as a carpenter at the Auckland wharves, because of a union dispute. So he went on the road, taking his little boy with him. By the hand."

"And this was Skye?"

"Yes. They arrived at the Bacchante vineyard, and there Peter Hamilton asked to be allowed to carve names and pictures into the round heads of their huge wine barrels. The Bacchantes are very romantic, and his story appealed to their romantic hearts, and so they gave Peter Hamilton and his little boy — Skye — a place to live on the vineyard, and allowed him to do what he liked with their barrel heads, just as long as he would do any carpentering needed, and would help out with the harvest."

Scarcely aware of the clicking of the camera, Kate described the Bacchanalian images Michelangelo carved — prancing goats, bare-breasted nymphs, cups of wine, garlands of leaves and bunches of grapes. "Then," she finished sadly, "he died. And so I never met him. But, meantime, the little boy, Skye, had been raised as one of the *famiglia* Bacchante — though he kept his own surname."

"Romantic indeed," said Waters.

"Yes. And Maggie and I — like all the teenaged Bacchantes — learned to tell Peter Hamilton's story, because it was the teenagers' job to guide the groups of tourists who came by the winery on Sunday tours. The story was a main attraction. I remember the faces of the visitors as they listened. A marvelous story, one that everyone loved. And that is the setting of my novel."

"Wonderful!" And the journalist dropped his pencil and notebook and clapped. The whole hour had gone by. Kate blinked.

When she and Jerry were back outside the hotel, she said, "That went quite well, I thought?"

"We shall see." Jerry was frowning. "He deliberately made you angry, *tesoro*, to goad you into telling more than you might have intended. I am glad I was there with you, very glad indeed."

Three

Jerry Giacomo was in bed with his ex-wife when the phone rang.

It was Kate, sounding far too bright. "What's the time in Manila?"

He rolled stiffly onto his side, peered at the clock, and groaned. "Five in the morning. Where the hell are you?"

"Pasadena, and it's two in the afternoon."

"No wonder you sound so awake. What's up? And why are you in California?"

"Second question first. I've just finished off a short West Coast book tour. Helen was with me, so we rested up here before flying back to New York tonight. The mansion here is lovely."

"I do remember that." From recollection, Pederson's Pasadena house was a very grand pre-gold rush building, designed, built and inhabited by dons in times immemorial; he remembered being particularly taken by the roof, which swept in a sea of golden-brown terracotta tiles to the white pilastered walls. But going down memory lane was the last thing Jerry wanted, not at this early hour.

He said grumpily, "You're still doing book publicity? But the book was launched six weeks ago."

There was a short silence, where Jerry thought he heard a sigh. "*The Barrel Carver* is not doing as well as the publishers hoped."

"How can they tell? It's early days yet."

"Everyone is more interested in the fire-fighting book. The reviewers rave about that one, and hardly mention the new one. The publicist thought a quick tour of the West Coast might bring the focus closer."

"I'm sorry, *tesoro*. But not every book can be a huge seller."

"True, very true. Most aren't, but I didn't expect *The Man Who Played with Fire* to be such a hard act to follow." Another sigh. "Answering your first question, Jerry. That journalist, Waters, he got in touch with me again."

Jerry was suddenly more awake. "Why?"

"There are people who want to meet me, one man in particular, but he won't say names. He said he is very influential and it could be very good for book sales and my future. But I feel uneasy about it."

"So do I. Waters struck me as a creep, and I am sure he is just after a story. But don't say no, just prevaricate. Put him off. Say you will think about it when the book promotions are over."

"He will argue about that. And, let's face it, the book promotions *are* over. He reckons the time to meet this man is now."

"I don't care. It sounds too vague. Your feeling is the right one, Kate"

"And the article he wrote for *Balustrade* is out. You should read it, Jerry."

"I'm in Manila, sweetheart!"

"It's online, Jerry. You really should read it — as it is all about you."

"What? Not about you and the new book?"

"There is a very big picture of you, and no picture of me, just a small one of the book jacket. And it is all about your army career and the fire-fighting, all great macho stuff with plenty of rave about *The Man who Played with Fire*, and just a line at the end saying that another book is coming out. He must have been prescient when he wrote it, as that's the way everyone feels about this new book, it seems."

"Wow." He grimaced. "I didn't mean to rain on your parade, pet."

"I know you didn't. It just seems odd that he has virtually passed me over as less interesting than a cynical soldier and fire-fighter of great repute, yet still wants me to meet these cronies of his."

"I agree with you. Keep him hanging while we think about it, and I'll do a little research."

And that was that. After an exchange of news about Maggie and Manila, Kate rang off, and Jerry rolled over in bed.

Rosita, to all appearances, was asleep. She had grown plump over the years, very comfortable to recline against. Jerry regarded her with vast affection. They had met in a London hospital fifty years ago, when she was a nurse and he was getting over his first brush with a bullet. It had taken only a month to get her pregnant, and six weeks to get married. She had left him two children later, declaring she was sick and tired of being alone while he was off fighting whatever and wherever, and never knowing if he would survive. The business of putting out oil rig fires had been even worse, as it got into the papers more often than the battles. The big check when he finally came home did not make up for the worry, or so she said.

She had gone back to Manila but, being an ardent Catholic, she had not made the divorce public, and Jerry had taken full advantage of that. Whenever he passed through Manila he had called in with money and presents, and incidentally had fathered two more children. Now they had eight grandchildren, and — oh God — she had just announced that the oldest, Alessandra, was pregnant, so he was due to become a great-grandfather.

Alessandra didn't happen to be married, but Jerry did not care about that. What worried him was the title of *great-grandfather* that came with it. Back when he was fifty he used to brag that he could beat any man twice his size and half his age at anything, including the conquest of women, and at the age of seventy-two he hadn't changed his mind about that. Consequently, he had spent much of the night proving to Rosita that he was certainly not old enough to have a great-grandchild. Which was the reason he groaned and moved stiffly when the phone rang again.

"Kate," he complained when he picked it up, but the grunt at the other end was unmistakably Harold Pederson's.

"*Storm Swept* will make port in Manila in the morning," he grunted. "Make sure you are down at the wharf."

And rang off.

There was a big party on the wharf when Jerry arrived next day. Colorful groups of very happy locals were singing and dancing, and drums were beating and music booming, while tables of food and drink were set out under an awning. Flags flew, and affectionate notices were tacked up everywhere. If Jerry had felt any doubt that most of the crew of *Storm Swept* were Filipino, this would have settled it. Obviously, families had come from all over Manila to greet their seafaring brothers, sons and cousins, and to make the most of the time they were here.

Jerry paused before heading up the gangway, studying the ship, sizing up the challenge. *Storm Swept* was a very pretty little vessel, eight decks high and painted glistening white. A color that made her a target, he thought. Low draft, too, judging by past itineraries — which he had got around to studying, meantime.

There was a marina at the stern, where boats could be launched and guests tipped into the sea in snorkeling and scuba gear. Without a deckhand on guard, it would be fatally easy for a pirate to board — and then, once the interior was invaded, the bridge and the engine control room would be vulnerable. Everything about the vessel rang warning bells. *Storm Swept* was simply a larger version of Pederson's luxury motor yacht, *Odyssey*, which Jerry knew very well indeed from last year's voyage — and which had been illicitly boarded by men with an agenda. Frowning as he looked up at the serried decks, he considered this ship just as vulnerable as the yacht had proved to be, back then. Like the *Odyssey*, *Storm Swept* in her present state would be very hard to defend. Pederson had been very lucky that the pensioners had been so resourceful.

The captain met him on the promenade deck, at the top of the gangway. He was Italian, which was a surprise, considering the poor record of the Italian skipper who had almost lost the ship to pirate attack. Then, because he looked so drawn and worried, Jerry wondered if he was the same man who had made such a botch of security off the coast of Borneo. But no, this was a different fellow. He introduced himself as Captain Francesco Calamari, and then confided that he hailed from Napoli, that fount of so many Italian captains. Considering his name, Jerry privately thought that it was no wonder he was a seafarer. He must have had a terrible time at school.

Calamari was very relieved to be able to talk in Italian — not that he wasn't fluent in English, but because he was able to talk more privately. Having been recruited in such a hurry, and after such an emergency, he was naturally nervous — "*è difficile,*" he confided, waving eloquent hands. He had to conduct himself with more expertise and energy than ever before, as he was taking over from such an embarrassing example of poor leadership. And this was quite a challenge, as Signor Giacomo must fully understand.

Jerry certainly did understand, but did not feel reassured in the slightest.

Calamari was also garrulous, talking non-stop as he led the way through heavy wooden double doors to a wide, carpeted corridor. The interior of this promenade level, which Jerry estimated as deck five, was surprisingly intimate, with paintings in pastel colors hanging on cream-papered walls. To his left, looking aft, there was a spacious lounge, and beyond that a restaurant, both of which had wide glass doors leading to the outside deck. To his right, beyond open flaps that revealed a lavishly appointed theater in the fore part of the deck, a stairway threaded up two levels to the bridge. And as they climbed the new captain talked, every inch of the way.

Times were hard for shipmasters, he declared, incredibly so, insupportably so — "The global warming," he elaborated; "it has made many angry wave patterns and furious storms, but do the shippers understand this confusion? No, Signor Giacomo, they do not. Captains are instructed to sail even when the good sense forbids it. We are not permitted to be deterred by dangerous seas! Container ships are the worst, Signor Giacomo, overloaded because of intense demand for goods, and so many containers are lost overboard, so many! More than three thousand last year! Containers holding cars, trucks, bulldozers, much heavy equipment go to the bottom, but there are other things that float. The prospect of collision is intolerable. A nightmare, truly, a nightmare for any shipmaster, but in particular the poor man in command of a small vessel."

Worse still for anyone sailing about in a yacht, thought Jerry, who had come to the rapid conclusion that Calamari was a nervous wreck. He meditated that Pederson's replacement captain could well be worse than the previous skipper, and wondered if he should phone the owner and have a little chat. But then, to his astonishment, Harold Pederson opened the door of one of the four suites set directly behind the bridge.

So he had phoned from the ship, Jerry realized. The shipping magnate looked much the same as he had in the New York restaurant, brisk and alert, his small blue eyes sharp under his hedge like brows.

Jerry said, "How long have you been on board?"

"Since Singapore."

"May I ask why?"

"There was a bit of damage — bullet-holes in bulwarks, broken windows, that kind of thing. I had business in Singapore anyway, and it worked out well for me to be there, to make sure that the job was done properly and thoroughly. Singapore is the base for Pederson Cruises, for the very good reason that it has very good haul-out facilities."

But of course, thought Jerry. Harold Pederson was a perfectionist. Like all Pederson's property, *Storm Swept* had to be pristine, even if it involved the large cost of an inspection of the hull. It was beyond him to guess why Singapore had been the essential choice for the repairs, though. Surely the windows and bulwarks could have been fixed by the crew, at sea? Wasn't there a decent bosun on this vessel?

He said to Harold, "So you are flying back from Manila?"

"I am not."

"No?"

"No. I want to be here for your presentation, and to see the pirate deterrent measures. Watch the installation of the equipment. And then ...”

Pederson paused.

Captain Calamari had made an unobtrusive departure, Jerry noticed, as if he were anxious to avoid conversation with the ship's owner. He waited for Pederson to go on, then got tired of standing about in the corridor and said, “What?”

“Have you read the latest issue of *Balustrade Magazine*?”

“Nope.”

“There is an interesting article about you.”

“So I heard.”

“I've had a lot of phone calls. It has aroused a lot of comment and some controversy. People are keen to hear you talk.”

“About fire-fighting?”

“And life in the army. So I want you to be our guest lecturer — our onboard expert — on the next cruise, after you have overseen the installation of the pirate deterrent measures. And maybe more after that. It will help the media forget the pirate debacle.”

Jerry laughed and shook his head.

“I'll make it worth your while.”

“That's what you always say, Harold.”

When a door to a second suite opened and Skye Hamilton walked out, Jerry supposed he should have felt surprised. Instead he merely observed, “So Harold summoned you, too.”

Skye grinned. He was a tall, lean man in his early forties, dark, with a few gray strands in his black hair, and with very pale eyes, paler than gray. Women called them wolflike. When he smiled, his tanned face creased up. As always, Jerry was pleased to see him, and on this day even more so. Not only was he another member of the *famiglia* Bacchante — being the son of the barrel carver, Michelangelo — but Skye was resourceful in an emergency.

"Joined the ship in Singapore," he explained when Jerry lifted a querying brow.

"You heard about the pirate attack?"

"Of course. But that's not why I am here."

They both looked at Harold Pederson. Skye, who had graduate degrees in business management from both Melbourne and Harvard, had been the first person to realize that one of Pederson's major ventures, Pederson Strategic, had been hijacked by money launderers. Obviously, checking his finances was an ongoing job.

Harold shrugged. "There is a lot on my plate."

Jerry winked at Skye. "Then I hope he makes it worth your while."

Four

Pederson led the way into his suite, which had a lounge that also served as an office. Through an open door, Jerry could glimpse a bedroom with an attached bathroom beyond, while another door led forward to the bridge. This, as Jerry knew from experience on the *Odyssey*, was Harold's habit. Because the tycoon liked to poke his nose into everything, the owner's suite always had ready access to what was supposed to be the captain's domain.

The settee was upholstered in pale green slubbed silk, and there was a large oil painting of the magnate's daughter, Jewel Pederson, hanging on the wall. It looked as if she had posed for the artist at about the age of sixteen, when she still had the glow of extreme youth, and it had much more movement than the usual portrait study. Pale blonde and remarkably lovely, she had been caught in the middle of a pirouette, with her arms outflung, and her skirt and long silvery hair spinning about her. Fine hairs lifted on the nape of Jerry's neck. What the hell was *that* doing here? It was as if beautiful, dangerous Jewel was lurking in the shadows of the ship.

Jerry sat beneath the portrait, so that he wouldn't have to look at it. There were busy computer monitors on the desk, with a tray of spreadsheets alongside a mega-sized printer. So Skye had been working already. Jerry said, "What's the latest with Pederson Strategic?"

Harold sat down on one of the matching armchairs with his knees wide apart. His tone was aggressive as he snapped, "There is nothing wrong with the way the *company* is spending money."

"All to eco-friendly projects," Skye said smoothly. "And some of them are making a lot of money — a lot." He nodded at Pederson, and then said to Jerry as if the tycoon wasn't there, "He has the touch of Midas, you know."

Jerry shrugged, unimpressed. "It's the way of the future."

"I agree. Investing in solar panels, wind farms, and wave turbines is working out well, though the initial cost is huge. It's the money *funding* the venture that is the major problem."

"Dirty money?"

"That's what the Justice Department thinks."

"But why would the Mafia or gangs or whatever want to launder their grubby takings by investing in greenie ventures?"

"That," said Skye, "is the question. We just have to make sure that it really is invested, and not being diverted elsewhere."

Which meant, Jerry mused, that Skye suspected there were upper echelon people within Pederson Strategic who worked with the launderers. He had more sense than to make a comment, but merely looked at Harold and waited.

Pederson was shifting in his seat, obviously impatient. "The issue at hand is the public face of Pederson Cruises — and that is what you're here to fix."

"The pirate attack that was foiled by pensioners?"

"Exactly. Have you done your research?"

"Of course."

"Do I need to put armed guards on my ships?"

"Absolutely not." Jerry spoke with perfect confidence. "Not

only are you getting into very difficult legal territory if you have guns on your ships, but do you really want people to be killed? Because that is what will happen, which is not a good solution."

Pederson winced. The publicity of a shoot-out would not be welcome at all. "What about armed escort vessels?"

"Same problem. Guns mean deaths."

"So what is the alternative?"

Jerry said, "Why not look at the basic problem first?"

"Problem?"

"It's implicit. What you promise to anyone who shells out for a couple of weeks on one of your lovely little ships is the freedom to swim, snorkel, putter off in a Zodiac to some secluded beach, or play on surf skis — right? They are paying to play with your toys."

"These are discovery ships," Pederson insisted, though he was looking uncomfortable.

"You can't tell me I'm wrong. According to the itineraries to the western Pacific, the ships stop at remote atolls so that the guests can play in the sea."

"We have been featured in *National Geographic* — and the Discovery Channel."

"So the guests trek on shore and boat up rivers, exploring beaches and jungles?"

"Wildlife photographers love us."

"The same applies. What happens if the ship is boarded while all these people are away?"

"Oh God." Obviously, Pederson had not thought of that.

"Exactly. So you have to make the ship *look* invincible. Not worth attacking, even with the toys out on the water."

"Tell me how to do that."

"Right now, there are acres of glass along the promenade deck

— glass that is not bullet-proof. Replacing all the glass with bullet-proof glass won't work as a deterrent, as no matter how strong it is, it will still look like ordinary glass. So you have to put up barriers. They could be quite artistic. A good designer will have ideas, I'm sure. And Manila is famous not only for great interior designers, but also for beautifully wrought iron. The same with all the glass doors. They need to be matched with grilles. And they all have to have strong locks."

"The ship will look like a Zanzibar brothel."

"Will it?" Jerry blinked. He had never been to Zanzibar, and had no idea what brothels looked like there, or even if there were any. He shrugged and said, "Consult with a designer."

"Do you have any better ideas?"

"Have plenty of deckhands in plain sight, always. The marina — that deck at the stern where the divers and swimmers and rubber boats slide away from the ship — is a very vulnerable spot. There must be two deckhands there all the time the ship is at anchor and the guests are playing in the sea or trekking in the jungle. Undoubtedly, they will be visiting primitive villages — and will look incredibly rich to the people in those villages. It wouldn't take much to stir up a few warriors into trying out piracy. And it would be a good idea to have the ship's tender patrol the sea around the ship, again with some muscular hands from the crew."

"But not armed?"

Jerry lifted his shoulders. "It's important that they look ready for trouble — but being armed with guns is not a good idea. If they were wearing helmets and Kevlar vests, they could look deterrent enough, though it could help if they were carrying something like belaying pins." He grinned. "Do you have belaying pins on your ships?"

"I would not have a clue," said Pederson, and laughed. It was perhaps the first time, Jerry thought, that he had heard the magnate laugh at one of his jokes.

"I am sure you know what I mean. You will also need to employ an electrician who is an expert in security."

"But there are security cameras throughout the ship already. They are constantly monitored down in the engine control room."

"It's no good knowing what is going on if you can't do anything about it."

Harold looked baffled, but instead of elaborating Jerry paused, thinking about how much he liked and respected Filipino seafarers. Then he reluctantly added, "And there is a second major problem — the crew."

"What? But that's ridiculous. Most of them have worked for me for years. They are salaried, not on contract. I treat them very well indeed."

"I am sure you do, and I know that being salaried is an unusual blessing. But it seems to me that the pirates off the coast of Borneo had an ally on board. I'll check this afternoon, but I don't see how those pirates managed to lodge a rope at the taffrail without some assistance."

Silence. Then Harold said, "You mean the rope was dropped down to them?"

"Exactly."

"Oh." He muttered what sounded like a Nordic curse. "So what do we do about it?"

"Have courses for the crew, and make it compulsory to attend them. If the crew don't know how to respond to a pirate attack, your preventive measures could prove to be useless. And the pirates should not — ever — be underestimated. They are poor, and they are desperate. Or they are terrorists with a mission. So the crew have to be prepared for the worst eventuality — the storming of the ship. Then, at the end of the course, they must pass some kind of test."

"Where could they be trained?"

Jerry shrugged again. "Here, if you wish. There are computer courses in both preventive security and crowd management — and if pirates do get on board, crowd management will be important."

"In Manila, you mean?"

"There are colleges here that do offer courses, and the coastguard would certainly help, as the government is very keen to have something done about the pirate problem, so many Filipino seafarers having been attacked, killed, and taken hostage of late. That could be an advantage, as so many of the crew are from Manila. But the local courses are biased towards armed guards. And we do not want guns."

Pederson shook his head and sighed. "So what do you suggest?"

"Take the ship offshore, and run exercises at sea. I've been qualified to run all kinds of safety courses, so I know I could do it, though I would need some consultation with the local maritime authorities first, to make sure of the law. At sea, it would be possible to have dry runs. Put out the tender, and have the men on the tender pretend to be pirates, so that the crew can practice fending them off. Then have a scenario where the men on the skiff — the tender, in the exercise — manage to board and seize the ship, so the crew can try out methods of defense and recapture."

"Without guns."

"Exactly."

"So you can draw up a plan of action?"

"Certainly. But I want to have a good look at the ship first, to see what can be done to make it look hard to invade. Is *Storm Swept* much the same as the other four?"

"The five ships are identical."

"Good. I'll make a thorough inspection right after lunch."

Storm Swept might carry only 120 guests, but the ship seemed very empty with no guests on board. There didn't seem to be many crew members around, either. Most were at the wharf side party, no doubt. The ship echoed as Jerry clambered down to the lower deck, accompanied by the senior engineer.

As was customary with Pederson ships, the engineer was Scottish, his accent so broad that Jerry had trouble understanding him. They spent a long time in the engine control room, which Jerry considered to be the heart of the ship, so wanted to get to know intimately. There were tell-tales and monitors running along the walls above the row of windows that overlooked the engine room, and a computer screen on top of a bank of cabinets under the windows, which conveyed information from the captain's bridge, so that the engineer on watch knew exactly the state of the ship.

On the other side of the after bulkhead, below the row of windows, the great engines crouched, pregnant with power. There was bulletproof glass in the door between the engine control room and the passage outside, and in the door between the engine control room and the engine room itself, both with code locks. The windows overlooking the engines were bulletproof, too. While the engine room itself would be very noisy during passage, the control room was sound-proofed and air-conditioned. It was also extremely clean.

Pleased with what he saw, Jerry said, "Could you take control of the ship from here?"

The Scot blinked with astonishment, and said stiffly, "Only after a direct order from the bridge, Mr. Giacomo — and then only with much limitation."

"But with all this modern technology, isn't it on the cards?" Jerry nodded at the myriad monitors and dials, along with the laptop and the array of buttons and levers. As he was perfectly aware, the engineer in the control room was in charge of not just the propulsion of the ship, but the lighting, the drinking water, the sewage system, the bilges, the ballast, the air conditioning, the security cameras, and the firefighting system. It was even possible for the ship's course to be steered from this room.

The Scot looked even more dour. "That might be all to the good, sir, but modern technology brings challenges, sir — challenges that take a lot of meeting."

Jerry kept silent. It was as good an answer as he could expect. The engineer was not a young man, and adapting to rapid technological change was naturally challenging. As an ex-soldier and fire fighter, he was a great believer in resourcefulness during emergency, however. If the worst happened, and pirates took over the captain's bridge, this could be a citadel, a place where key personnel would shelter, and hopefully respond with efficiency to the crisis.

Jerry looked around, judging the space. With five or six in the engine room, and another three or four in the control room, at least eight could shut themselves in here, safe from assault — ten, at a pinch. He nodded, and they moved on.

Working the big door that led to the open ramp at the bottom of the stern of the ship was even more reassuring. Extremely heavy, made of steel, it opened and closed with a motor. Certainly safe from pirate invasion when shut, though Jerry hoped all guests kept their arms out of the way when it was closing. The ramp itself could be tipped up against the door, also with a motor. If electricity failed, both could be opened or closed with a hand pump.

Jerry thanked the engineer, who merely nodded grimly, and then proceeded alone to the next item on his list — the windows and glass doors. The most vulnerable areas were the accommodation, dining and entertainment decks. There were twenty-eight balcony staterooms, each with a hinged glass door that opened to the outside. Jerry made a note, and then climbed up to the verandah suites, where the even better-heeled took their seaborne vacations. These had double-wide sliding glass doors.

There were also expansive windows to the restaurant and lounges, which ran the length of the promenade deck, directly below. Making more notes, and occasionally ruminating about Zanzibar brothels, Jerry headed for the stern, and studied the rail. There were patches of heavy varnish that evidently covered the scratches where the grapnel had taken hold. The result of a lucky throw? It was possible, and he hoped so. But that did not seem likely.

When he turned round, it was to find the ship's owner standing behind him.

He said, "Harold, I was not wrong — there are absolute acres of unprotected glass."

Harold winced.

"You're thinking about Zanzibar brothels?" When Pederson didn't respond to the lame joke, Jerry said, "Decorative wrought iron grilles would do the trick for the windows in the entertainment areas, though they might make the windows hard to clean. Because of that, they would be better set on the inside, with hinges, and good locks to secure them when they are shut. Folding grilles on solid tracks would work on all the glass doors, as long as they could be locked securely. But the crew would have to be trained in their use. It would be pointless and wasteful to install the grilles, and then have them folded back more or less permanently."

"Another part of the training session?"

"Yes. A crucial part, as the ship has to look hard to invade. But it doesn't need to be ugly. The designer will have ideas, I'm sure. On both counts — utility and beauty. After all—"

His phone rang. Jerry sighed, and picked up. It was Kate, in New York, sounding agitated.

He said swiftly, "Is everything okay?"

"I've just arrived at the apartment. Helen got an email that seems urgent, and she is busy booking a seat on the first flight to Mexico, and a cab to get to the airport. But it is Maggie you need to talk to — and please find Skye. We found poor Maggie in a state, and she is asking for him. She's frantic."

And frantic she was indeed. Maggie was crying so hard that it was difficult to work out what she was saying. "The creative director loved my ideas," she sobbed. "And someone was jealous — and planted cocaine in my bag. And you know I have never used, Jerry. But now they are saying I should not only be fired but charged by the police, too — and you know what it is like here. *They* are snorting all the time. And the gossip — the awful gossip. Why me? Why are they trying to wreck my career?"

"Have you talked to your mother?"

"Yes, of course. But she simply told me to forget it all and come home and start over again."

Typical, Jerry thought. Rachel Bacchante was a wonderfully caring mother to both girls, but had no imagination. There was no way she would understand that for Maggie it would be a humiliating defeat.

"I need to talk to Skye, Jerry. He always gives me good advice. I don't mean that you don't — but—"

"Yes, I know." But the answer was vague. The promenade deck overlooked the wharf, and Jerry, standing at the port rail, had an excellent view of the party celebrating the ship's arrival. The music was loud, and the dancing was energetic. There was no one like a Filipino to make the best of a good time, he meditated. And among them was Skye — dancing with Alessandra.

Alessandra — the granddaughter Jerry regarded with a jaundiced eye, being the one who was going to endow him with the humiliating *great*-grandfather title — was seductive even from this distance. Her abundant black hair tumbled down to her waist, her body, still trim, undulated seductively. She was wearing a dress with a tight black top that showed off her breasts, and a multi-colored skirt that spun out about her shapely hips. As Jerry watched, Skye subsided to a chair, and Alessandra laughingly perched on his knee.

Jerry shook his head in disgust, scarcely aware that Harold's phone had rung, and that the shipowner was talking into it, with long listening pauses.

"Wait a bit, pet," he said to Maggie. "I'll find Skye, and then phone back."

"Jerry, are you at a party?"

"You can hear music?"

"You call that music?" she said acidly.

"I'm at the wharf, and the crew are reuniting with their families, with music and food and dancing, and all that good Filipino stuff. And, *tesoro*, it is not even teatime yet."

He shut off his phone, ready to set off for the quay, but Harold gestured for him to stop. "That was Helen. She has spoken to the creative director at Bellissimo, with good results. He has decided that Maggie will be an out-of-house designer until things settle down. They are certainly not firing her, or contacting the police. It's a simple matter of jealousy. Typical, of course."

The expression on Harold's face spoke plainly of his poor opinion of top-end fashion houses. "So," he said, "both Kate and Maggie are flying here, and Helen will join us when she can, but she has sudden business in Mexico — one of her charities, perhaps, but she didn't have time to explain. The cab arrived as we were talking, and so she had to rush away. The girls can stay on the ship while we are fixing it to be pirate-proof. Maggie can work perfectly well at sea — after all, she managed on the *Odyssey* last year."

Then, with a nod, he was off, looking busy. Jerry hoped that he was about to contact wrought iron screen designers, but left him to it, heading for the gangway instead.

He was almost at the bottom when his phone rang again. It was Kate.

He said, "Is Maggie settling down?"

"Not Maggie this time," said Kate. "It's me, and I am angry."

"What is it?"

"That ghastly journalist just phoned me again — about that man he was talking about — the one he wants me to meet."

"What journalist? Waters?"

"Yes! "

"So who does he want you to meet?"

"He now says it's a man from my mother's past!"

"*What?* Someone who knew Kelly?"

"Yes!"

"Who?"

And she told him the man's name.

Five

"So who is it?" demanded Skye.

Jerry studied him as he drank beer. It had been an effort to prise Skye away from Alessandra — who declared herself in love yet again — but now they were at Rosita's house, which was strangely quiet. He could hear his ex-wife singing to herself as she worked in the kitchen, but the rest of his extended Manila family was either at work, or at school, or at sea, or at the party on the wharf.

He said, certain that it must be an alias, "The *Honourable* Adrian Blackwell."

Skye stared. *"Who?"* Then he said in a lower voice, "Why would he want to meet Kate?"

"A man from Kelly's past, or so Waters claimed."

Skye frowned. "But how would Blackwell be involved with Kelly?"

"Kate did say that she thought the reporter was lying."

Jerry got up, went to the kitchen, kissed his ex-wife on the smooth nape of her neck, and fetched two more bottles of San Miguel from the refrigerator. He felt as if he and Skye needed it.

The lounge he returned to was typical Manila, with wrought iron bars on the windows, white-painted walls, plushy settees sprouting many colorfully embroidered cushions, and lots of religious icons hung here and there, along with pictures of the family. After sitting down and wriggling his bottom to get comfortable, he said, "The last thing we want is a fortune-hunter coming after Kate, particularly one with a fake name and a fake title who pretends to be rich and powerful."

"He's not fake, unfortunately. Blackwell is his real name. And he really is rich." Sky grimaced. "And you say that a journalist is trying to connect Adrian Blackwell with Kate?"

"Yes. Waters, Graham Waters. The same character who wrote that article about me for *Balustrade Magazine*."

"But you have no idea why Blackwell wants to meet her?"

"Not a notion."

"What is Graham Waters like?"

Jerry thought back to the interview, which now seemed a long time ago. "English, of course. It's an English magazine. Not as upper-class as the publication he works for, but an educated accent, and more intelligent than he looks. Obviously, he's dogging Kate for another story. Damn it, Skye, I warned her after the interview that he had deliberately made her angry so she would reveal more than intended, but thinking back, he played exactly the same trick on me."

Skye pried the cap off the beer bottle, and drank deep. "Whatever Waters has in mind, it could be a hell of a story."

"Why?"

"Because the *Honourable* Adrian Blackwell is the CEO of Pederson Strategic."

"Dear God." Jerry stared at him, his mind racing. "The man who could be behind the money laundering?"

"Could be. Yes."

"You've investigated this Blackwell?"

"Not me — though I wanted to, as the man is a business mediator with political connections. Powerful political connections. For whom he has done big favors. How do you think he got his title? It wasn't inherited, you know. When Harold hired a private detective firm, his brief to them was to investigate the entire upper echelon of Pederson Strategic. Now, in view of this new information, I intend to focus on Blackwell. With your help."

"Me?" Jerry laughed. "I'm a fire-fighter, not a detective."

"And you were a major in the British intelligence service."

Whoops, Jerry thought. How did Skye know that?

"That was centuries ago," he protested. "All I learned was how to wear a stiff uniform, say yes sir, no sir, three bags full, sir, to lieutenant colonels, and drink stiff whisky sodas. As for intelligence, I passed on far too much suspect information, and put far too many of our lads in harm's way. That's why I transferred to a real fighting unit."

"Rubbish."

"And I'm not a forensic accountant, either — that's your job."

"I know." Skye drank beer, and sighed.

"So you reckon that this *Honourable* is the kingpin behind the skullduggery that is going on in Pederson Strategic?"

"I won't go so far as to say that — not yet — but it's definitely possible."

Jerry paused. Rosita was creating cooking noises in the kitchen, as only she knew how to do, and the smell of sizzling chicken wafted into the room, along with her singing. It was hard to think of high finance and terrible publicity when surrounded by warm aromas.

"Tell me what you do know."

They were interrupted. Alessandra sashayed into the room, fresh from the wharf party, pert of breasts and hips, and looking mischievous. "Skye, so there you are," she said.

"Go and help your grandmother," said Jerry. "This man is far too old for you."

"I am not pregnant," she proudly announced, and made the

situation clear in Tagalog. *"Isang pagkakamali lang* — big mistake."

"I don't care," said Jerry, though he did care. A lot. Relief washed warmly through him, but still he ordered, "Go into the kitchen."

She pouted, but undulated away.

Skye laughed and said, "And how old were you when you had that fling with Kelly?"

"Alessandra's only sixteen — and she's my granddaughter, so my wicked past don't signify. And you have to get serious, Skye. If I am going to help with this investigation, I need background."

Skye sobered. "The story goes back twenty-five years — a short history, considering the size of the operation today. That's when Saudi Oil got up and going."

"In London?"

"In Geneva, as it happens, but that's only incidental. Blackwell was in the profitable business of expediting meetings between businessmen, princes, and politicians when an old friend persuaded him to find him an office with a name-plate and a business card — which Blackwell did, with no hesitation at all, according to the story. And it makes sense, for that old friend was a Saudi national by the name of Zaid Feisal. So Blackwell found him a place in the Geneva office of a senior British diplomat. And that is how Saudi Oil got started."

"How the hell did Blackwell manage that?"

"As I said, he had many, many political and business contacts. And Feisal and Blackwell went back a long way, as they were both at Eton and Oxford."

Jerry frowned. " Saudi Oil is the last business I would have expected to have such an insignificant start."

"Feisal was remarkably effective at getting established — not just fast, but convincingly, too. What he offered to oil-rich states was the middle-man, the person who would help the sheiks and sultans invest the money from the oil bonanza, and the little Gulf states, in particular, took him up on it. Using the Saudi name was inspired, as it carries such a promise of huge riches. And Blackwell was the perfect conduit for Feisal, as he already had an impressive record in the mediating business. Within a handful of years, the company occupied a high-rise in London, as well as one in Geneva, and was worth close to three billion."

Jerry whistled. "Wow."

"That's what Harold thought," Skye agreed. "A couple of years after Saudi Oil got started, another middle man by the name of Brooke introduced Harold to Blackwell and Feisal, who proposed that Pederson should start up an operation called Pederson Strategic, to be backed by Saudi Oil. The stated aim was to invest in eco-friendly ventures — wind farms, tide turbines, solar panels, that kind of thing."

"But was it meant to be a non-profit operation?"

"No, of course not. Blackwell and Feisal are entrepreneurs, not philanthropists — but from Harold's point of view the idea looked good, as eco-friendly was increasingly the buzz word of the day. All the pension plans were — and still are — looking for that kind of investment. And the finance was all laid out. Saudi Oil's initial input — meaning money that Feisal would organize — was to be close to two billion, which would buy Saudi Oil sixty percent of the company. Pederson, by investing nine hundred million, would have a forty percent share."

"That is a hell of a lot of money."

"Indeed."

"You are sure of all this?"

"Of course."

"And Harold went for it? Even though he was lending his good name to a venture where he was not the major partner? That part is the hardest to believe."

"You know how Americans respect British titles, and that *Honourable* would have impressed him out of his little cotton socks. Whether Harold knew Feisal and Blackwell personally is debatable. He probably did, but I doubt it would have made much difference if he hadn't, as Brooke was good at what he did. Anyway, the deal with Feisal and Blackwell was beaten out on Feisal's luxury motor yacht *Masha'Allah*."

"Good fortune, in Arabic."

"Is that so? Good fortune it proved to be — for them, but not for Pederson, who has only recently had to face the brutal truth that they are using his eco-friendly foundation as a money-laundering operation."

"How long ago was this?"

"Just over twenty-two years."

"Why so long to suspect what was happening?"

Skye shrugged. "Harold was at too great a distance from what was going on. Right from the very start, Blackwell and a board of directors were in charge, and though Feisal was not on the actual board, he acted as a prime associate. Harold was present at important meetings, of course, but it looks as if a lot more meetings were held without letting him know. As we have found out over the past year, a lot of the action flew under his radar, mostly engineered by Feisal."

"They borrowed money?"

"Billions, mostly from private sources, most of which came via a Cyprus bank. And, as we now know all too well, it looks as if that was the money that was being laundered. When the loans were repaid — out of the profits of the eco-ventures — the money was clean. God knows what it was spent on after that. And money is being siphoned from the actual fund itself."

"Much?"

"About four billion, so far. Probably into cryptocurrency, as we can't track any lavish purchases."

"But that's more than the original investment! How the hell are they doing it?"

"Quite easily, as I've found out. One of the ploys is to get governments to lend or subscribe huge sums to produce the wind turbines, or whatever. With that money, the subsidiary buys factories in Europe where the materials are expensive, and the workers are highly paid — and then closes down those factories and replaces them with plants in Third World countries, where the workers are paid badly and treated shockingly, and the raw material is cheaper. So, while the product — whether it be a solar panel or a huge wind turbine — looks as good as promised, it has cost much less than the estimate in the proposal. And the money scooped off the top is sent to some private bank account in Switzerland or Cyprus."

"It almost looks legal."

"Oh yes," Skye agreed. "But it is not ploughed back into the foundation, the way it should be. Which is why the Department of Justice started poking around last year, and Harold hired me to track the cash. It could be just a hint of what has been stolen. And not just by one man. All the board members and senior officials are under suspicion. Harold made a huge mistake when he allowed his name to be used by the company, particularly since he was never the major shareholder."

"Did the detectives find out anything at all?"

"Plenty of dirt, but nothing relevant. Blackwell and Feisal have a history of hedonism that goes back to university days. They haunt London West End and Geneva nightclubs, and there are rumors that a few escorts have disappeared, over the years."

Jerry frowned, feeling a shiver creep up the back of his neck. "Murdered?"

Skye shrugged. "We simply assumed that they were paid to go away."

Jerry paused for thought. "So we have two questions that need urgent answers."

"Yes?"

"Why is Blackwell having anything to do with a sensation-hunting journalist like Waters?"

"Indeed. It opens all sorts of options."

"But, more importantly still, why does Blackwell want to meet Kate?"

Six

Helen Pederson complained, "This village is really remote. It's pretty enough, but I had no idea it was such a long way from anywhere."

Her first husband stared up at her from his wheelchair, saying dryly, "I'm so glad you noticed."

"Very pretty, but very hard to reach," she went on, the sarcasm ignored. "This morning I had to board a local bus that was really, really crowded, quite totally so, and even though I protested, they made me take the prime seat at the front, and that made me feel very uncomfortable. After all, it was their bus and their country, not mine. You probably don't remember, but I am a very democratic person. I chair charities, you know. I suppose they aren't used to tourists this time of year, and felt as if I should be pampered."

The man in the wheelchair silently studied her, matching the memories in his head to what he saw now. His ex-wife wore loose pants and a loose top, but still managed to look amazing. She had put on a few pounds over the years, but it suited her, as the little extra padding was just enough to keep her face smooth, almost youthful. No wonder, he thought, that the locals gave up the best seat on the bus. That combination of cool elegance and sex appeal was as fascinating as it had been when he had first seen her, craved her, and seduced her, more than two decades ago.

It had been at a soirée in Manhattan, run by that ghastly socialite, Claudia Vermeeren. Helen had been just twenty-two years old, and at first glance he had felt sorry for her. She had looked so lost and alone, and terribly young, and evidently had not been warned about the style of the occasion, as she was wearing a most unsuitable dress. And then, as he scanned the slim body that the tight, short garment scarcely hid, and then lifted his eyes to look into hers, the sexual attraction had hit.

He remembered the jolt, deep in the gut, like the sudden flare of a primitive flame. Pheromones, the thought objectively now. Rampant hormones. He had once watched two preying mantids in their mating dance — the male drawn fatally to the predatory female, who had turned round when he had finished his job, and bitten off his head. Now, Brooke thought that he knew exactly how that male insect felt.

But at the time the flash of desire had been over-whelming. He had worked his way through the crowd to the girl's side, simply intending to dance, but when he pulled her into his arms, the spark had flared to a blaze. He had rushed her out of the room, into a taxi, into his apartment, into his bed. The gossip, undoubtedly, had started then, but neither of them had cared. The lust had been mutual.

The memories were as vivid as ever, but that sexual spark had gone, thank God. His fault or Helen's? Hers, Brooke decided. She looked too poised, too confident. He had expected her to be tearful and intimidated, certainly not like this. She was behaving as if this were a normal social occasion, prattling away to fill the conversational gaps with small talk.

"Tell me about this arduous journey," he jibed.

Again, Helen ignored the sarcasm, if she even noticed it. "I had no idea it would take so long to get here, Pierce, but I did do my best. As always, you have absolutely no right to feel angry at me. I had only just come off a book tour, you know, a tour for a writer I sponsor. I flew from New York to Mexico City, and then had to book into a hotel while I arranged a flight to Loreto, but you have no idea how few planes were flying – because it is the low season, I suppose. Then I waited for the plane, and when I finally got there, I had to stay for three more nights, as I needed all that time to work out how to get to you. I never believed I would see so much of Mexico."

"Lucky you."

Another dismissive glance. "And there was no way to get to this village except by bus. I had to catch it at an unholy hour in the morning, and then we drove off into the desert. The windshield was a mess – full of cracks and splinters, with a few icons bobbing around. I don't know how the driver could see his way. Every now and then he would stop and let off someone who simply walked off into the mirage and the sand and the cactus, and I felt so bad for them, because they weren't even carrying bottles of water. Then we arrived at some sort of terminus, so I asked my way to your village, but had to stop overnight. In a rather awful hotel. With cockroaches. But at last, this morning, I found a bus that would bring me here."

"Well," he said, still very dry. "I am so glad you managed it." Silently, he wondered if she had always rattled on like this, but did not think so. Was it because she was nervous? She certainly didn't look it.

"And here I am," she said. She glanced around the room, and then perched on a small settee that was mostly covered with a worn serape.

"You live here?" she asked. "Is this your house?"

"Yes, and yes. It is a poor place, but mine, and yes, I live here.

I have lived here for the past twenty years."

"Why so bitter? You look comfortable, and it is an interesting place. It could have been worse. I was informed that you were dead, you know."

"And you don't think I don't wish that I was?" He looked down at himself, the wheelchair, the rug that covered his helpless legs, and the paunch that hung over his belt, because he drank too much and had no exercise.

"Self-pity does not become you, Pierce."

"Oh yes. I could have been crippled in the United States, where I would not be able to afford this house, or the care."

"So you want me to pay the difference? Is that why you summoned me with enigmatic threats? Is that why you went to so much trouble to find my email address? I feel a certain responsibility, because we were married, once. I am known for the people I sponsor, you know. As I said, I am a liberal person. But you can't blame me for the state you are in, Pierce."

"So it was not your idea for your lover to pay me off with one hundred thousand dollars?"

Her fine brows arched. "I had forgotten about that. It was a generous gesture. Harold said that you needed the money – which you did, no doubt, as your expensive life style did not match your means. That, incidentally, is why I had to start up the etiquette and deportment business in Washington that you hated so much, to get our bank accounts out of the red. And they were definitely our *joint* accounts that I am talking about, not your personal ones – the ones I wasn't supposed to know about. Harold didn't need to pay you. Face it, Pierce, our marriage was over. My little business was doing quite well, but not well enough to support you and your mistresses in your globetrotting lifestyle. I was going to leave you, whatever happened. I just happened to fall in love with Harold along the way."

"The money was a taunt," he said bitterly, and with abrupt movements wheeled his chair to the tiny kitchen. He looked back over his shoulder. "A drink?"

She shook her head.

"Well, I need one." He found the tequila bottle, filled a glass, and then wheeled back into the lounge.

She said nothing, just waited. He stared at her, looking as composed as if she had not made the long, strange journey. He said coldly, "I spent the check on a Porsche – did you know that?"

"I was told that at the time, or so I seem to remember. They said you had failed to take a corner, and had been killed in the crash."

"I bought the car in Mexico City, right after I signed the divorce papers and sent them back to your sugar daddy. And I crashed it the first time I took it out for a drive. But, though I broke my back in five places, and had to spend several months in hospital, I did not die."

She paused, studying him with her head on one side. "And you blame me for that silly decision to squander the money on an over-powered car?"

"Of course."

Helen stood up. "This is pointless," she said, and picked up her bag.

"Ah, Helen, but you have come all this way."

"I did, and I'm here, but still can't see the reason why you wanted to see me so urgently. Your email read like a threat, you know. It was designed to get me off-balance. But I see no reason to be shaken."

"Oh, but the reason is obvious – once you know about it," he said. "Sit down, and I will show you."

Helen looked around impatiently, but perched again on the sofa, not sitting back but leaning forward, ready to get up and go.

He had the old photograph close by, on a little table at his elbow. He produced it, and said, "My mother, when young. So, do you see the reason now?"

He grinned humorlessly at her, his expression challenging. Helen frowned, looked at the picture, then back at his face. "See what? I don't have a notion what you are going on about, Pierce."

"You don't see the resemblance?" he demanded, and produced the magazine, the page already turned to the photo of Helen with Kate by her side.

"Look at the girl with you," he said.

Helen looked and shrugged. "Is the magazine story about her book? I don't read Spanish, so what does it have to do with me?"

"You don't see the girl's resemblance to my mother?"

"How could I? Lots of people look like other people. Your mother was obviously a very pretty woman, but she died long before I met you, so no, I do not see any resemblance to Kate. How could I? It's just an old photo, Pierce, and I have come a long way for nothing. It has been an utter waste of time and effort, not to mention the cost. We used to be married, so I felt responsible, but now I am here, I do not. You might be a bitter, hurt man, but too many years have gone by for me to make any kind of a connection."

He paused a long moment, studying her, wondering why he had ever loved her in the first place. She was so cold, so ... *owned* by another man. But it hadn't been love, he remembered; it had been lust. He had been trapped in a loveless marriage by overwhelming sexual desire. Anger seethed inside him.

"I know that girl is our daughter. And I intend to make it plain to Pederson – unless you make it worth my while to keep quiet."

"What?"

"The family likeness is unmistakeable. Helen, I *know* that girl with you in the picture is the girl I fathered the last time we had sex."

Helen stared, her mouth falling open. For the first time, he had shaken her composure. He stared back aggressively, certain that she was gripped by the same memories: of that night when he had barged into the apartment; the night when she opened the door after he had hammered on it repeatedly, too angry to find his key.

Yet again, the old, humiliating memory dragged through his brain. He had flown in from London, furious every moment of the way, staring at the divorce papers, and taking the check that had come with them as an insult. Helen had been wearing a diaphanous nightgown, and he had been nuclear with rage. He had rushed her into the bedroom and they had coupled like the first time, impelled by pure animal lust. Had it been rape? No, he did not think so.

She shook her head, staring at him with disbelief. "You think *Kate* is your daughter?"

"*Our* daughter. And I will let Harold Pederson know. Copies of the two photos should be more than enough to convince him."

"Oh my God," she said, and suddenly laughed. "I came all this way for *this*? Your attempt at blackmail is pathetic, Pierce. Kate Giacomo isn't my daughter. She belongs to a different family altogether. And I have a picture of my own to prove it."

And she produced a picture – of a beautiful blonde and blue-eyed girl. She was twinkling into the camera with a mischievous smile, on the verge of a wild dance.

Pierce took it. And looked. "*Jesus*," he said, and shut his eyes. His stomach clenched and he felt sick. He hadn't had the nightmare for weeks, but he knew he would be tormented again tonight when – if – he slept. Surely it was a mistake? But when he looked at the picture again, it was the same girl who haunted the nightmares.

"What are you doing to me?" he demanded. His voice was high with hysteria, but he couldn't control it. "Are you threatening me? *But I didn't do anything wrong!*"

"Pierce, just what are you raving about?"

"How did you get that picture?"

This time, Helen looked properly rattled. "I don't know what you mean."

"That's a picture of a high-class escort you couldn't *possibly* know. Someone I met in terrible circumstances; an experience that I've tried very hard to forget. So how the *hell* did you get it? And *why* are you showing it to me now?"

Seven

Maggie and Kate were later getting to Manila than expected, as they had stopped off at the vineyard for a few days. They were greeted with relieved hugs from both Skye and Jerry at the airport, then rushed off to *Storm Swept*, where Harold met them at the top of the gangway.

He simply said, "At last — so now we can get away," and then turned back inside. As he went he jerked his head at Skye, and barked, "A meeting in my suite in ten minutes. All of you."

Accordingly, after dumping the girls' luggage in the suite on the bridge deck that had been assigned to them, the four Bacchantes assembled in Harold's lounge. He was not there, but they waited.

Maggie looked at the full length, life-sized portrait of Jewel Pederson, visibly flinched, and said softly, "Oh boy. Do you remember…?"

"Oh, yes," said Skye.

"Why has he hung it in here?"

"God knows. If Harold had had his way, Jewel would have been put into an institution at the age of ten, when the specialists decided her mental illness was untreatable. Incurable."

Maggie grimaced. Then she looked at Jerry and said, "What is that terrible noise?"

"A gang is putting up wrought iron to make the ship look pirate-proof. Hopefully, it won't finish up looking like a Zanzibar brothel."

"What?"

He laughed. "Harold's little joke. At least," he added, "I think it was a joke, but who can tell with Harold? You will enjoy the designer."

"What do you mean?"

"You'll see for yourself, as he is coming with us."

The wrought iron screens and folding grilles had been delivered in double-quick time, and now four men from the design studio were assembling them, supervised by the designer himself. It was a huge job that would take several days, so they were coming along on the jaunt. A specialist electrician and an equally specialist locksmith were finishing off the instalment of the electronic locks, before heading back to the wharf.

As he spoke, Jerry could feel the engines start up. With the petty thrift that characterized many billionaires, Pederson was saving money by having *Storm Swept* fortified at sea, thus avoiding wharfage.

He lifted a brow at Maggie, and said, "What's the latest with Bellissimo?"

She grinned sheepishly. "I don't know why I made such a fuss. When it came down to it, there was no way they were going to contact the police, or even fire me. The publicity would have been awful for them. I'm happy to work off-site until the silly jealousy settles down. I don't know why the junior designers hate me so much, but they do."

"Helen fixed it?"

"I suppose so." She sat down opposite the portrait of Jewel Pederson, and gazed at it thoughtfully. "I said ages ago that Helen was my fairy godmother, just because I was born the same day, in the same place, during the same storm as Jewel."

Then her eyes shifted, so she looked directly at Jerry. "There was someone in the airport who looked familiar. He must have been on the same flight."

"Probably someone whose picture you saw on television or in a magazine," Jerry said, and she laughed.

"Of course. Why didn't I think of that? Kate didn't notice."

Kate, who had been frowning at the portrait instead of listening, said, "Where are we sailing? And why, may I ask?"

"Away from nosy journalists," Jerry said. But there was something that was puzzling him. "I know it's a great idea for Maggie to have seafaring holiday while the silly business at Bellissimo dies down. But you?"

"So you wish I had not come?"

"Don't be ridiculous."

She laughed, but then sobered. "It's odd. I would have stayed back to be handy for the publishers, but Helen made me come."

"What? Why?"

"While Helen was talking to the Bellissimo people, something arrived that upset her."

"A letter?"

"An email, on her phone. I think it was from a lawyer . . . though I can't be sure about that. It was about someone or something that was really vague but also worrying. I had a weird feeling it was about me, because Helen kept on glancing my way. She frowned a lot, and muttered to herself, but I couldn't hear what she was saying. When the idea of Maggie flying to Manila came up, she said that I should come with her, that it would be good for her to have the company."

Understandable, Jerry thought, as Maggie had been in such a state at the time. He said, "So what happened after Helen read the email?"

"She bought a seat on the first flight to Mexico City, then

booked a cab, which came right away. She had her suitcase with her, as we had just arrived from Pasadena, but she just shoved some things out of it into a shoulder bag. So I guess she expects to be back soon. But as she rushed off she was really insistent that I should come to Manila, and said she would join us after she had sorted it all out. But," she finished in a murmur, and shook her head.

"But?"

"Whatever was in that letter, it troubled her. You could see she was shocked."

They were interrupted by a tap on the door. A darkhaired man walked in, looked around, and then focused admiringly on the girls. He was about Skye's age, as lean, tall and broad-shouldered, but with a lot more film star quality. The tropical white uniform he wore with conscious flair was perfectly ironed and creased in all the right places, and the black epaulettes on his shoulders were proudly embellished with three broad gold bars and a gold fouled anchor.

"*Primo Ufficiale* Marani," said Jerry, with a half-hidden grin. "Our chief officer, who is undoubtedly delighted to be acquainted with Kate Giacomo and Maggie Bacchante."

"Charmed, very, very charmed, infinitely so and indeed," Marani said in cutely accented English. The smile was melting as he gazed first into Maggie's eyes and then into Kate's, clasping their hands in his. "Call me Carlo," he invited.

For a moment, it looked as if Kate and Maggie would dissolve into giggles, but they managed to greet Carlo in Italian, which sweetened his seductive smile even further. Then Marani came back to earth, saying, "I regret to say that you are on the crew list."

"We are crew?" Maggie was innocently wide-eyed. "You mean we have jobs?"

"No, of course not." Call-me-Carlo laughed indulgently. "You are all supernumeraries."

"Is that a problem?"

"*Ovviamente no!* But you and Signorina Giacomo must complete the induction before twenty-four hours."

"Induction? What is that?" Bad girl, thought Jerry with hidden laughter; she was flirting outrageously.

"Safety measures, Signorina Bacchante," said Marani. "You have to be shown how to put on and wear the life vests, how to operate the fire extinguishers, and the correct behavior in emergencies. This is including the opening and closing of the fire doors, which needs some physical power, but I will be at the ready to assist you. It is a regulation, you understand, which must be completed by every member of the crew every thirty days. As the regular crew of *Storm Swept* completed an induction the day we left Singapore, it is only necessary for you and the four men from the design studio of Manila, with, of course, the designer. And," he added, "Signor Giacomo too."

"Why not Skye? And what about Harold? Didn't he want to see us?"

Skye shook his head. "Harold and I went through our own induction coming out of Singapore. Obviously, something came up and he is busy. When he gets here, I will explain why you're not waiting." He winked as he waved them away. "Enjoy yourselves, girls."

First Officer Marani took them down to the engine control room, where one of the Scottish engineers took over. As Jerry noticed, this one managed to be much more charming than his senior. After listening, watching, and admiring his detailed demonstration of how to lock the bulletproof doors to both the engine control room and the pit where the engines grumbled, the girls followed Marani along the lower deck to the marina. Here was a different kind of door, which worked, if necessary, with a hand pump, as well as a motor. That, explained Carlo, was in case the electricity failed. It took some strength, but Carlo, as promised, lent his shoulder to both Kate and Maggie, who accepted his help with exaggerated modesty.

Also in the group was Carlos del Rosario, the elegant young designer. Though del Rosario was just his surname, he insisted on being called Del. Dark and willowy, and unusually tall for a Filipino, he was spectacular in his dress, with baggy calico pants and a loose yellow blouse under an embroidered brocade vest.

"Just like the sultans used to wear," said Maggie with professional interest. As a modern statement, he also wore a panama hat with a bright feather stuck in the band. As Maggie confided to Kate, she couldn't help but approve of that feather. A dashing touch, which she admired – as a fellow designer, of course.

"That was definitely more fun than I expected," she said to Skye when they got back to the owner's suite. "I worked the hand pumps for the fire doors, and was almost allowed to push an alarm button. Call-me-Carlo was most helpful, and definitely cute. And so was Del. It wasn't nearly as boring as I expected."

"My turn comes tomorrow," Jerry murmured, coming along behind. "And this time I hope you behave yourself, girls."

Eight

The lecture was staged in the theater at the bow end of the promenade deck. Here, in more normal times, guests were entertained with music, dance, and lectures. The lounges were upholstered in claret-coloured velvet, and each had a little table. It was easy to imagine the men in tuxedos and the women in expensive long dresses who normally relaxed there, but now, as Maggie looked around, it seemed rather odd.

Every crew member who was not on essential duty was there, plus del Rosario and his men from the Manila design studio. The deckhands were wearing greasy jeans and t-shirts, and the stewards were in casual clothes, instead of uniform. The crew shifted about restlessly, chatting quietly to each other while they waited, as if they were uncomfortably aware of their contrast to the usual audience. Apart from the engineers and chefs, they were all Filipino.

Harold took the podium first, in order to announce that *Storm Swept* was on the way to the northern coast of Borneo, the site of the attempted hijacking. Then he introduced Jerry in glowing terms as the cruise line's trouble-shooter and security expert.

Jerry, looking cynical, took over. First, he described the attempt to board the ship, and then he related how the pirates were foiled by the actions of the passengers. "Going back to northern Borneo was suggested by me," he went on, "because I want to scout the territory and size up the threat. In a nutshell, I don't think the pirate attempt was a casual one. Instead, the evidence suggests that it was yet another attack by Abu Sayyaf militants."

Maggie, sitting at the back with Kate and Skye, had never heard of Abu Sayyaf before. The Filipino audience, however, came to full alert. She saw the deckhands and stewards look at each other with eyebrows high, and there was a definite sense of alarm. The installers from the design studio looked grim, as if they wished they had not come along on this jaunt.

"I see that the name is a familiar to many of you." Jerry flicked a switch, and a map of northern Borneo appeared on the screen behind him. "For the uninitiated, Abu Sayyaf is a Jihadist group operating out of the southwestern Philippines that is allied to al-Qaeda. Daesh, in other words."

There was a murmur from the back. "Daesh? What is that?"

Maggie looked around. It was one of the engineers. Jerry seemed surprised. "It's a Jihadist group, but you may know it under different names. Americans refer to it as ISIL. They call themselves Islamic State, but most of Islam would not recognize them as such. Instead they refer to them as '*al-Dawlal-Islamiya fil Iraq wa al-Sham*' — meaning 'trample underfoot.' The Islamic State hate it, and so many Western journalists enjoy using the term, though they shorten it to Daesh."

There was a small ripple of laughter, while several heads nodded.

"Abu Sayyaf, the local arm of Daesh, are not Filipino," Jerry went on, "though most of their victims are Filipino. Their base in the Philippines is favorable to them because it is so handy to northeastern Borneo, where they are intent on establishing an outpost."

There was a comment in Tagalog from the body of the

auditorium, and Jerry nodded. "Yes, I know that Borneo is largely Malaysian, and Malaysia is largely Muslim. In the state of Sabah, where Daesh aims to set up a control center, Islam is the official religion, though other religions are freely recognized. Personally, I have nothing against Islam. I have worked for many years with Muslim people in the Arab states, and have nothing but respect for most of the ordinary citizens there. And the Malaysian authorities, no matter what the religion, feel the same as I do about Abu Sayyaf. They have a zero tolerance of their methods of kidnapping and ransom. I should add, also, that there are far-right fundamentalist Christian churches in the Americas that are funded by the same kind of gang warfare. Evil is not confined to just one religion."

The scene on the screen was now a group of men with guns, a cluster of Filipino hostages sitting crouched at their feet. None of the gunmen wore a mask, though a few had headbands. Some were in jeans and shirts, while others were barechested, their hips wrapped in sarongs. They were all grinning, while the captives looked miserable.

"Basically," Jerry went on, "they are thugs hyped up with crack and methamphetamine. While they claim to be Jihadists, and treat their hostages with the same cruelty, including filmed beheadings, religion means little to them. They are gangsters, pure and simple. A number of prominent Muslim leaders have condemned them for bringing infamy onto Islam."

The image on the screen shifted to the picture of a round-faced, olive-skinned man with plaintive eyebrows and a narrow beard, who was wearing a white skullcap and was dressed in a long white *dish dash* gown. "This," said Jerry, "is Mohammed Jamal Khalifa, at one time head in the Philippines of a so-called charity, the International Islamic Relief Organisation. In reality, it was a funding pipeline for terrorist activities in the South China Sea. He was a Saudi national backed by al-Qaeda, and his second wife was one of Osama bin Laden's sisters. Which means," he added with emphasis, "that he was bin Laden's brother-in-law."

There was a patter of comment from the audience, and Jerry nodded. "You are right. Of course there was an agenda. Over his eight years in the Philippines, his charities funneled many hundreds of thousands of dollars to terrorist cells, along with manuals for bomb-making. Then, at the age of forty-nine, he was murdered, perhaps by special forces from some Western power. And that kind of funding dried up."

A few muted cheers, and he grinned. The image on the screen changed back to the map of Borneo, though this time the word PIRATES in large red lettering was imposed over the coastline.

"But Daesh are always resourceful, even after the loss of the local leader, along with his financing. As is traditional in this area, the Abu Sayyaf turned to the sea. Now, they specialize in seizing passengers for ransom – journalists, in particular – and seamen for recruits. Many captives have been beheaded, while others have been ransomed. And it hasn't just happened to ships like this one. Fishing trawlers, small freighters, and cruising yachts have all been attacked, some of them successfully."

Another slide, this one of a ship on fire. "They do not believe in suicide bombing, as they consider it cowardly, so would-be martyrs have been infiltrated from the Middle East. They have also planted bombs in hotels and cathedrals, but their most notorious feat was the bombing of a ferry in Manila, where over a hundred passengers were killed, including a number of children. It was a ship about the size of this one."

Having made his point, Jerry turned to the program for

making *Storm Swept* look as invincible as possible, and then the tests that would follow. "It is imperative," he stressed, "that we turn *Storm Swept* from an easy target into a hard one, and my job is to show you how to do it. And if you pass the tests, it will add to your qualifications."

He then introduced del Rosario, who took over with descriptions of the wrought iron fittings. Maggie studied him with professional interest. Today, he was clad in purple leggings with sneakers, and a very loose knee-length Indian-style tunic in bright patterns that were outlined in gilt. He was again wearing his hat, and again she approved of the feather. He smiled often, and looked winningly at Harold Pederson as he stressed that, as the designer, he had the appearance of the ship in mind as well as its safety.

"Not one of our seafarers should be in danger, and my task is to make sure of that," he said, and then repeated it in Tagalog, for the benefit of the Filipino audience. "But," he added, "still I must make the ship look beautiful."

Pederson took the stand again, to talk about the necessity for the grilles to be kept in place, except for cleaning the windows.

"There will be many guests who forget to replace the sliding grilles over their balcony or verandah doors when they head off for dinner or cocktails or a show," he said. "So it is up to the room stewards to make sure that the grilles are drawn across and locked. If the glass doors are left exposed, that is an invitation for pirates. And, as Mr. Giacomo has demonstrated, what would happen after they boarded the ship would not be nice. And," he added in ominous tones, "anyone who fails to complete and pass the computer courses in security and crowd control will no longer be employed by Pederson Cruises."

The image on the screen became a timetable, copies of which

would be posted in the crew quarters. The entire audience nodded cooperatively as the ship's owner glowered down at them, and the presentation came to a close.

Nine

Helen Pederson looked about the crowded waiting room of the clinic. There were several patients in wheelchairs, some with walking frames, the rest with canes, all bowed down with pain. She felt guilty about being straight and healthy, and tried to be as insignificant as possible, sitting huddled about herself on a chair in a corner. It was a hot, dusty room, but she felt cold, still chilled by the shock of Pierce's reaction when he had seen the picture of Jewel.

She had not been able to ask any questions, as a woman had come in during Pierce's outburst, and had looked around suspiciously. Her name was Maria, and she was Pierce's housekeeper and carer. A woman in late middle age, she had heavy brows, and an intimidating presence. Though she spoke only Spanish, and Helen could not understand a word, she had made it obvious that she was very possessive where Señor Brooke was concerned, and blamed his visitor for the distressed state he was in.

Helen had been summarily shown the door. She hadn't blamed Maria, as Pierce had looked truly awful, but it had left her in a difficult position. If it had been possible she would have left the village, but there was no bus. She was stranded. As far as she could tell there was no cellphone service, so she couldn't phone Harold or Skye or Jerry to ask for help. Obviously, she was stuck here for the night, and what on earth was likely to happen in the morning? She felt out of control, and wasn't used to that.

Somehow, she had found her way to a lodging house, along the street from Pierce's cottage and opposite the clinic. The room had been primitive, but clean and colorful, but though the bed was unexpectedly comfortable, she had not slept much at all in the night, despite her exhaustion.

There were far too many questions revolving in her brain.

The picture of Jewel wasn't a photograph, but a small print of the full-length portrait she had commissioned when her daughter was sixteen. Helen had loved the painting, but Jewel had hated it. It was impossible not to remember the tantrum, and how the artist had cowered under Jewel's shrieked attack, just as it was impossible to know what had triggered the manic outburst. Jewel had screamed that it made her look like a common whore – which did not make sense, because the artist had captured both her breathtaking beauty, and her winsome, mischievous air. But it was all part and parcel of Jewel's mental disorder.

Harold had been there at the time, unfortunately – and most unusually, because he had grown cold and distant ever since the year that Jewel's illness was diagnosed. He had paid the artist and then taken the painting away, silent and grimfaced. Helen had never seen the painting again, though Harold did deign to tell her that he had had it hung in one of his ships. Why? It was a mystery, and he did not explain.

At least it was out of Jewel's sight, avoiding another meltdown, and Helen did have the small print that the artist had sent her. But why had it sent Pierce into a similar frenzy? At the renewed memory of his hysteria, a nervous tremor ran down her neck.

The clinic was so hot, but Helen shivered. She should have been on her way to Loreto, set to make a series of flights to Manila, but there had been a tap on her bedroom door. It was a woman dressed in a nurse's uniform, with a message from Pierce's physician. It was imperative that he see her. So now she was here, and waiting.

Why did the doctor want a meeting – and so urgently, too? Was it to tell her that Pierce was mad? That he was imagining dreadful things? His doctor might have something like a diagnosis of dementia to reveal. The psychiatrists had thought that Jewel's condition might have been inherited . . .

Helen shut her eyes, pushing the thought away, because it led inevitably to Pierce's accusation that her daughter had been conceived the night he had slammed into the apartment. She had moved into Harold's Washington mansion the very next morning, and had slept with her current husband for the very first time. A month later, two weeks after the signed papers had arrived, and she and Harold were married, she had realised she was pregnant – but to which man?

Helen shuddered, taken back to the moment when the Washington obstetrician – who also happened to be Harold's cousin, and therefore naturally jealous of a prospective heir to the Pederson fortune – confirmed her condition. He had studied her clinically, his smile chilly. "Harold will be thrilled," he'd said. Two previous marriages had been childless, and at the age of forty-eight he had given up hope.

"But let's pray the baby's eyes are blue," he had murmured. And had smiled, his own blue eyes icy with the whispers and gossip that he must have overheard.

She had stared at him with silent horror. Both she and Harold were very fair with blue eyes, and her mother had also been blonde, though her father had been darker. Pierce Brooke had brown eyes with golden lights and long black lashes – almost girlish, but his most attractive feature.

That her baby would have sherry-brown eyes had been a nightmare that had stayed with Helen throughout the pregnancy – but she had been saved in the most unexpected way. Because Harold's yacht had been overtaken by a tremendous hurricane, her baby had been born in a clinic in a remote part of New Zealand. Two other babies had been born at the same time, and the nurse who should have filled in the forms had been killed by the storm. So any one of the three infants could have belonged to any of the three mothers. All three had been screaming when she had found the three cribs, eyes wide open and little arms threshing in the air. And just one was fair, with Harold's blue eyes and her own pale skin, while the other two were dark-eyed and black-haired.

Helen had felt no doubt at all which baby was hers; she had felt so joyously confident when she claimed the tiny girl with blue, blue eyes. Even though the terrible storm was raging about the clinic, putting that baby to her breast had been one of the most wonderful moments of her life. She had nursed that child, watched over her obsessively, and had loved her without reservation, even after the diagnosis, despite the . . .

Dimly, she heard a name being called. *Mrs. Brooke?* Then she realised that the nurse was looking at her. A mistake had been made, but Helen supposed it was understandable. She stood up, and walked through the open door into the consulting room.

Dr. Dominguez was a small man with a large presence. He didn't rise when she came into the room, but looked at her from under a great thatch of white hair. He had a small beard that rimmed his chin, and small, dark eyes that nailed her from under his frown.

He was seated on the far side of a desk, and there was a chair in front of it. When he nodded, Helen pulled it out, and sat, facing him. Then he watched her in silence.

She said, "I'm sorry, but I don't speak Spanish." As Harold's hostess, she had visited many foreign cities, and had learned to speak a few words in many languages, but learning to hold a proper conversation in any of them had been pointless, because his meetings always moved on to somewhere else.

"No problem," he said. His English was almost unaccented. "I believe Pierce Brooke is your husband?"

"No, there has been a mistake. My name is Helen Pederson."

Dr. Dominguez frowned as he made a note, and she had the impression that he was deeply disappointed.

She said, "Is that why you sent the message?"

"Yes. He appears to have no family at all, so I was relieved to hear that a woman that his housekeeper claimed was his wife had finally arrived."

Helen sighed, and looked down at her hands, clasped in her lap. "I'm sorry," she said. "But I am of no use to you. I was indeed married to Pierce Brooke, but that was a long time ago. We were divorced, and I have been married to another man for over twenty years."

"But you came?"

"Yes." Now, she wondered why. The email from Pierce had been in the nature of a threat, saying something had come to his attention that would interest Harold Pederson greatly, and that it would be most advisable for Helen to come and find out about it first. But it had turned out to be a pointless attempt at blackmail, just because a photograph of his mother greatly resembled Kate Giacomo. She had come all this way for nothing.

But why had Pierce reacted like that when she showed him the picture of Jewel? Helen's mind jerked away.

"I am glad you did," the doctor said. He was looking down at a folder of notes. "Because I need a family member – or someone like you – to take responsibility for this poor man."

"Responsibility?" Helen tensed.

"Yes. He is soon to die."

"Well, I am sorry about that, but what is it to do with me?"

"He has liver cancer, and maybe a month or just two to live."

She thought of the tequila bottle, and his paunch and blotched cheeks, and was not surprised.

Again, she said, "I am sorry. But what can I do?"

"He needs family for that little. He tells me he has a daughter. Can you deny him a last meeting with her?"

She stared, and had to bite down a small hysterical laugh. "I should be in Manila," she said. "My husband – my husband for more than two decades – owns a ship, and he wants me to come and join him. There is some kind of emergency."

"I can supply the medications, which is all he needs now, but please keep him with you."

Helen was silent. It was such a ridiculous request that she had trouble not shaking her head. Dear God, she thought, and stood up and slung her bag over her shoulder.

"I can't," she said. "I am so sorry, Dr. Dominguez, but it just isn't possible."

"But his daughter?"

"His daughter," she said coldly, "is just a figment of his imagination."

Ten

The training exercise started amusingly enough. Jerry's first instruction was for the crew to search each other and the ship. When his audience of deckhands and stewards laughed, he grinned tolerantly.

"I do have my reasons," he said. "Just pretend that you are the nosiest customs officers on this planet, and that the ship is full of guests who might not be behaving themselves. So what do you look for?"

"Drugs."

"Of course."

"Guns."

"Most definitely."

Silence, as the hands pondered. One said, "Tobacco?"

"Only in suspiciously large quantities. And the same goes for currency."

"Do we check laptops?"

Jerry hesitated. In many countries it was illegal, and he could be prompting them to break the law. Finally he prevaricated, saying, "But what would you be looking for?"

"Pornography, gambling, Jihadist sites."

Jihadist sites. That was not a bad idea at all, Jerry thought, and wondered if it would be a good idea to have the internet monitored on board Pederson ships. But maybe that would be illegal, too, so he shook his head. When they got back to Manila, he would check it out.

"Nope, not sure we are allowed that," he said. Then he sent them off, after instructing the room stewards to wait outside the cabins they normally tended once the search was finished.

Maggie and Kate were both watching, their expressions highly interested. "That last man was thinking of yesterday's lecture," said Maggie when the three were alone.

"I know," said Jerry.

"Did you really need to scare the daylights out of them?"

"Yep."

"Well, you gave *me* nightmares, and Del said he couldn't sleep, either."

"That man phoned again," said Kate, who hadn't been listening. "I thought it wasn't possible to get cellphone calls at sea, but he managed it somehow."

Jerry looked at her sharply. "Waters?"

"Yes. *That* man."

"Did he mention Blackwell again?"

"Yes! That *other* man. The one Waters reckons wants to talk with me – and this time he told me why. Blackwell wants to know where Debbie Parkin is now."

Jerry went very still. "What did you tell him?"

"Nothing."

"Good."

"What do you think he is after?"

"He's fishing for another story, and I don't want you to talk to him any more. I mean that, Kate. Block his number, if you like."

Both girls looked shocked.

Maggie said, "You make him sound dangerous."

"He made me angry during the interview," Kate said,

frowning. "But he didn't come across as threatening."

"It's not him I'm worried about."

"You think *Blackwell* is dangerous?"

"I will make up my mind about that if and when I find out why he's asking about Kelly – Debbie Parkin," Jerry grimly said, and they silenced as Harold Pederson came into the theater.

The small blue eyes studied them, as bright as a bird's. Then he demanded, "What the devil have you got the crew doing?"

"Searching the ship for guns and drugs. It's the first part of the exercise, something that they will need to do before every cruise, and before every arrival at port." Jerry ruminated again about searching laptop drives, but decided not to mention it. Not yet, anyway.

Harold nodded. "Yesterday's presentation went very well, I thought."

"Thank you," Jerry said, assuming it was a compliment. "Which reminds me," he said, and handed an envelope to Harold Pederson.

It contained an invoice for a significant amount of money, and a letter he had composed over the previous week — just to make sure that Pederson made good on his promise to pay him well.

"*Dear Mr. Pederson,*" it began. "*Re: your contract to estimate the vulnerability of* Storm Swept. *I have examined your ship, the engine rooms, the holds, the marina, the entertainment areas and the guest accommodations. And I must say that I am impressed by the measures you have taken to make them safe for the passengers you carry. However, when pirate incursion is considered, there are a few issues that I noted, and which need fixing.*"

After that, he outlined the problems with the glass doors, and the large area of glass on the promenade desk. Then he described his recommendations, such as the training of the crew, and the supply of mentored computer courses, accompanied by a series of lectures.

High-power fire hoses were strongly advised, along with specialized audio equipment that emitted focused noises so painful that it would stop invaders in their tracks, with plans of where they should be placed. Night vision equipment was also recommended, along with laser guns, camera-bearing drones, security screens, and door access control

Then, as usual, he added the warning that the letter should be kept in a safe place, and certainly not copied, as it would give ammunition to anyone who planned to invade the ship. "*And, according to your information, the same inspection should apply to the other vessels of your luxury small ship line. As always, I assure you that I am at your service for any security issues that might arise,*" it ended.

The envelope, when he handed it to Harold Pederson, was sealed, but the world-weary look the shipping magnate cast indicated that Pederson knew very well what kind of message it contained.

Jerry grinned, and stood up. "Room stewards next," he said.

He started with the verandah suites, where the more well-heeled spent their seaborne vacations. As instructed, the room stewards for this deck were standing in the corridor, each pair in front of one of the four cabins they butlered. Jerry had a list, which he checked, looking from one alert brown face to another. Again, he noted that all of them were men. It must be Pederson policy not to employ women on the discovery ships, he thought.

He said, "How did the search go?"

They grinned. He knew them all, as they also looked after the owner's suite, and the three owner's guest cabins, upstairs and aft of the bridge. One of them could be a traitor, but he didn't want to think about that. Not yet.

The one called Lester looked at Ryan, and said, "Too much tobacco, too many cigarettes in his room."

"Bad for the health," Jerry said, and shook his head in mock severity. Lester was joking, of course. Pederson allowed no smoking on board at all, definitely not in the crew quarters. And the steward's intelligent eyes were dancing.

Getting down to business, Jerry checked the grilles covering the sliding glass doors to the verandas, finding them secured and locked. Nodding with satisfaction, he returned to the corridor, and proceeded to put a small, scarcely noticeable sticker on four of the doors.

"These," he said, "are the citadels for the guests. Do you know what I mean by *citadel*?"

They looked at each other, and then shook their heads.

"On a ship, it is a refuge in a crisis. Hopefully, we won't need them. If we see likely skiffs approaching, we will sound the alarm. Your job is to assemble all the guests who have cabins on this deck, and keep them in this corridor. Tell them to sit on the floor, against the inner wall. Then make sure that all the grilles are pulled shut and locked, and that all these inside doors are locked. That should be enough, but if the worst happens, and the pirates get on board, you usher the guests to the marked rooms. Issue them with life vests, make sure that all doors are locked from the inside, and stay in the cabin with them. Talk calmly and reassuringly, but make sure none of them try to get out. If the pirates start trying to break down the door to the corridor, usher the guests into the bathroom, and lock that door, too."

Then he went over it again in Tagalog, just in case some of the English had been hard to understand. Questions followed, which they readily answered, proving to Jerry's satisfaction that they had understood the instructions, and would hopefully remember them, too.

"Any questions?" he said when he finished.

Lester nodded. "What about the engineers and officers?"

"They have their own citadel in the engine control room."

"What about the bridge? Wouldn't that be the pirates' first objective?"

"You are absolutely right, but if the bridge is compromised the management of the ship is then taken over by the men in the engine control room."

"What if they threaten to behead the captain — or whoever else they capture?"

"It will then be a matter of hostage negotiation."

Jerry's tone was confident, which seemed to reassure them, because they all nodded. Inwardly, however, he was wincing. Hostage negotiation had been one of his tasks when he was in army intelligence.

And the results had been very mixed indeed.

After reminding the veranda suite stewards that they would be tested on this, Jerry moved on to the balcony staterooms, one deck below, where he went through the same process with the room stewards there — who, again, were all men. Meantime, the deckhands had assembled on the promenade deck, where Del's team were checking the window screens.

Marani joined them, along with the Filipino bosun, and Jerry consulted his list, while they all watched attentively. Beyond the rail the sea shimmered under the late morning sun, the breeze lacing the tops of limpid wavelets. It was a very calm day, so that only the breeze and the motion of the ship stirred the air. The water under the ship was perfectly clear, taking on all shades of green and blue about their long wake. The misty horizon was empty.

"Okay," Jerry said at last, and looked up at the attentive faces. "The first part of the job is to make the ship look a hard target. That is why screens have been installed behind all the glass areas. It is also important that you guys look tough propositions. Not that you aren't already," he added, to laughter. "But if we are transiting a high risk area — like the northern coast of Borneo, where we are headed — you will be issued with Kevlar vests and helmets, which are to be worn by those on deck duties. I know they will be hot and uncomfortable when carrying out your normal tasks, but it is important that you look ready for trouble."

They all nodded. He scanned them briefly, noting that they were muscular enough to be impressive from a distance, even when not wearing body armor. Keeping a ship like *Storm Swept* clean and well maintained demanded both strength and stamina, and these men had been doing it for years.

"Then, if they do decide on pursuit, there are things we can do to prevent them coming alongside. Obviously, abrupt changes in course and speed can be managed by whoever is on the bridge." He looked at the first officer, Marani, who nodded in enthusiastic agreement. Hopefully, Jerry mused, Marani was more efficient than his gaudy appearance suggested, and would pass this on to the captain and any others who were likely to be on watch on the bridge.

"There is much that can be done on deck, too. Lines can be trailed out into the water, where they are likely to tangle with outboard motor propellors. But, if the pirate skiffs manage to get alongside, there are other recourses, such as fire hoses and sirens that are aimed directly at the intruders. Laser beams, to dazzle them as they try to come over the gangway, are becoming popular, too. We also have night vision glasses, so you can see skiffs arriving close in the dark."

The pensioners' response — simply throwing deck furniture at the skiff — had been unexpectedly successful, so Jerry mentioned it, though with a wry smile. "Pouring a heavy soap solution onto the deck is another good recourse, as it makes secure footing impossible. But it is slippery for you as well, so care has to be taken."

And then, with a flourish, he produced his *pièce de résistance* — four small drones, triggering huge enthusiasm in his audience. Everyone clamored to have a go at operating the buzzing gadgets, and there was a great deal of comment and laughter. Which meant that it was not a good moment for the owner of the ship to make an appearance.

The bristling of the hedge-like brows reminded Jerry that this was supposed to be a serious business. His audience silenced, and Jerry continued, saying, "The modern recommendation is to have small-target radar, the pirate skiffs being such small craft that they can sneak under the ship's counter. However, the cameras carried by the drones can keep a better watch on the water close by. They can also be used to zoom back and forth over and around the skiffs, buzzing the pirates and distracting and confusing them, which gives them a double purpose."

Another babel of comment, but this time Harold looked approving. Jerry had had no trouble talking the tycoon into buying the toys, though he'd had to persuade him that armed drones were not a good idea. Probably, Harold would not be able to resist trying out them himself.

When they had silenced, he said, "Citadel."

Puzzled looks. "If the pirates evade all the foregoing, and manage to board the ship, the crew all need a panic room —

somewhere to hunker down so the pirates can't get at them. The engineers and off-duty petty officers will use the engine control room as their citadel, and will be able to control the ship from there. The room stewards have been allotted staterooms where they will usher the guests, and stay with them. The table stewards and chefs will have to select a room near the galley that can be locked, and does not have a vulnerable porthole."

He paused, looking from one attentive face to another. "Deckhands, being the force confronting the pirates, will be exposed to danger longer. However, you should have to have a plan of retreat, and a secure place to hunker down. Today, I want you all to think about it, and write down suggestions, which you will hand to me in the morning.

"And that," he said with a smile, "is it. Tomorrow, I will be giving five of you the chance to pretend to be pirates. You will take out one of the ship's tenders, and pretend that it is a skiff. And the rest of us will do our utmost to destroy you."

Eleven

Helen walked to the spot where she had come off the bus, and then turned left, heading for the beach. It was late, near sundown, and it was dim and blessedly cool. Dusty palms rustled alongside her shoulder, stirred by a faint breeze.

The bus had come this way after she had left it — but not very far, she saw. She had arrived at a paved circle, where the bus evidently turned to go back to town. It was also the end of the paved road. After that, there was nothing but hard black sand.

She kept on walking, and then stopped, facing the sea. A curve of low black hills enfolded the big bay, with the lighted fish factory at the far end. The water was calm, and very dark, with a mirrorlike surface. There was no surf at all. The evening air smelled ammoniac, as if the fish guts that were dumped from the factory washed ashore here. She saw ripples a few yards out, as if some kind of life was moving just beneath the water. This was a whale-watching place, she remembered, where the gray whales came to give birth. Right now, the ripples were probably sharks.

She shivered, then took out her phone. As hoped, there was reception here, perhaps because of the factory. The mobile was her only link to the outside world, as she had not been allowed to bring a satellite phone into Mexico — because of the drug trade, she had been told. Back at the lodging house there was no signal, and her tablet had not been able to get online at all.

When she dialed Harold's private number, the line was dead, just the way it had been for the last few days. Harold was probably at sea, out of reach. He had mentioned it the last time she had talked to him, when she had been able to talk to him from the hotel in Loreto. The ship was going to sea for exercises, or so Harold said. Jerry was on board, and was going to coach the crew in safety measures. And, because of the laws of some of the countries where they were sailing, he wasn't carrying a sat-phone, either.

She waited, staring out to sea, where there were lights in the distant mists. Fishing vessels, she supposed. When she tried again there was a hum on the line, but received only the chance of leaving voice mail. She simply said, "Harold, I love you and I miss you, and I really, really need to talk to you. I will keep on trying, though the reception is awful here. When you are close enough to land to get a decent signal, phone me, please. If I can't answer, please, please leave a message."

Then she put the phone back in the side pocket of her pants. She had no idea of the time over there, and thought it might be the small hours of the night. Here it was evening, and the sun was about to set, so it was time to get back to the village. She walked back across the darkening sand to the end of the road, where, to her surprise, she found a small group of men.

They were dressed in clean jeans and t-shirts, and all except one were young. When they hailed her, she produced the only sentence in Spanish that she knew, one that she had been using a lot lately: *"Yo no hablo Español, lo sento."*

The older man said, "That is no problem, madam." His English was fluent, with an Australian accent. "I worked in Darwin for four years," he explained.

"Nice," she said, though she had never been to Darwin. "I was born in New Zealand," she added, but was not sure why she had told him that, as it was over twenty years since she'd last been back.

"I once visited New Zealand," he said. "Good fishing. I would like to work there, but it was not possible."

She supposed there were strict rules. "So where do you work now?"

He shrugged, and said something in Spanish to the others, who was gazing at her raptly, as if the sight of a middle-aged blonde was a big novelty round here. Then he said, "We all work at the factory. During the summer."

"And in the winter?"

"That is when the whale-watching happens, and we work on the tourist boats. It's much better money, so we wish the whale-watching boats were here all the time."

She considered him. He had the usual bushy moustache, which curled round his mouth. It was black, though his hair was gray. He, like the others, looked fit. None of them looked poor, so the tourist season was very good money, she thought, or else the factory paid them enough to live decently through the summer.

Driven by curiosity, she said, "How do the tourists get here?" It was a puzzle, because the only way she had been able to get to this primitive little village had been by that bus.

"Many drive in the motor homes, you know. But it is a long way from anywhere. Most come by boat."

"By cruise ship?"

"Not big ships, as the bay is too shallow." His expression was indulgent — because she was just an ignorant woman, she supposed, though he was certainly not being offensive. "But there are many small operations sailing from further along the coast. Those are the boats we work on — and also the rubber boats for viewing the whales. We are good seamen who do not gut fish all the time."

The same kind of wildlife-watching operation that Harold ran with his discovery ships, Helen supposed. She tried to imagine the bay with crowds of tourist boats clustered about the whales, and motor homes lined up along the shore. It was impossible. The whales, she thought, must get very irritated, even if the local people liked the invasion.

"So why are you here, at the end of the road?"

The older man translated what she had said, and they all laughed. "We wait for the bus," he said. "And go into town. It is our time off, you understand."

Helen hadn't known that there was a bus in the evening, as she had arrived on the morning bus, and had assumed that it was the only one scheduled. But, sure enough, the bus ground into sight in the distance. It was the same bus, with the cracked and starred windshield that all buses seemed to have around here. If she'd had her bag with her, she would have been able to start the long journey back to Manila. Back to Harold. Away from the problem with Pierce Brooke.

She said, "Do you stay the night?"

"Yes, and then we catch the bus back in the morning."

She didn't ask what they did in town, as it was obvious. But it was a miserable existence, she thought; very boring outside of the season. She watched them clamber aboard, and felt sad for them. Maybe she could found a charity for this remote Mexican village, she thought, and wondered if the children had any chance of an education — not that she had seen any children.

Once loaded, the driver carried on to the paved circle, turned his vehicle, and came back. As the bus passed her on the way to town, the men all waved, and Helen waved back. It was no wonder they were friendly, she meditated; talking to a foreign woman in this place at this time of year was indeed a novelty. For the first time, she fully realized what a strange fate had been in store for Pierce after she had thrown him out of the Washington apartment.

It was another reason for him to be bitter, she supposed.

Twelve

Storm Swept was lying almost still, alone on the sea on a tropical late afternoon. The sky was an ethereal blue, unmarked except for the clouds that were clustered in the south. Hanging over the jungles of northern Borneo, Kate imagined; she had read that a cloud cover was often the only indication of land lying just beyond the horizon. The sea was as smooth as a slow-flowing river, heaving just a little on the surface, all shades of blue and green at the top, bottoming to indigo and purple. The afternoon had been very hot, which was why Jerry was holding live exercises in the early evening. Already, it was getting cooler.

It had been a busy day. She and Maggie had been rehearsed in what they should do if the ship was invaded. Jerry had established four citadels down in the crew quarters, on the same deck as the engine control room and as far from the bridge as possible. Evidently, the bridge was the most vulnerable part of the ship, being the logical target for pirates. Being close to the engine control room was desirable, too, as Jerry said that the whole ship could be operated from there, if necessary. The engineers had been reluctant about the idea, but had agreed that shutting down the engines, the steering, and the air conditioning was a good idea — in an emergency. And only in an emergency, the senior engineer had stressed.

Trying out the citadel that she and Maggie had been allotted had been fun. The chefs and Del, along with his four hands, had been in there, too. Maggie and Del had had their heads close together, or so Kate had noticed. She wondered if they had been quarreling, as usual. For two people with a common interest in design, they seemed to have a lot to argue about. Today, Del was wearing distressed jeans under his Indian tunic, with pink sneakers on his bare feet. And, of course, he had on his straw hat with a colorful feather.

Maggie was wearing one of the long silk shifts that she had designed herself. Was she enjoying herself? Kate certainly was, much to her surprise. She herself was just wearing shorts and a sleeveless t-shirt. It was a lot more like playacting than getting ready for an emergency. The table stewards were having great fun, too. They had rehearsed shutting and locking the grilles, while the room stewards practiced ushering guests into the allotted safe staterooms.

And now they were onto the live exercises. The climax of a very interesting day.

The ship's tenders had not been suitable to use as pirate skiffs. They were also the ship's lifeboats, so were enclosed, with roofs and windows. Now, the tenders were out on the water, buzzing around like beetles, while the four pretend pirates were in one of the rubber boats.

To Kate's amusement, the deckhands playing the part had costumed to suit, with bandannas tied around their heads, a Jolly Roger flag to wave, and toy weapons to brandish. They were threatening the ship one moment, and drawing off the next as the tenders raced close. Along the deck, four even more enthusiastic deckhands were controlling the drones, sending them zooming about the heads of the would-be attackers. Kate couldn't see how pirates could possibly get on board the ship. Even Harold was smiling. Then, just as Jerry was going to change the deckhands about so all of them could play an active part, the show was brought to a halt.

There was a radio call from the bridge to the ship's owner.

It was Captain Calamari at the other end, sounding most apologetic.

"There is a British frigate nearby and coming this way," he said. "A warship. And an army officer needs to speak with Major Jack."

"*Who?*" In his usual fashion, Harold shouted deafeningly into the radio receiver on his collar.

"I think he means Signor Giacomo, sir. And he is very urgent."

The radio call went on for a long time. The two girls and Skye were sitting at the dinner table when Jerry finally joined them. Harold wasn't there yet, so Kate said quickly, "Have the army top brass read the piece in *Balustrade Magazine*? Are you in big trouble?"

To her relief he grinned as he shook his head. "It's something else," he said, but did not go on to explain.

Skye regarded him over the rim of his glass. "Something to do with a British frigate creating a highly unusual military presence in the South China Sea?"

Jerry looked evasive for a minute, and drank wine. Then he nibbled at smoked salmon on a cracker while they all watched and waited. Finally, he said, "The Brits do have interests here, you know."

"I thought those days were over."

"They have bases in Brunei and Singapore."

"No, no, it's something more than the old colonial instinct. Come on, out with it, Jerry."

At that moment Harold arrived, looking alert. His piercing

blue stare scanned them all, one face at a time. He sat down and thanked Ryan as his glass of wine arrived, and then lifted his brows at Jerry. "So, why is a British frigate patrolling this area?"

Jerry said very reluctantly, "It's an exercise – an initiative from the Philippines. It's led by the British, but is at the request of the Philippines government. And I am not sure how much has been released to the press."

"And the reason?"

"To keep the sea route free to all. They reckon that keeping the South China Sea open is vitally important."

Harold was scowling. "Agreed. Of course, and absolutely. I have freighters as well as the discovery fleet, you know. So how is it threatened?"

"It's a matter of borders. Right now, all the countries bordering the South China Sea allow free travel in their territorial zones, which benefits your companies and all others, too. That the sea stays a major trade route is beneficial to all. But, if the sea is taken over by just one of those nations, that trade will be crippled."

"You're talking about China."

"Yep."

The word was flat.

"So how does the Chinese government plan to take over the whole sea?"

"By creating artificial islands, some of them many miles from the homeland. That part of it has been in the papers often enough. They started with barren reefs, and have raised them, and fortified them. It's like stepping stones, and so they are extending their area of control. They are asserting what they consider historical rights."

Harold snorted. "I have already heard that, over and over, and have never heard the logical argument. Just ask Captain Calamari what he thinks of global warming. A few more years, a hundred more storms, and the artificial islands will be inundated. And all their work and money will have gone down the drain."

"I am sure that is absolutely true," said Jerry. "But the Brits would say it is immaterial right now. The Chinese takeover is a current threat, not a future one, and the Philippines government is very unhappy about it. Filipino ships have been harried and shadowed by Chinese craft. This includes efforts to sink their ships by blocking them. And much radio interference. The People's Liberation Army are demonstrating military power by dropping missiles into the ocean, so Taiwan is getting nervous, too. So they presented a very good case."

"How big is this exercise?"

"It's the biggest British deployment since the Falklands affair."

Skye whistled. "Is it going to turn into a shooting war?"

"I very much doubt it. I definitely hope not. But a few ships have been rammed, and if one incident leads to fatalities . . ."

Harold sat back as their salads arrived. His expression was both shrewd and thoughtful. "All very good, Jerry," he said at last. "But what has it to do with you, me, and my ship? I'm sure they didn't just want to talk about the political situation."

Jerry grimaced, and then said, very reluctantly indeed, "They want to requisition *Storm Swept*."

"*What?*" Harold's voice was a roar, and they were all staring at Jerry in disbelief.

"You must be joking," Skye said at last.

"I am afraid that I am not. We will meet up off the coast in the morning. And then, no doubt, we will learn a lot more."

Thirteen

Pierce wasn't there when Helen arrived at his cottage, but the door was open, so she went in. The silence was warm and dusty with the remnants of the hot afternoon. Helen hadn't seen her ex-husband since his strange reaction to the picture of Jewel, so she waited.

Should she tell him what Dr Dominguez had said? That Pierce had only a short time to live, and needed family support? Probably not, as there was no way she would take responsibility for him. She had enough on her plate with the girls. Maggie's problem with Bellissimo had been easily solved with a phone call to the right person, but Kate's disappointment with the launch of her second book was more difficult to handle. And the very thought of taking Pierce to Manila was appalling. Quite, quite impossible

Without knowing she was going to do it, Helen picked up the magazine Pierce had thrust at her, and turned to the story that had triggered this strange reunion. She sat down, and turned the pages slowly, and then took out her phone, and studied the photos of Kate she had taken during the book tour. Jerry was on Harold's ship, she remembered. When she was back on the beach, she should try to phone him. Then her thoughts were interrupted when the door opened wide, and Pierce wheeled in.

He just glanced at her, as if he expected her to be there, and she wondered if he had been at the clinic. If so, she thought, he probably already knew about the doctor's crazy suggestion.

He said, "Drink?" She shook her head, and he went into the kitchen.

By the time he got back she had replaced the magazine. She sat down, and when he was facing her, she said, "Who was that escort you were going on about?"

"What?"

"The girl you thought you recognized when I showed you the picture of my daughter."

"Daughter?" He frowned, and she realized that she hadn't identified the print when she had shown it to him, as she had been so rocked by his violent reaction. Then his eyes went wide. "That blonde girl is your *daughter*?"

"Yes," she said shortly, not wanting to go into detail. "She reminded you of someone — of a very unpleasant experience. Was it one of the escorts you spent our money on when you were overseas? One of your mistresses? An affaire that went bad? Did you get her pregnant and have to pay her off?"

He stared at her, his drink raised to his mouth. Then he set the glass aside and shouted, "It was not like that, Helen! She was hurt, very hurt, but it was nothing to do with me! I would never, ever, drug a girl and torture her!"

Oh God. Over the years of being Harold's hostess, it had been impossible to avoid whispered stories about how certain powerful, out-of-control men showed off their so-called virility when they lured young women away from the boardroom. And the fact that the victim resembled Jewel made the thought of what this unknown girl might have endured even more painful.

She said quietly, "Tell me about it."

"I don't want to go there."

"Believe me, I can make a very good guess at what was happening to that poor girl. Was it in London? Paris? Moscow?"

"Geneva, if you really want to know." Pierce's expression was fraught. She didn't expect him to elaborate, but he added, "She was an English girl. From East London."

Helen's heart bumped. Kate's mother — Debbie Parkin — had come from East London, or so Jerry had told her. But why was she thinking that?

She said, "So what was she doing in Geneva?"

"They had taken her there. She thought she was going on a glamorous holiday, and had been excited about it."

"*They?* There was more than one man?"

"Two men. Blackwell was one. He had invited an old friend to join him for a party weekend, and the old friend brought the blonde with him."

"Old friend?"

"Dating back to university days. Blackwell had an apartment on the top floor of his office in Geneva. *Very* top floor. A luxury penthouse. When I say luxury I mean *luxury*. The girl must have thought she'd arrived in heaven when she stepped out of the elevator."

"Blackwell?" Helen frowned. Harold had mentioned the name quite often. "This surely wasn't the Geneva office of Pederson Strategic?"

He shook his head. "Saudi Oil. It was over twenty years ago, and there was no Pederson Strategic back then."

This wasn't as reassuring as Helen would have liked. Harold had never discussed his business with her, as she had been too taken up with the demands of raising their daughter, but she had a feeling that Pederson Strategic and Saudi Oil were closely connected.

Pierce confirmed it with his next few words. "But the two operations were linked — or were going to be, back in the day when I was involved."

"So you went to the building on business?"

"How did you guess?" he said dryly. "It was Sunday, and late, but the wheels of commerce and diplomacy never stop, as I am sure you know already. And your current husband was making unexpected demands."

This was becoming more complicated that she expected. What did Harold have to do with it?

She licked her lips and said, "So you were keeping an appointment."

"I was not." The words were sharp.

Again, she thought he had come to a stop, but then he put his empty glass to one side and looked at her again. His eyes were distant, and his face deeply creased. "I needed to discuss the latest development with Blackwell, and I had the codes to all the doors. So I was looking for him, as he wasn't answering his phone. The office levels of the building were empty, but I had the code for the elevator."

"But surely not the key to the penthouse?"

"I didn't need it. The elevator stopped in the apartment lobby, and I was going to knock until Blackwell heard me, but the door to the apartment was open. That's when I heard her."

And he shuddered.

Helen's mouth was dry. "Screaming?"

"Worse than that. A whine of pain and exhaustion and never-ending terror. So I went in, and ..." He broke off abruptly, picked up his glass, and wheeled into the kitchen, calling over his shoulder, "Are you sure you don't want a drink?"

"No," she said. She was not sure she could handle alcohol right now.

"You might need it."

"We shall see."

She waited until he was back by his little table, and then said, "What did you find?"

"I am *not* going to go into detail. Even thinking about it gives me nightmares."

"They were in the bedroom?"

"Not even that. They were in the lounge, on an expensive rug. It was a valuable Persian rug, I remember that, because at the time I had the weird thought that it was a shame that such a nice rug would have to be destroyed. It was ruined."

She thought perhaps she should have had the drink. "Blood?"

"And worse. They were treating her like a dog — only if she was a dog, the SPCA would have been called. They were doped to their eyebrows, of course."

"Cocaine?"

He shrugged. Pierce had never been a user, or even taken much alcohol, she remembered. He had taken pride in his healthy, perfectly toned body, which made his present state even sadder. So it was logical that he wouldn't know.

"It had been going on for two days, since the Friday night," he said grimly.

She shut her eyes, trying not to imagine it. "So what happened then?"

"I told you — I rescued her. It wasn't hard to shove those two sick sadists away, because they were both completely crazy, out of their minds with sex and drugs."

"You did more than shove them away, I'm sure," she said. Pierce had been fit and strong back then, and she knew what his firecracker temper was like. He would have taken out his disgust by pounding them into insensibility.

"They were going to kill her, I am sure of it. There was no way, after what they had done to her that they were going to let her go. There were other girls — other escorts … I had heard rumors of other high-class prostitutes who disappeared without trace, who were never located again."

She swallowed sickly. "And then?"

Pierce gulped down half of the drink, then set down the glass. "I wrapped her up in a blanket, grabbed her bag and her clothes, and took her to a hospital. They patched her up and monitored her as the drugs leached from her body. After they discharged her, I took her on the next plane to London, and cabbed to my apartment there. Gave her my bed. But I did not sleep with her," he said with emphasis.

"Are you sure?"

"Oh for God's sake, Helen. Do you really think so badly of me? Believe me, I did all I could for her — I arranged medical care, a nurse to come in every day. But then," he added in a snarl, "I found the divorce papers that were waiting for me, my dearest ex-wife. So I had other things on my mind. Such as getting on the first flight to Washington."

Oh God. No wonder Pierce had been insane with rage when he arrived at the apartment. So why did she feel guilty? He had always been expert at manipulating her.

Helen pressed her lips together. "So, what happened to the girl?"

To her surprise, he laughed and waved a hand.

"You know, I do not have a notion. I left her the key to my apartment, and gave her full access to everything there. There wasn't a mortgage, just the levies. I gave her money before I left, lots of money, more than enough to keep body and soul together. She might even be there, all these many years later. If she found a proper job, she could have managed in style."

"Work? What kind of proper job could she do?"

"She told me she had trained to dance, and loved it, so she might have grabbed the opportunity to become a dancer. She would have had to be really, really stupid to go back to her old way of life."

A dancer? Helen's breath caught.

She touched her lips with her tongue, and said, "What was her name?"

And Pierce told her.

Fourteen

At dawn Kate was out on the promenade deck, watching the sun leap up from the horizon in its usual tropical fashion. *Storm Swept* was now very much closer to the coast, but Borneo was still mostly unseen, veiled by a cloud bank that was broken only by the sunlit crest of a single mountain, which floated above the clouds like an ethereal body.

Just as predicted, the frigate materialized out of the west. It was much smaller than Kate expected, but nonetheless looked vastly powerful. To her surprise, too, it was beautiful, as perfect as a dart. There was a pause while its wake caught up with it, and then the warship lay perfectly still, sitting on its reflection between *Storm Swept* and Sabah.

She heard a step and looked over her shoulder to see Jerry joining her. His expression, she saw, was dour, as if he expected the worst. When she turned back to the rail the frigate was putting down a boat, which puttered briskly up to them. It was open, unlike the tenders of *Storm Swept*, so that she could see the men who were in it – six of them, with one who was obviously an officer.

He was much younger than Jerry, but as they came near she said, "Have you seen him before?"

Jerry shook his head. "Never in my life."

"What is his uniform? It doesn't look like navy gear."

"Army," he said, more grim than ever.

Oh dear, she thought, remembering *Balustrade Magazine*. "Do you outrank him?"

Jerry barked with laughter. "I left the army long ago."

"But it counts still, I'm sure. What rank is he?"

"Captain," said Jerry, but shook his head.

"So you do outrank him."

He laughed again, and shook his head.

"Does he belong to a regiment?"

Jerry shrugged. "I have never seen that badge before, either."

The bosun barked an order, and the raptly watching deckhands came to life, producing a rope ladder that was swiftly unfurled. The army officer climbed up nimbly, and strode up to Jerry without hesitation. To everyone's astonishment, he saluted. Jerry merely nodded.

The captain's shoulder badge, Kate saw, was very fancy indeed. It carried not just a fouled anchor, but also crossed swords, an eagle, and a gilt crown. There was a green beret folded neatly across his close-cropped head. It was all a bit too pretty for a soldier, she thought, and wondered what Maggie would make of it. Where was Maggie, anyway?

The uniform wearer stepped back, and shouted, "Sir! Captain Crawford, sir! Frank Crawford. Intelligence officer with the combined services on the Brunei station, and seconded to the navy for this operation, sir."

Jerry grunted, unimpressed. "What the devil are you doing here?"

"The commander wishes very much to have an interview with you, sir. On board the frigate." The added words were deliberate.

Kate winced. If Jerry went on board the warship, would he ever come back? Would he be detained to explain away his subversive comments?

Jerry was still quite unmoved. "The commander of your

operation is Commodore Hilton, right?"

"Sir."

"Well, I don't know him, and don't particularly want to get to know him, if you want the brutal truth. I have already spoken to him by radio, and feel as if that is enough. His request is impossible."

Crawford looked quite scandalized. "But he is a comrade in arms, sir."

"You must be joking."

"Despite certain recent publicity, sir, you are still highly respected by the military."

"Which means you want something from me. Personally," Jerry added on a deliberate note.

A pause, then Crawford said, "Commodore Hilton very much wishes to have the advantage of your expertise."

"What bloody expertise?"

"Your languages, sir. We believe you talk Bahasa."

"Tagalog." Jerry drawled out the *ga* . . . part of the word, so that he sounded really quite native.

"Well, just the same, sir."

"You say you are in the intelligence corps, but can't speak any of the local languages?"

"The custom now is to use local translators, sir."

"So you need *me*?" Jerry snorted. "Unbelievable."

"Nevertheless, sir. Our commander thinks your presence at his operation would be beneficial. Indeed, it could be critical."

"But I left the army thirty years ago!"

"But you are still a major, sir. It is a rank that doesn't die, sir."

"So how did the intelligence corps know I was on board? Even that bloody reporter doesn't know where I am."

"The Pederson Discovery Cruise Line posted an advertisement

naming you as their guest lecturer and head of security, sir."

Jerry muttered under his breath. Meantime, Pederson had arrived.

Jerry faced him with a scowl. "I did not expect this, and I did not ask for it."

Harold merely nodded, his own stare expressionless. He stepped forward, introduced himself, and shook the captain's hand. The handshake was typical, or so Kate thought. Pederson's hand was huge, and his strength intimidating, particularly when his age was considered.

He said, "No doubt you haven't had breakfast yet. Please let me offer you a meal."

Captain Crawford looked uncertain. "I do need to speak to you, sir, and pass on an urgent request from my commander, and I thank you for the offer, but my crew . . ."

Everyone looked down at the frigate's barge, where five men were sitting in the thwarts, and the five men looked back. They were soldiers, Kate guessed, as they were wearing tropical fatigues, and were heavily armed. They were either wearing bullet-proof vests or were extremely muscular. Probably both, she thought.

"My steward will find them some sandwiches and coffee," Harold said briefly, and led the way to the double doors that opened into the restaurant. Kate quietly followed them. Though it was early the day's humid heat was descending, and the cool air inside was a blessing.

Ryan, with the sixth sense that all Pederson stewards seemed to acquire with the job, had already set another place at the table. As he poured coffee and produced fruit juice, his expression was the usual smoothly helpful one, but it was obvious that he was highly intrigued. Kate felt no doubt that he would be listening to the conversation, and would pass it on in the crew mess.

They all sat down, with Crawford opposite Kate. They still had not been introduced, but when she smiled nicely, he smiled back. Then Skye, Maggie and Del arrived, and he smiled at them, too. Obviously, he felt that a big part of his job was being charming.

Harold was not charmed in the slightest, as he immediately made apparent. He planted his elbows on the table and barked at Crawford, "Now, tell me exactly why a Royal Navy frigate is accosting me off northern Borneo."

"We are here on exercises, sir."

"Nonsense. This is nothing to do with the exercises, the Chinese, or the Philippine government. I have already heard more than enough on that subject from my head of security. I did not ask what your frigate is doing here, I asked why you are bothering me! And for God's sake stop calling me sir!"

Crawford took a deep breath. "A freighter has been hijacked, along with a British pilot who is based in Brunei, and we want to get it back."

"Which freighter?"

"*Star*."

"Which *Star*? There are thousands of them."

"A popular name, I agree, sir – Mr Pederson, sorry. This one freights goods between Singapore and Sabah – foodstuffs, mostly. They were just off Kota Kinabalu and had taken on the pilot when they were boarded by pirates. After taking control the pirates forced the captain to sail to the estuary that lies just south of here. According to our sources, they dropped anchor a few miles up the estuary, left four of their number to hold the ship, then took the captain and crew upriver to their lair."

Harold considered, and then said, "And they are demanding a ransom?"

Crawford shrugged. "Of course."

"Of course." Pederson was quiet for a moment, frowning down at his plate as he forked scrambled egg. Then he looked up. "So what is this favor I am being asked?"

"Our frigate can't get to the freighter, because of the bar at the mouth of the estuary. It depends on the tides, but the whole of the watershed is too shallow to risk our ship. But, according to our information, *Storm Swept* often sails up the estuary so that your guests can photograph the wildlife. The pamphlet often mentions the advantages of the ship's shallow draft. Well, that's what it says in your promotional literature," the captain added. "I am quoting correctly, I think."

Pederson exploded. "You expect me to risk my ship on a crazy mission to retrieve a pilot?"

"It's not quite like that, sir."

"So what the devil do you mean – and stop calling me sir."

"If you would consent to carry a squad of men and some rubber boats up past the anchored freighter to the head of the estuary, it would be possible to paddle the boats to the pirates' lair without being detected beforehand. It all has to happen in the dark, of course. And the presence of Major Jack – Giacomo – is urgently requested, as translator. The crew of the freighter are mostly Malay, you see, and their testimony could be most valuable."

Pederson looked at Jerry. "Do you speak their language?"

Jerry paused for a long, reflective beat, but then nodded. "My Tagalog is more fluent, but I do understand Bahasa."

"Would you be willing to do this?"

A long pause, while Kate waited, breathheld

"Yes," he said

Fifteen

Skye was in the owner's suite when Jerry's phone rang. It was sitting next to the computer where he was working on some spreadsheets. It was an unusual sound, as they had been out of cellular range for some days, and it was a sound he had not missed at all. He left it three times, but at the fourth insistent ring, he finally picked it up.

He said shortly, "Jerry is unavailable right now. Please leave a message."

A woman's voice exclaimed, "Is that you, Skye?"

Skye's eyebrows shot up. "Helen?"

"Yes, it's me. Oh, thank God that I can talk to one of you at last! I can only get a signal if I am standing on the beach, and *Storm Swept* has been out of cellphone range for *ever*."

"So where are you?"

"Mexico, in Puerto San Alvaro, which must be the smelliest seaside village in the world. And so primitive! There is no internet at all, and the only cellphone signal comes from a terrible fish factory. I don't know what they do with the fish – turn it into fertilizer, perhaps, because that is how it smells. I am amazed they have electricity!"

Skye paused to think. He had a vague idea that Jerry had mentioned that Helen had gone to Mexico, but remembered no details at all. Then he wondered why Helen hadn't carried a Sat-phone. She had certainly had one on the yacht *Odyssey*. But satellite phones were illegal in many countries, and she might have had trouble getting one through customs.

Finally, he said, "If it's so awful, why are you there?"

"I had to see someone, but that's not as important as talking to Jerry. Where is he?"

Skye paused. Both Jerry and Harold had gone with Crawford to the frigate, and because of security, the captain had made them leave their mobile phones behind. He wasn't sure how much he should reveal, so said cautiously, "He is on board another ship."

"So you are not back in Manila?"

"No, we are still at sea, though close to northern Borneo."

"Oh God." She went quiet, and then said, "I have to know, and it seems you are the only one I can ask. Skye, does the name Debbie Parkin mean anything to you?"

This time, Skye replied without thinking, caught off-balance by the completely unexpected question. His talent with numbers relied a lot on his photographic memory, and the name was etched so clearly on his mind that the reply came automatically.

He said, "That was the name on Kelly's passport."

"Kate's mother's real name was Debbie Parkin?"

"Yes."

He heard her breath suck in sharply, and then she muttered, "*Oh God.*"

There was a pause, in which it was obvious she was gathering her thoughts, then Helen said, "This is awful. I really do need to talk to Jerry. When will he be back?"

"I don't know. Sometime soon, I hope. But it's complicated. He's in the middle of something important. Is this because Kelly was Jerry's girlfriend?"

He heard her swallow. "Yes."

"Which means that you have to tell us more, Helen." His words were urgent.

"It's complicated, Skye." She paused again, then said, "I'm here with my ex-husband, the man I thought was killed in a car crash. He's crippled – his back was broken in five places – and he's in a bad way. He emailed me because he had the crazy notion that he could blackmail me for the money he reckons I owe him."

Skye frowned, his mind running over past conversations with Jerry. "You mean Pierce Brooke."

"Yes." She sounded surprised. "How did you know that?"

Skye didn't answer. Instead, he said, "And what did he hope to blackmail you about?"

"I told you, it was crazy. Don't ask; it's ridiculous. It's going nowhere." Her voice was a snap.

"So why do you need to talk to Jerry about it? Obviously it is something to do with your past, so shouldn't you be talking to Harold?"

"Listen to me, Skye. It is something else entirely."

"Well, I can't help you if I don't know what's going on."

"It was what Pierce had to say about *Kelly* that's important."

Skye's breath caught. "Because your ex-husband knew Kelly?"

"Yes!"

And the signal was lost.

After five failed attempts to phone back, Skye tried to carry on with the spreadsheets, but it was impossible. His thoughts were running so fast he couldn't make sense of the data he was tracking. So he sat back, and concentrated.

Mentally, he made a big circle around the word *blackmail*, and another around Kelly's name. Everyone else believed that 'Kelly' – Debbie Parkin – was Kate's mother; it was only he and Jerry who suspected that Helen and Harold had claimed Kelly's baby by mistake. Which meant that the beautiful, dangerous girl called

Jewel Pederson was really Debbie Parkin's daughter, and one of the other two girls was Helen's. But he and Jerry were not likely to tell the world about it, as it could destroy the Pederson marriage. Was that what had been in Pierce Brooke's mind when he set out to blackmail Helen?

It had happened so long ago, yet the threat was real enough to make Helen travel to a small Mexican fishing port to see him. But now she reckoned the meeting had been a waste of time. She had been insistent that whatever threats Brooke had made were baseless. If really so, she would have been on her way to Manila by now. Instead, she was staying on in Mexico, in a village she appeared to despise – but why?

It was something to do with Kelly. Skye knew for certain that Helen had never met the dancer, though it seemed that Brooke had known the girl. But in what connection? And what did it have to do with Helen?

Pierce Brooke, he remembered, had been some kind of middle-man. Like Blackwell, he arranged meetings between politicians, financiers, highflying businessmen, sultans and princes, many leading to lucrative deals. Skye supposed it must have been a profitable job. Even if the fee had not been huge, the mediator could rake off a percentage, or even risk insider trading. But, while Brooke had been the man who originally arranged the meeting between Blackwell, Feisal and Pederson, he not featured at all in Skye's investigation of the Pederson Strategic records. No contacts, and no payments. Nothing.

He turned back to his computer, but hunting Brooke down on the internet was equally unrevealing. It was all too long ago. Exercising in the ship's gym did no good either; the hard exercise that reliably cleared Skye's mind did not work its usual magic this time. Jerry and Harold weren't back yet, and neither of their phones had rung, so he took a shower, grabbed a beer from his minibar, crossed the corridor, and tapped on the girls' door.

Kate answered. She was alone. There were marked up pages alongside her laptop, so she had been trying to work, too.

Skye settled on the small settee, and said, "Want to join me in a drink?"

"Why not? It's past lunchtime. I wonder if or when we will eat?"

There was a half-bottle of sauvignon blanc in the room refrigerator. She sat down in the desk chair, lifted her glass in a salute, and sipped.

Skye did the same. "Having a problem to concentrate?"

"Keep wondering about Jerry."

"He will be fine."

"He is seventy-two, Skye! And," she said in a lower voice, looking down at her drink, "I'm not sure what life would be like without him."

"You are thinking about all the times he left the vineyard to fight another fire?"

She shook her head, but nevertheless Skye said, "Jerry is a survivor – and smart and quick. He always came back."

"But I have a bad feeling about this one."

"Why, what do you think is going to happen?"

"He committed terrible indiscretions when we were interviewed by that awful journalist, and I worry that he will be detained for subversion."

Skye, who had read the magazine story, had trouble not laughing. "Journalists write that kind of rubbish all the time, honey. They think of it as breaking news, though I think the latest term is 'impact journalism'."

"Well," said Kate wryly, "it certainly had an impact on me."

"And it did nothing to harm your novel about firefighting."

"But," she said, and sighed instead of ending the sentence.

Skye waited, then said, "Where is Maggie?"

"Last I saw of her, she was drafting designs in the restaurant, and squabbling with Del."

He laughed. "There is certainly a spark there – a meeting of creative minds, perhaps. If she ever takes him home to meet the *famiglia* Bacchante, I hope I am there to see the expressions on their faces."

"Me too." Kate shook her head with a grin. Then she sobered, "It's so quiet."

Skye listened, and she was right. Hammers tapped as the studio hands put up the last of the grilles, and there was the occasional rumble as the engines worked to keep them in the same spot, but there were no other sounds.

She said, "What do you think will happen, Skye?"

"I wouldn't be surprised if Harold decided to go along with it. Not because of the pirate threat, but because of economics."

"Just because of *money*?"

"Well, that's Harold. He's a money man, let's face it, and the issue is a lot bigger than the rescue of one British pilot. Cooperation would seem a good idea. All his freighters sail through the South China Sea, and his cruise line depends on the freedom to carry guests about southeast Asia."

"But what difference would it make if the Chinese took over?"

Skye shrugged. "Up until now everyone has been able to send ships freely through other nations' territorial waters, just as Captain Crawford explained. By long tradition every nation has the right of free passage through the South China Sea, but if the rules change, Pederson shipping is in very big trouble. *All* non-Chinese shipping will be in big trouble."

"But can they do that?"

"History, Kate, history. China has dominated the South China Sea on and off throughout the ages, and the Chinese have long memories."

"But no other country is going to recognize past history, surely?"

"You are so right, *tesoro*."

"Surely it benefits the Chinese, too, that the sea route should be open?"

"It's more than that. The twelve-mile agreement covers just the surface of the water, and what travels upon it. There is also the two hundred-mile law, which covers what lies beneath the sea – mining and fishing. And the current estimate is that there are over ten billion barrels of oil under the South China Sea, and perhaps two hundred *trillion* cubic feet of natural gas."

"That's not very green!"

"The world needs energy, and fossil fuels will dominate for a long time yet, I'm afraid."

"Oh dear." Kate looked at her watch. "I think I hear the call to lunch," she said. "And I need the sustenance. You are straining my brain, Skye."

He laughed, and they went down to the restaurant.

It looked quite different with the decorative grilles installed over the wide expanse of windows. The wrought iron patterns cast mysterious shadows, and the light was more diffused, more intimate. Del was a good designer, Skye decided, as well as being personally flamboyant.

Mack, with marvelous seventh sense, brought glasses of wine right away, and they sipped in isolation for some moments. Then Maggie and del Rosario joined them, still arguing. There was a definite spark between them, Skye thought again, and wondered what Jerry thought about it.

Harold arrived at the table, which surprised Skye, as he had not heard the boat return.

Kate said, "Where is Jerry?"

"Still on the frigate. He will lunch there while they confer."

"But why?"

Instead of answering, Harold said, "I asked them to bring me back early. Urgent business."

Skye stared at him, wondering if Helen taken his advice and had managed to contact her husband, somehow. By radio, or the internet? Had something come up concerning the Department of Justice investigation? If so, it would definitely be urgent.

No explanation was forthcoming, however. Harold merely added,"Jerry will come back with the squad in an hour or two. And then he will accompany the force to the pirate lair, once we reach the head of the estuary."

Maggie exclaimed,"So you are going along with their plan?"

Harold spread his hands.

"Risking this lovely ship?"

They all waited, but Harold merely nodded.

Ryan arrived with their salads. There was also French bread and French cheeses, smoked salmon garnished with capers and lemon juice. Mack filled wine glasses.

There might be no menu, but the provender was very good. Skye paid little attention to what he was eating, however. He was staring at Pederson, his head tilted as he tried to work out what was going on in the man's mind. Harold was determined to keep the small talk going, though, even though the Bacchantes were watching him in suspense.

When he had eaten, he said. "When you have finished, Skye."

"In your office?"

"Where else?" And Harold strode off, having eaten almost nothing.

"Where else," echoed Skye. He grabbed up some bread and cheese, and followed.

Sixteen

The military arrived mid-afternoon. Kate had no way of telling who were sailors and who were soldiers, because they were all wearing jungle camouflage. Maggie arrived at the rail alongside her, but said not one word. Instead, she took a long, comprehensive look, then retreated to the restaurant and her sketchpad, so Kate was alone on the promenade deck when Jerry came over the gangway.

He was dressed as usual, in cut-down jeans and sweatshirt, and looked enlivened.

"Did they give you lunch?"

"They did indeed. Proper military grub, baked beans and all. We are all set for action." And then, without another word, just a big wink, he was gone.

Captain Crawford came last. Like the others in his squad, he was wearing tropical fatigues in camouflage colours. Kate darted up to him, and he stopped and looked pleased.

"Is it really necessary for Jerry to go?" She looked around to make sure Jerry wasn't listening, and then hissed, "He's very old, you know."

Hi grin widened. "We do not plan to put him in harm's way."

"Are you sure? He can be impulsive."

The captain merely laughed, and gave her a playful salute before following the rest inside. They were headed to the big reception foyer on the lower deck, where she had seen a white board set up for the briefing.

He thinks I am behaving like a mother hen, she thought resentfully, but couldn't help but remember how animated Jerry had looked as he followed the soldiers – or marines, or whatever they were – into the briefing room. As if he had suddenly dropped ten years. It was no wonder Rosita had left him, she moodily mused. It must have been awful, waiting in London for him to come back from Iraq or Afghanistan or wherever – and then, when he gave up the army, he had taken on even more dangerous work. Rosita would have been a lot happier with her family in Manila.

It was all so bloody *macho*, Kate thought, male stuff, with all that bonding and violence. Thay had no idea how remote it was from ordinary life. Good for novels, but nothing else. When she looked over the rail, rubber boats were being dragged up the ramp at the stern. They were pushed inside and stowed, and then she heard the clang as the marina door slammed shut.

Seconds later, she felt the ship shudder as the propellors gripped the sea. The water swished as they wallowed, and then *Storm Swept* straightened up on her course to the shore. The frigate also started to move, first of all getting out of the way, and then darting off with amazing rapidity, heading for the northern horizon. Within minutes it was just a dot on the sea. Why? So the pirates would not be forewarned, she supposed.

The land profile looked distant, veiled in fog, and as the minutes and then an hour trudged by, did not seem to come any closer. She gave up, and went back through the heavy wooden doors into the restaurant.

Maggie and del Rosario were leaning over a cleared table, sketchpads between them. Maggie was drawing rapidly, while Del watched her. Today, he was wearing baggy cargo pants in an indigo color, and a lime-green tank top. There were fluorescent pink trainers on his bare feet. As usual, he was wearing his feathered hat, and as usual, they were squabbling in low voices.

They quarreled a lot, Kate thought, and wandered over to see what Maggie was drawing. As always, she had started with a long upright triangle, the apex being the neck of her model, and the two slanting downward strokes the legs. She had filled in the legs first, with baggy pants like the ones del Rosario was wearing.

The difference was that they were white, and patterned like wrought iron in black. No wonder Del was objecting, Kate mused. It was outright artistic theft.

"But it's a compliment," Maggie protested. "And let's face it, you don't design clothes."

"And you should not steal the work of other designers," del Rosario growled.

"But why not? I don't work here; I work in New York, where good clothes are important."

"Why New York?" he said, still combative.

"It's only there you will find a pure distillation of modern style," she countered with a superior sniff. "The only city where you get uncomplicated urban dressing with overtones of executive aggression."

"You are not making sense," he argued, and Kate could not help but silently agree with him.

"It's the biggest city where women can take executive positions and really make a difference. So why not design a wardrobe for them?"

Del shook his head. "What kind of wardrobe?"

"Smart, but comfortable. Lots of stretch, and lots of pockets, so they are not hampered by awkward handbags. Black, or stripes, and geometric lines."

"If you're so mad on geometrics, why not triangles?"

"Why not?" said Maggie, and settled to sketching jackets with enormous triangular lapels. "Needs those stripes," she said with her head on one side, and del Rosario set to sketching, too. They made quite a team, if a bizarre one, Kate thought with amusement, and wandered back to her stateroom.

At the end of the corridor the door to the bridge was open, and she could hear Captain Calamari agitating inside, and Call-me-Carlo reassuring him. All in Italian. They would be in trouble if Harold heard them, she thought. He insisted on English being the language of his ships. Captain Calamari had never navigated the estuary before, but Carlo assured him that he had done it many times. Kate hoped he was as good as he thought he was.

It was hard to settle back to writing. Maggie seemed to find inspiration in everything; she wished it were the same for herself. An hour later, when Skye came out of Harold's suite, she was glad to see him.

He was frowning, looking harried, as if the job Harold had set him was troubling.

"I need a break," he said.

"So do I."

"And we are getting very close to land."

When they walked out onto the promenade deck it was to find that the scene was opening up. Kate could see the tops of palms, and the white fringes of beaches. Then *Storm Swept* nosed her way past two capes into the muddy estuary. The engines slowed as they approached the bar, and then with a growl of the engines and a swish of mud, the ship was over and into deeper water.

Brown water and jungle surrounded them. The sky was low, looming with cloud, and it was suddenly very humid and hot. It was very tropical, with cries of monkeys and birds coming and going, far off and then near. The air was electric with an impending storm, and Kate could feel the hairs rising on her arms.

She said to Skye, "There's grass – is it grass? All along the fringes of the water, very close cut. Or cropped. I wonder why it is kept so short?"

"Snakes, I imagine." Skye was leaning over the rail. He pointed, and she joined him in time to see an enormous crocodile slide down a stream of mud into the water. Even when it was submerged, she could see the tip of its snout, and cold bubble eyes. "They walk along the bottom," he said. "Did you know that?"

"No." She shivered, but it was fascinating. It was terribly hot, like a sauna, but she stayed by the rail. She could understand the attraction of these discovery cruises, because it was so easy to imagine passengers with fancy cameras catching these exotic surroundings.

Monkeys were running along the edge of the water, plucking up something from the mud, and darting back when menaced by unseen things. They shrieked to each other, and sat up to scratch at their rumps. There was strange howling from the trees, and she saw huge branches bounce up and down, weighted by whatever animals were jumping up and down. Orangutans? Men of the forest, or so she thought she remembered from school. Large apes with tails, native to Malaysia, now endangered. She wished one would come out of the leaves, even though she did not have a camera.

All of a sudden it was twilight. Kate saw bright birds with harsh voices flicker over the water to roost in the trees. There was an overriding smell of mud, leaves, rot, and growing things. Then the sun dived below the horizon, accompanied by a crack of thunder that made her ears ring. With equal abruptness the rain slashed down. It was like a high pressure hose, but the wrong temperature. Too warm, like a shower. The wind gusted, and some of the rain fell horizontally, slanting under the promenade roof.

"Better get inside," said Skye. The night was abruptly as dark as a grave.

Just as Kate was about to step through the glass doors, she looked back, stalled by a crack of thunder. In the flash of lightning she saw a bulky shape in the distance, dimly lit with lanterns.

"The freighter," said Skye. "The ship the pirates hijacked. They are showing riding lights, so some of the pirates must be on board."

How did he know that it was the right freighter? Because of the session with Pederson that afternoon, she supposed. Harold must have been told a lot during the conference with the men on the frigate. Was that why he had set Skye to work? Something Harold had learned – or a lot of what he had learned – had triggered a frenzy of activity. She had heard the phone ringing many times, and the quick clatter of computer keys.

But of course she could not ask, because Skye was too discreet to answer. Instead, she said, "Why would there be some pirates still on board the freighter?"

"Left as shipkeepers, in case anyone tries to retake it. And also as a forward lookout for the pirates upriver. They are bound to have cellphones, and maybe even radio, and can send a warning if they see anything threatening coming up the estuary. That's why it is such a good idea for the military to requisition *Storm Swept*, as she is a familiar sight around here. This way, they get up to the mouth of the river without raising the alarm."

"But in such weather – wouldn't it seem strange that a cruise ship is coming here?"

He laughed. "This weather happens all the time. It's just part of the territory. And this is a discovery ship, remember."

The ship kept on going past the anchored freighter, through the dark and the murk and the rain,. They bumped on another bar once, churning unseen mud with a roar from the engines. Obviously Carlo, up on the bridge, was hard at work. *Storm Swept* was a kettle of noise – the rush of the water along her sides, the thump of the engines, and the rattle of grilles being shaken by the rising gale.

Inside, there was no one in the restaurant. The four men who had come with del Rosario were in the crew mess, Kate supposed, and Maggie and the designer were in their respective staterooms, or so she hoped. Captain Calamari was maybe panicking, but Carlo should be guiding the ship.

Skye took a seat at the table that Maggie and Del had cleared, and like magic Ryan arrived with biscuits, grapes, cheeses and wine. An hour later, just as Kate was wondering whether there would be any dinner, there was a big shake, and a rumble that reverberated throughout the interior. The anchor was being lowered.

Skye said, "This is as far as we go."

"This is where they launch their rubber boats?"

"Yep."

More noises – thumps, and splashes in the water. It was still raining hard, and the wind was kicking up, but Kate went outside to look. The night was as black as before, and the raindrops dashing around the overhead lights were like golden splinters.

The ship's engines kept running, and their sound increased as *Storm Swept* was slowly brought around. A great wave rushed along the hull, and then was gone. Still the engines roared – louder, louder. It was a grinding noise, augmented by the wild water that sucked and dashed along the hull.

Skye's voice said, "They are making a lee, so the boats can be safely manned," and when she looked round, he was standing right behind her. Kate could see what he meant, as the wind flicked the top off the next wave, flattening it, and there was a smooth hollow between the ship and the wave. "Whoever is conning the bridge is a good seaman," he said.

Was it Call-me-Carlo? Amazing, she thought.

The first boat appeared from around the stern quarter, towed by a line from somewhere amidships. It lifted on a crest, and a bunch of men leapt into it from the gangway door on the lower deck. No sooner were they in the boat than it sank dizzily into a trough. Up it surged again, and three more men joined the first lot. Was Jerry with theim? She couldn't see. Then it puttered away, making room for the next boat. And all the time the rain poured down.

Two more boats followed, to vanish within instants. "It will be more sheltered when they get into the river proper," Skye's voice reassured her. "The banks there are very high, and it is overgrown with trees, in parts."

And there were crocodiles, Kate thought, and shivered.

"How long will they be?"

"Oh, we won't see them till the morning," said Skye.

Seventeen

Jerry got back to *Storm Swept* just four hours later, proving that he had not lost his talent at leading a squad in and out of battle. He was utterly drenched, smeared with mud, but feeling very pleased with himself. Not only had he acquitted himself well, but the operation had gone much more smoothly than expected. The rain had stormed throughout their raid of the pirate camp, which made it all so much easier.

There had been just seven terrorists there, which was a surprise. Had some run away? Surely not. The seven had been hunkered down when the British force had arrived, almost as if they were cowering, and Jerry had never known an enemy force give up so easily. He was amazed that the freighter captain, the British pilot, and the six surviving seamen had not made their escape, despite the rain and mud. The numbers had certainly been on their side.

So now the pirates were tied up, and their stockpile of AK-47 rifles had been seized. Pathetic, he thought now. Their camp had been a revelation, a simple bamboo hut on stilts in the jungle. Stone-age living with modern arms. Horrible people, though. Three of the freighter's crew had run off into the jungle, and so three of their shipmates had been beheaded as a punishment.

In other places and other times, no prisoners would have been taken. Instead, the seven terrorists had been brought on board *Storm Swept*, to be imprisoned in one of the cabins and kept under guard until they could be handed over to the frigate. Or so Jerry supposed.

Then, as Jerry stepped into the interior passage, he saw Skye pushing through the crowd of incoming soldiers, mouthing words. Then he was close enough to hear when he hissed, "I need to talk to you. Urgently."

His expression was definitely urgent. Jerry frowned, instantly concerned for the girls, but then spied Maggie and Kate standing in the restaurant, nearby.

"What?" he said.

Skye looked around. "In private."

"Of course." Jerry really wanted a hot shower and a drink, but Skye looked insistent, and his voice was still low.

They waited while Crawford and the remaining men pushed by, on the way to the lower deck. The captain of the freighter was with them, a resigned looking Chinese man with the six survivors of his crew trailing behind him. But just as Jerry turned to Skye, he was accosted by the British coastal pilot, who had evidently hung behind.

The Englishman was elderly, probably too old for the job, and he was grizzled and weather-beaten, too, but the determined set of his mouth spelt trouble.

"Major," he said. "Your attention, please."

Jerry said shortly, "What?"

"I need to get to the bridge."

"Why?"

"I have to talk to the captain of this ship."

"Why? If there is something to warn him about, I can pass on a message. And the first officer has sailed this estuary many times."

"The freighter has to be recaptured *now*. If we wait until

morning, the freighter will be gone. There are four pirates on board, and they have the engineers captive. It would be an easy matter for them to weigh anchor and escape."

"But why would they do that? They don't know that we have seized the pirate lair, so have no reason to do it."

"They have cellphones and radio, we saw them," the pilot argued.

Jerry had seen them, too: they had been confiscated, along with their rifles and jungle knives. He sighed and said, "Have you talked to Captain Crawford?"

"You are the senior officer, right?"

"Retired," objected Jerry, though that sounded rather odd in his own ears, as he had just led a successful exercise. "And Captain Crawford is the one who will decide whether to retake the freighter or leave it till morning." And he would have to be crazy to try it right now, Jerry thought.

"He would do it, he told me he would. He's keen to finish the job properly. So I need to see the captain of this ship."

Jerry sighed. He didn't believe that Crawford had agreed to the mad idea, not for an instant. And Captain Calamari was a nervous wreck already, so would certainly not be up to a challenge of this magnitude.

The pilot's attitude was nothing unexpected, however. The old codger was not even the captain of the freighter, let alone one of the owners, but he had all the obstinacy of the sea, where a vessel that was under his command – even temporarily so – was his territory. That the boat had been seized by pirates was a personal insult, one that he was determined to reverse.

"We shall see what the captain has to say," Jerry said. Skye was grimacing, but the pilot's obstinacy was beyond mere logic. Surely, however, he would give way in face of Captain Calamari's flat refusal, Jerry thought, so led the way up the stairs.

When he knocked on the frame of the door to the bridge, the captain and the first officer were conferring, and the helmsman was hard at work keeping the ship up to the anchors, in the teeth of the tide and the gale. There was a tiny concrete wharf, but that was just another hazard. Two deckhands had binoculars, and were scanning the murk, while *Storm Swept* surged up and down on the swells. All of them looked extremely busy.

Captain Calamari turned, but before Jerry could say a word, the pilot barged past him, and strode up with perfect confidence. Then he made his demand, while Calamari's expression became progressively more appalled.

"*Stai scherzando!*" It came out as an expletive.

"He thinks you must surely be joking," said Jerry.

Neither were listening. Captain Calamari was waving eloquent hands and vowing that it was far too dangerous for the ship to leave her anchors, but at least he had reverted to speaking English. "The rain – the gale – the constantly changing of the bars in the estuary!"

"It's clearing, Captain Calamari," the pilot said in his gruff voice.

Jerry peered through the bridge windows. It was not.

"The rain is not as heavy."

"*Nessuna differenza,*" Calamari argued, and Jerry couldn't see any difference, either.

"And the time to recapture the freighter is now — not tomorrow, but absolutely right now. Otherwise when dawn arrives the freighter will be gone."

"Why would they sail? They do not know that we approach, so why? To approach is madness, and even those brainless brigands know that."

"Naturally they are on guard, and will get away at dawn, as a precaution. It's imperative, I tell you. Why don't you listen?"

"You expect us to recapture the ship now? In the dark? In the rain? And in the gale? *È impossibile!*"

First Officer Marani was much more sanguine about it, which Jerry supposed was unsurprising. Perhaps Call-me-Carlo thought that the dramatic recapture of a pirated ship would look good on his record. Looking animated, he called out, "It is certainly clearing. I can see a light."

They all looked. It was one of the two beacons that marked the head of the estuary. As Marani went on to point out, the depth sounder showed clear bottom forward, and there were no other vessels recorded on the automatic vessel finder. It was logically possible for *Storm Swept* to blunder on into the storm.

For the first time Jerry realized that Skye was on the bridge, too, because he heard him say clearly, though quietly, "Perhaps it would be a good idea to let the owner of this ship have a part in the decision. Because it is not a small one."

"Yes, yes, *si*," cried Captain Calamari.

Harold arrived. He looked rumpled and grumpy, so evidently had managed to sleep. "What is it?"

Captain Calamari explained. With elaborate courtesy, he introduced the British pilot. Harold looked impatient, and so did the pilot.

"So?" said Harold.

"I want the *Star* recaptured," said the pilot.

"Now? Why not tomorrow?"

"Right now. There are four of the pirates on board — only four. We have enough fighting men to take her within minutes. It's just a case of coming up in the night and boarding her."

"Why should I commit my ship to something so dangerous?"

"Because I am British, sir!"

"I am American, sir."

"But don't you have an arrangement to meet up with the frigate in the morning? Do you really want to keep the soldiers and their captives on board for longer than necessary?"

That was a good point. But still Harold hesitated. His little blue eyes were very sharp as he glanced from face to face. His broad chest was thrust out, and the short sun-yellowed curls on his head were tousled. He stood akimbo, his feet apart, and his legs strongly muscled. Jerry mused that he looked a hell of a lot like his Viking ancestors.

Then he grinned, and said, "I do keep my promises. So let's go for it."

Looking animated, First Officer Carlo spoke to the engine room, and the ship trembled like a greyhound on the leash. The anchor inched up and twisted into the hawsehole, landing with a loud clang. Slowly, *Storm Swept* gathered way, heading north into the stormy night.

There was a tap on the door frame, and Ryan came in with a tray of mugs of hot chocolate. Jerry grabbed one gratefully, and the captain took a mug too, but the old pilot didn't seem to notice. In his intense preoccupation with what very little that could be seen through the bridge windows, he didn't even seem aware of his saturated condition.

"We are sailing, sir?" said Ryan to Harold Pederson, and the owner nodded.

The pilot had overheard, because he said, "And we will take the bastards, along with the ship." He was talking into empty space, however, as the steward had gone. "Port," he barked, looking forward again. "Haul the ship to port."

Against all logic, he was hugging the lefthand bank. The delta was splitting into a number of mouths, the entrance to each one marked by a huge clump of elephant grass, which passed by fleetingly in the beam of their spotlight. There was another heavy rain squall, blocking out whatever the spotlight might reveal, but just as Captain Calamari was beginning to panic the squall passed on, and Jerry could glimpse the banks on the lefthand side.

He saw more than that, as the spotlight swung from one section of the riverbank to another: breaks in the jungle, tiny villages, little rice padis created with unimaginable labor, strings of betel nut palms. An hour, he thought — just sixty minutes, and they would be up with the anchored freighter.

But then the weather closed in, and the rain swallowed up the light. The pilot and Carlo were left with the monitors for navigation, while Captain Calamari agitated at the chart desk, his fingers clutched about the edge. His mug of chocolate was forgotten, even when it fell to the deck with a slop and a crash. Jerry kept on sipping his, but he was as tense as the captain, and only vaguely aware of how wet and bedraggled he felt. And then *Storm Swept* got stuck on a bar.

Everyone on the bridge felt the thump as the bottom hit mud. The engines roared as the ship dragged mud along with water, and the angry sounds of the wash slashing the side of the hull were distinctly audible.

With another thud, the ship lifted. Jerry could only imagine what their wake would look like in daylight — yellow and brown, rather than flecked white. It was impossible to see the rush of the water, but it was a roar in the ears. Twenty minutes had gone by, but the ship was free.

Moving very slowly, though. Somewhere in the murk ahead

the anchored freighter loomed. Jerry was conscious of movement in the decks below, as the squad prepared to board the other ship. So this crazy idea had been in Crawford's head all along, he fleetingly thought. On they crept, with Marani and the old pilot barking directions. Thirty nail-biting moments later they were close — but too close. The shape of the freighter loomed up like a cliff, and Captain Calamari shouted out in alarm.

Jerry could see the hull — not just black, but red with rust, too, and he realized that the spotlight was aimed at the freighter. The pilot muttered a warning in Carlo's ear, and Jerry realized that *Storm Swept* was hemmed in by a shoal on the other side. Getting to the flank of the freighter was going to be like threading a needle.

The spotlight was too bright, dazzling them all. The pilot shouted as he called for helm hard-a-starboard, and *Storm Swept* brushed gently along the side of the other ship. With a yell for hard astern the engines growled. Water washed loudly, and *Storm Swept* stopped. The engines were still thrusting, but just to keep the ship in position.

Jerry heard the cries as the squad poured out of the open promenade deck, flung up grapnels and clambered onto the other ship. Like boarding an enemy in the old days, he thought — a pirate-like boarding of a pirate-seized ship. Then he frowned, as he heard rifle shots. Then screams. Surely the pirates had not been ready and waiting? There had been the spotlight, and the thuds as *Storm Swept* came alongside, but the Abu Sayyaf on board should have been as confused and badly led as their comrades back up the river.

The spotlight moved, to focus on the open deck of the freighter, and Jerry could see struggling shapes. One man went down under the blow of a cudgel — one of Crawford's party? He hoped not, but then saw the man heave himself to his feet again, and the brief flash of a shot. The shape that had attacked him fell down, and the shooter ran out of the beam of the light, headed for the interior of the ship. Then, shockingly, more shots rang out, but not from the freighter. They came from within *Storm Swept* — from the lower deck!

Then a lot of yelling— in Arabic, by the sound of it. Bloody hell, Jerry thought, the captured terrorists had broken free. Someone on board must have freed them while Crawford's lot were preoccupied with seizing back the freighter. Hadn't Crawford left a sufficient guard? The capture of the lair upriver had been too easy. It had made Crawford and his men over-confident.

As feet came pounding up the stairs, Jerry shoved Harold towards the door to the owner's suite, jerking his head at Skye to follow. Pederson resisted for a few seconds, but urgency pre-vailed. To Jerry's relief, Skye was close behind. He slammed the door shut, locked and bolted it, and then they all stilled, listening.

Stamping and shouting in the bridge, where the captain, the helmsman, the lookout, the first officer, and the British pilot had been left behind. The voice that echoed from the other side of the door was speaking Arabic, making a threat that was emphasized by the click of a rifle being readied.

Jerry pushed Skye and Harold towards the bathroom, then yelled in Arabic, "If you kill the pilot or the captain, there will be no ransom."

"Who are you?"

The terrorist's Arabic was halting, and strongly accented. Indonesian, Jerry thought. He said, "Major Jack," and then added in Bahasa, "There is nothing for you here. The soldiers will reassemble, and their force is much greater than yours. You should surrender while you have the chance."

The pirate laughed, and there was a series of thuds as several shots slammed into the heavy wooden door. Jerry heard movement in the passage between the four suites, and headed that way. Over his shoulder, he barked, "Lock the door behind me, and then get back to the bathroom."

Harold exclaimed, "But what about the girls?"

Jerry grimaced. If Maggie and Kate had followed the instructions given in the exercises earlier, they would have headed for their allotted citadel in the crew quarters — which meant that they would have blundered into the escaped captives.

He said, "I will find them, I swear." And opened the door to the corridor — to face the girls.

Both had their hands up, and were being herded by a grinning pirate with a rifle, evidently with the aim of adding them to the count of hostages on the bridge. Maggie was white-faced and silent, but Kate was screaming at their captor.

The bathroom door crashed open, and Harold shouted, "Kate! Oh God, Kate!"

The girls turned, and the pirate with them. Beyond, Del stepped silently out of the doorway of the girls' suite. His face was a mask of fury. He held a bottle high, and with an athletic swing he smashed the bottle down on the pirate's head. It shattered, and the terrorist collapsed in a sudden spurt of blood.

"My God," said Jerry, impressed. There was a strong smell of aged Scotch whisky.

Del looked down at the splashes of blood on his tunic, and the dark puddle that was flowing onto the floor. His face went white, and his voice shook as he said, "Is he dead?"

Jerry crouched by the crumped form. The pirate was definitely dead. When he stood, he said, "Of course not. Just knocked out.

You did well, Del. Now would you please take everyone into Harold's bathroom, and lock the door. And until the moment that you are absolutely sure that I have the situation under control, *do not come out.*"

To his relief, when Del beckoned imperatively, the girls followed him. Not a word was said. Perhaps, Jerry thought, they were shocked into obedience by the designer's unexpected resourcefulness.

He heard the click as they locked the door, then hefted the rifle the dead pirate had dropped. It was military issue, he grimly noted, expertly maintained by some British soldier, who could well be lying dead on the lower deck. Having readied it, he opened the damaged door to the bridge.

Back in the bathroom, a phone rang.

Eighteen

It was three in the afternoon, and the sun was almost directly overhead. It was terribly hot and sweaty standing on the black sand of the beach, but Helen had been summarily shown the door by that awful Maria. Logically, she should have gone back to her lodgings where at least she could lie down, or go to the one convenience store to buy a cool drink. But she was too angry and frustrated for that.

That *confounded* housekeeper seemed to be obsessed with her charge, and had become furious when she arrived to find Pierce in the bathroom, vomiting. Helen put it down to his liquor intake, as when she had left the night before he was settled with the tequila bottle, moodily drinking himself into oblivion. The stomach upheaval was just a bad hangover, she told herself, though she did remember Pierce saying that the terrible old memories gave him nightmares and made him sick.

But even though she couldn't understand a word of the tirade, it was obvious who Maria blamed. Helen herself. So Helen had flounced out, then marched down to the beach with her phone in her hand. To her relief there had been a signal, but when she dialed Harold's private number, there had been the usual message.

So where the devil was he? She tried Jerry's number with the same lack of result, and finally Skye's — and, thank God, he answered. But that was even worse, as a voice in the background said, "Sir, please turn off your phone."

And the phone went dead.

When she tried Harold's number again, his phone was turned off too. Then, to her utter frustration, the signal was lost. She tried a few more times but with no result, so she walked, head down, back to Pierce's cottage.

What the devil was happening on board that ship? It sounded as if it had been a steward who told Skye to turn off his phone, as there was an accent that she picked as Filipino. It was earlier than her usual attempts to call, so perhaps it was the wee hours of the morning — which might explain why Skye had been told to turn off the phone, as it was disturbing the guests, but somehow it made the worry worse. Was Jerry not back on Harold's ship? And why had Skye not passed on her message that she needed to talk to him urgently?

Helen's steps slowed as her thoughts revolved. Was it necessary for Jerry to hear the dreadful story about the girl that he was fond of, and had adopted as a holiday partner? She certainly wouldn't want Kate to know the horrible things that had happened to the young woman who had given birth to her.

There was also the possibility that she was mistaken, and the girl Pierce had rescued was not the same Debbie Parkin Jerry had known as 'Kelly'. Up until the last few days, Helen had had no idea of what Kelly looked like — not until Pierce had mistaken the picture of Jewel for Debbie Parkin, and Skye had identified Debbie Parkin as Kelly. Because of the name in her passport.

That implied that Kelly — Debbie Parkin — was blonde and blue-eyed, which was news to Helen. Up until then, the sum total of her knowledge was that Kelly was a dancer who had vanished the day after giving birth. The same day that Helen had given birth to her own baby, Harold had come on shore and carried them both back to the storm-battered *Odyssey*. It was safer there, because the hurricane was tearing the hospital into murderously flying fragments.

And so, though she had seen all three babies yelling their heads off in three identical cribs, she hadn't seen the two other mothers.

When Helen arrived at Pierce's cottage the front door was open, and Dr. Dominguez's nurse was there. Helen knew it was the nurse, as she recognized the voice, even though the words were in Spanish. The nurse, the carer, and the patient were all in the bedroom, so it was impossible to see what was happening, but when the nurse came out she gave Helen such a reproachful look that she immediately felt guilty. It wasn't her fault that the picture of Jewel had set off this episode, she defensively thought, but it brought home the possibility that Pierce might really be as sick as the doctor had said.

When both carer and nurse had gone, and Pierce wheeled out into the living room, she said quietly, "Is there anything you want? A cup of tea might be nice."

"The society hostess," he sneered.

She looked at him. He was white-faced and more haggard than ever. It was hard not to compare the wreck she saw now with the charismatic man of her memory. Back then, he had been tanned, fit, and vital. Black-haired and olive-skinned, with flaring black eyebrows, and those amazing eyes.

Suddenly, with strange discomfort, she realized that he could have fitted in with the Bacchantes. That he could have been Italian. Those eyes … They were still as luminous and eloquent as they had been all those years ago, dark brown, and with golden lights. Fringed with inky black lashes. So different from Mexican eyes, which she found opaque and uncommunicative. It was the penetrating stare from those eyes that had riveted her in the first place.

Shaking herself mentally, she said, "It's too early for tequila, and you need something substantial in your stomach. Tea and a biscuit? Beer and a tortilla?"

"Oh, for God's sake!" he exploded, and then said more mildly, "Chicken."

"What?"

"Chicken and a tortilla."

"Are you sure? The tortillas here are the best I have ever eaten, but the chicken is old and still has its feathers on when they cook it! Feathers — and feet!"

He stared, and then for a second she thought he might actually laugh. He said, "How do you know that?"

"I don't starve, you know. I eat in the restaurant over the road, in the same old building where I rent my room. The staff are *nice*," she said with emphasis, thinking of the appalling Maria, "and though we don't understand a single word of each other's language, they do their best to get me whatever I want. Within reason. But the chicken is truly awful. They boil it whole, and then dump it in a big bowl with all the soup it was cooked in. It floats, and it has pools of oil and feathers on top, and looks disgusting."

"Then that's what I will have."

Dear lord, she thought, but as she went over to the lodging house, she wondered how Pierce normally ate. Did Maria bring him meals? If she did, she was going to be more hostile than ever when she found that he had already been fed.

Then, when Helen arrived back at the cottage with two warm tortillas wrapped around bits of chicken, with a bowl of the soup, it was to find that Pierce had rummaged out the tequila bottle.

"Are you trying to kill yourself?"

He shrugged. "Why not?" But he did eat the food, while she perched on the settee and watched. He ate quickly, as if he wanted to get it over and done with, then picked up his tequila glass, and stared at her over the rim.

His expression was aggressive, almost accusing. Again, she felt defensive, but said nothing.

He said, "The nurse had something interesting to tell me."

"Yes?"

Did he know about the diagnosis of liver cancer? And had only just been told? It didn't seem likely, as Dr. Dominguez had struck her as the kind of man who would prefer to tell Pierce himself, instead of leaving it to his nurse.

"The doctor has ordered you to take me with you when you go."

It was so unexpected that she almost gasped. "I most certainly have not agreed to that! What on earth would I do with you in Manila?"

"Manila? Is that where you live now?"

"It's where Harold is currently based." When she saw him lift a sardonic eyebrow, she said, "On one of his ships."

"That sounds most enticing."

"I have definitely not agreed to take you away."

To her alarm, he grinned. He was in a mood, she saw, working himself up for a confrontation. He drank deeply, then waved the empty glass at her — which she ignored — and said, "Maria read me the article about you."

She said acidly, "I am surprised she can read." Then chided herself for the uncharitable comment.

"Well, it was fortunate, as I can't read Spanish. But I found it very interesting. Tell me about those two girls you sponsor."

"What? Who?"

"Kate Giacomo and Maggie Bacchante. The writer gossiped that in New York they are known as the Cinderella girls, and that you are their fairy godmother."

Helen quelled a grimace. "I sponsor a lot of people. And causes. I am known for my charities."

"But these girls are special."

Helen paused, her mind racing. What had the article actually said? She wished she had taken more notice of the name of the magazine, and had an internet connection so that she could look up the English version of the story.

Finally, she answered, "They are special, I agree."

"And I wonder why, I really do."

She shook her head, saying nothing. He stared at her for a moment, and then, having given up the idea of having his glass refilled by her, he wheeled into the kitchen. By the time he got back a third was drunk, and she said, "You'll be in the same sad state tomorrow, if you keep on like this."

He waved his free hand. "I had a very bad night, that's all."

"And you blame me."

His grin was tight. "Of course."

She couldn't help adding, "Because I showed you a picture of my daughter."

"Your daughter?"

"Who apparently looked like someone else."

He shut his eyes and shook his head. "Don't remind me." She saw him take a deep breath, then those compelling eyes focused on her again.

He said, "Those two girls — the Cinderella girls — were they really twins?"

"Not biologically. Kate was taken in by the Bacchantes as a

tiny baby. Her mother had disappeared the day after the birth."

"Just disappeared? That sounds strange."

She shrugged. "They were strange circumstances."

"So why does everyone think they are twins?"

"They were both raised by the Bacchante family. Maggie's mother nursed them both, and they were treated absolutely equally. They look alike, and because of their upbringing, they behave in the same ways, too."

"You haven't explained why they are so special."

"Both girls are very talented. What is this? A cross-examination?"

"Why would I cross-examine you, my dear ex-wife?" He laughed when she scowled, and said, "You haven't read that magazine story, have you?"

"You know that already, Pierce."

"Oh, that's right. I do. Because if you had, you would not have fallen for my pathetic attempt at blackmail."

He finished off the drink, and wheeled into the kitchen, and she took her chance to grab the plate and bowl, and leave.

On the way across the street she realized that she was moving fast. Running away? Surely not. But instead of ordering her own meal when she returned the plate and bowl to the restaurant, she went into her room, and sat down, breathing rather hard.

What was wrong with her? But she couldn't help remembering that throughout her pregnancy she had been haunted with memories of Pierce's eyes. That blackmail he had planned could have worked — she had had sex with both Pierce and Harold the month she fell pregnant. The obstetrician had tormented her with sly hints about the importance of the color of her baby's eyes. Harold was very fair, and came from a fair-haired, blue-eyed family, and the doctor was Harold's cousin. He would have been in line for a very nice legacy if Harold hadn't married her, and fathered an heir. And, if her baby happened to have brown eyes…

She remembered the utter relief when she had found the blue-eyed baby. She had woken from a drugged sleep after giving birth to find three cribs in the ensuite bathroom … three cribs, none with labels, holding three baby girls with no identification bracelets. But when she found the blue-eyed baby she had felt no doubts whatsoever. It had been the most wonderful moment of all her life, she emphatically thought, and braced herself to go down to the restaurant to have a meal that did not involve chicken with feathers.

It was an attempt at something like normality. But that night her dreams were about Kate's dark, sparkling, black-fringed eyes.

Nineteen

Jerry was still asleep when Skye barged into his cabin and shouted at him to wake up. Stiffly, he turned over to face him.

"I've only just got to bed," he groaned, and struggled to open his sticky eyes.

"It's three in the afternoon, and you have been asleep for hours."

"Where are we?"

"Nowhere. We're still hanging about while Harold lets the commander of the frigate know his opinion of the debacle last night, but we'll be back underway the instant he returns."

Jerry blinked. "He's registering a formal complaint?"

"Yep — at length, and he's in a state of incandescent fury."

Jerry sat up, scrubbed at his wild hair, and grinned. "Good."

Crawford deserved every ounce of the official disapproval coming his way. When Pederson had agreed to allow *Storm Swept* to be requisitioned for the operation, the understanding had been that the ship would be well guarded. Instead *Storm Swept* had been saved by a passenger — yet again. Del had definitely had killed the terrorist, whose body had been quietly dumped over the side for the crocodiles. Unlikely as it was, Del had turned out to be a hero.

"But once Harold comes back it won't be long before we're out of cellphone range."

"So?"

"So Helen wants to speak to you."

It was then than Jerry saw that Skye was holding out his phone. He winced, and said, "Oh God, what have I done now?"

Helen exclaimed, "You haven't been answering your mobile, that's what!"

It was so loud that they both could hear it. Jerry sat up straighter, jolted into paying attention. Skye perched on the bedside table, obviously intent on hearing the conversation, too.

Jerry took the phone with a cautious hand, looked at it as if it might bite, and then said, "We've been at sea, Helen. And doing really important things."

"It's easy for you! I have to stand about on this beach to get any kind of reception, which isn't any fun at all. I've been doing my utmost — my absolute utmost to get in touch! — and every single time I have managed to get through, you have not responded, Jerry. Didn't Skye tell you that it was urgent?"

Jerry looked at Skye with his eyebrows high, and then said, "Are you alright?"

"I'm fine. I just wish I wasn't in this horrid place."

"Why? Where are you?"

"Hasn't Skye even told you *that*? I'm in Mexico. In Puerto San Alvaro, which is a really tiny village, in a sort of whale-watching place, only it is not the season for watching whales, because they come in the winter. There is a beach, but the sand is black and the place really stinks of fish fertilizer. I rented a room in a sort of lodging house across the street from the clinic, and while the room is clean and quiet, the hotel is truly awful. The privies are all *outside*, and they stink, too. Unbelievable. And though the tortillas are good, being incredibly fresh, everything else is awful. They serve chicken with the feathers and feet still on! And the only thing fit to drink is beer."

Jerry grimaced. He could vaguely remember someone — Kate? — telling him that Helen had flown to Mexico, but it felt like ancient history.

He said. "I've been just too busy. Sorry about that."

"Doing what?"

"I'll tell you about that later. Meantime, why are you in this Mexican village, since you hate it so much?"

A deep breath at the other end. "I got an email from Pierce Brooke — my first husband — with a demand."

"Wasn't he supposed to be dead?"

"The report was wrong. He's in a wheelchair, but he survived the crash."

"But it was over twenty years ago. Why contact you now? And why the devil did you go?"

"It was a threat, only a veiled threat, but Pierce said that if I did not turn up within ten days, he would send evidence to Harold, and I would then have to face the consequences."

"Evidence? Of what?"

"That's why I went, because I had to find out."

"So?"

"He had this crazy idea that he could blackmail me about the time I moved in with Harold."

"After all these years? It doesn't make sense."

"He had seen a fashion magazine with pictures of me."

Through the suite window, Jerry could see the frigate putting out a boat. He said, "Do get on with it, Helen. There are pictures of you in glossy magazines all the time. So why was this one so different?"

"Because Kate was in the pictures, too."

Jerry looked quickly at Skye, who raised his eyebrows and shook his head. This was news to him, too.

Jerry said as lightly as he could, "And?"

"And he claimed that Kate was his daughter. Apparently, Kate looks a lot like his mother, when his mother was young. I wouldn't know, because she was dead when I married Pierce, but he seemed very sure about it."

Jerry pursed his lips in a silent whistle.

Skye said, "Why did he think he could blackmail you about that?"

"Are you listening, Skye? I didn't give you permission, and I don't remember being asked."

"Kate is a Bacchante, remember. We are all Bacchantes, even if we have different names, so of course I am listening."

Helen was silent a moment, then said, "Okay. He thought he could blackmail me because he had jumped to the crazy conclusion that Kate is my daughter, too. That she was *our* daughter, Pierce's and mine."

Again, the two men looked at each other. Jerry said carefully, "He was basing this on a magazine photo of Kate? It certainly does sound farfetched."

Another deep breath. "My baby was conceived the week I left Pierce and moved in with Harold. That's why the timing is so crucial."

A long pause, and then: "So either man could be the father of your daughter?"

A long sigh. "Yes. I know it sounds awful, but I wasn't cheating on Harold, because I was still married to Pierce at the time. That I didn't know which man was the father troubled me throughout my pregnancy. But as soon as I saw my little baby, that fear went away. It is simply not possible that Jewel was Pierce's daughter. She was not like my first husband in the slightest."

Jerry looked at Skye with his brows raised very high, but he simply said, "I see. So what happened after he revealed this theory?"

"Well, that was the threat he had alluded to in his email."

"That the baby was his, and not Harold's?"

"Exactly! He thinks I owe him for the years of pain and penury since the divorce. So he threatened to tell Harold that he, not Harold, was our baby 's father! On such flimsy evidence! Just a couple of pictures, one very old. He had just assumed that Kate was mine, without any effort to make sure! How mad. To tell the honest truth, I laughed. Then I showed him a picture of our real daughter, of Jewel, a little print of a painting that was made of her, one that I carry around in my purse."

"So?" The frigate's barge was coming near.

"When I produced that little print of Jewel's portrait, his reaction was so strange. Really creepy. Pierce was horrified — no, more than horrified. Hysterical. For a few minutes he was totally out of his mind. I truly am not exaggerating, Jerry. He reared back and virtually hissed at me, and put his hands over his eyes and raved about nightmares. Today, when I got back to his cottage, a nurse was with him, as he was vomiting. Badly. And *that's* why I needed to talk to you so urgently."

There was a shout from outside as the barge arrived, and then a distant thump as Harold came back on board.

Jerry said, "Helen, please explain."

"He demanded to know why I was tormenting him with a picture of Debbie Parkin."

Dead silence. Below, the engines rumbled into life, and the ship wallowed, and then began to move.

Jerry said carefully, "Are you sure this was the Debbie Parkin who called herself Kelly?"

"If we are talking about the girl who was Kate's mother, yes! I have thought about it a lot, but Parkin is not exactly a common name, Jerry."

"So how did Brooke know her? Was he one of her clients?"

"No, no — he *rescued* her."

"What? How?"

"He found her being raped and tortured!"

Jerry's breath hissed between his teeth. "Raped?"

"Yes! And drugged, though I don't know what drugs, and neither does Pierce, because he was never a user. I mean, he takes medications now, because he is in constant pain, but never hard drugs, not when I knew him."

Jerry's voice was shaking. "Was it your ex-husband who raped her? Because if it was —"

"No, no, it wasn't Pierce, he was adamant about that. Very passionate, in fact. He told me how he rescued her. In great detail, though he said he was holding back a lot, because it was so awful."

"So just how did he rescue her?"

"He had gone to this penthouse on an urgent business matter, and found the poor girl in this appalling situation. He went ballistic at the scene, and I think he did a lot of damage, though he didn't tell me much about that. Pierce always had a firecracker temper. Then he wrapped the girl up in a blanket, grabbed her bag and purse, and took her to hospital. After she was discharged, he took her his London apartment. That's how he found out her name was Debbie Parkin, because that was the name on her passport. Then — then, when he got to the apartment, he saw that papers had arrived, meantime. They were the divorce papers that Harold had sent. So he gave her the apartment — gave her the keys and lots of money, and flew back to Washington. He never saw her again."

Jerry pushed the phone at Skye and then turned away, wincing with rage and grief. He had lived and travelled with Kelly over the last four months of her pregnancy, and had become fond of her. She had been so beautiful, and so vulnerable, despite the risky way she made her living…

When Helen spoke next, her voice became quieter. "I feel bad about it now, because that was the night I threw Pierce out. The next morning I moved into Harold's apartment. And Pierce flew to Mexico City and crashed his new car."

Skye said, "Don't blame yourself. It was Brooke's own recklessness that landed him in this fix. But is that why you have stayed on in Mexico? Because you feel guilty?"

"No, no." Helen sounded definite. "Pierce has a housekeeper — a Mexican woman who is very possessive. She got angry with me for upsetting Pierce — well, that's what I assume she was shouting, because I don't speak Spanish. I've learned a few words since I have been here, but nothing useful, except for a bit of shopping. I didn't bring many clothes, just a shoulder bag, and some of the local skirts and tops are fun, as well as very cheap. But the housekeeper reported it to Pierce's physician, and the doctor sent for me. And he has made it very difficult for me. Pierce has liver cancer, and not long to live, and the doctor told me that he is now my responsibility."

Skye shook his head, even though she couldn't see him. "Don't listen to him, Helen. It sounds as if your ex is well set up where he is. To ask that of you is ridiculous. You have to say goodbye, and get to Manila, where we will make port in about three days. That gives you plenty of time to be there to meet us."

"I can do that, easily. But Dr. Dominguez says I have to bring Pierce with me."

"For the good lord's sake, why?"

But before Helen could answer, Jerry grabbed back the phone. "Just who was the bastard who did that to Kelly?"

"Not Pierce, definitely not."

"And he doesn't know the man."

"Of course he does — he went there on business, to deliver an important message. And he blundered onto that awful scene because he had a key card to the elevator, and the door to the apartment had been left open. And there were two of them, not just one. Oh, that poor, poor girl. I know that the sex trade is a very risky business, but no one deserves that. My heart breaks for her."

"I need names." Jerry's demand was both hoarse and loud. The engines roared. They were moving fast, and the phone was on the verge of losing the signal.

"They were arrogant young men with far too much money, of course. Drugged out of their minds, just animals, really, except animals would never behave like that. It is mankind that commits true evil."

"Helen!"

"Oh, sorry. They were Saudi Oil men. And the terrible thing is that I think they do business with Harold."

"*Who were they?*"

"Oh, didn't I say? Adrian Blackwell and Zaid Feisal."

And the signal was lost.

Twenty

Kate said to Harold, "Do you think Captain Crawford will face a court-martial?"

"I doubt it," said Harold. "Unfortunately, that kind of blunder is usually swept under the carpet. Only one soldier was hurt, and no one was killed except for that terrorist. And his body was dropped over the side, so there's no evidence."

"That's a pity."

"Why? Didn't you like Crawford?"

"I didn't get to know him well enough to decide."

"You were both flirting with him."

"We were not!" But she saw that Harold was teasing, and laughed. "I thought he was condescending, to tell the truth, but I guess all soldiers tend to be like that. Superior in their macho world, armed and dangerous. Not Jerry, of course," she hastily added.

The ship was gliding back to Manila, and they were sitting in deck chairs at the after end of the promenade deck, watching Maggie and Del. The two were playing a game that Maggie had made up and probably called deck tennis. Both were laughing uproariously. If the murder of a terrorist had disturbed Del when he was first told he had killed the pirate, he was certainly over it now.

Normally, Kate would have joined them, but she had spied Harold sitting alone, and on impulse had sat alongside. Now, to her surprise, she was enjoying his company. It was unusual to see him taking any kind of relaxation, and his expression was warmer than usual, too, quite indulgent.

It was a tranquil scene, to suit. *Storm Swept* was smoothly surging along, and the sea seemed limitless, aquamarine, azure and all shades of green, almost purple where the few clouds cast shadows. The deck was sheltered from the direct sun, and a small, kind breeze was whipped up by their passage.

Harold said, "Does Maggie always behave like this?"

"Always." Kate dimpled. "She got us into terrible trouble at school."

"She told me once that she drew caricatures of the nuns."

Kate laughed. "I had forgotten that. We all hated the physical education teacher, and when we were out on the field and her back was turned Maggie would change the rules of whatever we were meant to be playing. We would all go along with it, managing to keep straight faces, and the poor woman used to get so awfully confused."

"Are you like that?"

"Of course not. I am much, much more serious. I was just one of those who went along with her mischief."

Harold was smiling. "And yet you are so alike."

Kate smiled back, thinking that she had never believed that this powerful. intimidating man could be so companionable. "It's because we are both Bacchantes," she told him. "And not having actual Bacchante genes doesn't seem to make any difference. Skye is a Bacchante, too, even though he was adopted when he was small. Yet he looks so like Bacchante men his age that people get muddled. There is something magical about that family. They somehow implant Bacchante looks and nature into those they enfold into the *famiglia Bacchante*. By osmosis, perhaps."

"So I have learned." His tone was unexpectedly wry.

"You must visit the vineyard some day."

"I definitely will."

"With Helen."

"Of course."

Kate giggled. "Maggie has already invited Del."

"Good lord. I would like to be there when she produces him, just to see their faces."

"I do wonder what he will be wearing — though undoubtedly that hat, whatever the rest. But they will take it in their stride, I'm sure, though Rachel might object in private."

"Rachel?"

"Maggie's mother. Her husband was killed by the hurricane on the same day that Maggie and I were born, so I never met him. I wish I had, for he must have been lots of fun, quite flamboyant, really. They said that he fell in love with Rachel the day she tumbled off a stool while taking something off a high shelf, and he was there to catch her. Rachel was just a shy country girl who worked behind the counter in the general store, went to church, sang hymns, and made beautiful quilts, but she fell in love, too, so much so that she even converted to his faith. She still talks about him, and mourns him, even though they were married for less than two years. Everyone loved Stefano, or so I was constantly assured. He laughed and sang all the time, and played practical jokes on everyone, but was a hard worker, too."

"So we know where Maggie gets her aptitude for mischief."

"Oh yes. And she loves anything flamboyant, too — which is why she and Del have struck up such a friendship, I suppose. Del is definitely flamboyant! But he was so brave," she soberly added. "He saved my life, I know it."

Harold said, "I saw him hit the pirate over the head. Tell me what led up to it."

"We were supposed to hide in the crew quarters if the ship was invaded by pirates — but the pirates came from inside, not outside, as you know. They were confined on the lower deck, the same deck as the citadel, so when two of them escaped, we thought it was best to hide in our suite. Del came with us — mainly because he was desperate to go to the bathroom." She laughed and shook her head.

"Go on."

"So when the pirates broke into our cabin, he was out of sight. They had no idea that he was there. I was mentally telling him that he should stay inside the bathroom — a mental shout! And he must have known it, because he obeyed. Or maybe it was just his good sense. Both of the terrorists were horrible. They yelled at us in a foreign language, and made rude, aggressive gestures. I was sure they were going to cut off our heads, because they are notorious for that, but one ran ahead to seize the bridge, while the other held us back with his rifle. When he heard his comrade shout out, presumably telling him that he had the bridge under control, he prodded us out of the cabin and along the corridor to the bridge, intending to make us two more of the hostages, I suppose. But Del came pelting out with that bottle of Scotch — a full bottle, I'm afraid. I am sorry your expensive whisky was wasted, but it was terribly brave, because Del isn't macho at all."

"I had noticed that," said Harold. He was sober-faced, despite the twinkle in his eye.

"In fact, I do believe that he would have fainted or thrown up if he had realized that he had actually killed the terrorist, but Jerry didn't tell him that until much later, when he could stand the shock."

They were interrupted. Skye came out with a print-out in his hand. One eyebrow quirked when he saw them together, but he didn't comment. Instead, he said, "Harold, you have to come in to see this."

Harold stood up. The conversation was over.

The computer Skye had been using was open to an image of the front page of *The Straits Star*. The single word of the headline, in a huge, blaring font, read SCAM.

Harold set down on the chair without a word, and began to read. The story revealed that the hundreds of millions of dollars which were supposed to fund a solar energy research project in Malaysia had been diverted to a bank in Cyprus. The hundreds of millions had come from Pederson Strategic, and the brain behind the fraud was alleged to be a major figure in Saudi Oil. Lists of facts and figures backed this up, all in damning detail.

This was followed by an interview with a spokesman for Saudi Oil, who claimed that the money must have gone to minor entities, as the headquarters in Geneva had no record of these transactions. Were these entities owned by Saudi Oil? The spokesman refused to answer, saying that research was needed. Would there be an investigation? Most certainly.

Harold sat back, twirling a pencil, his expression abstracted and his eyes remote.

Skye said, "Have you noticed the byline?"

Pederson looked at the screen again. "Graham Waters. So?"

"The same journalist who interviewed Jerry and Kate. Just before we sailed from Manila, he phoned Kate to say that he had been interviewing the *Honourable* Adrian Blackwell."

"Why phone Kate?"

"No idea." Skye tapped the computer monitor, and said, "But what is important is that it seems very likely that Waters is getting this story from Blackwell."

Harold thought about it, then nodded.

"So it looks very much as if Blackwell got wind that he is being investigated, and is covering his back by leaking to the press. He's a whistle-blower, but very selective about the stuff he is revealing."

Skye leaned forward and refreshed the page. The story was being constantly updated, as new details were rolling.

"Look," he said, pointing with his pencil. "It's more than a panic reaction after learning that he was being investigated. Blackwell is angry, and this time he has named the major figure in Saudi Oil – Zaid Feisal."

"My God," said Harold, and pulled his chair closer to the monitor. The updated story alleged that the deal between Saudi Oil and Pederson Strategic was an elaborate pretense, as was soon demonstrated by a fraudulent transfer totalling many millions of dollars to a Swiss bank account owned by a minor Saudi prince named Zaid Feisal, though that man held no official position with either Pederson Strategic or Saudi Oil.

So where was Mr. Feisal? On his yacht *Masha'Allah*, apparently, somewhere in the remote western Pacific.

"Interesting," said Harold. He puffed out his lips as he thought, and then plucked at the lower one. "It certainly does look as if the devils have fallen out."

"But why? What could have happened? According to all the accounts, Blackwell and Feisal have been tight cronies since university years."

"Who cares? What is important is what Blackwell might tell the journalist when he gets around to naming me."

Skye was thinking hard and speaking very carefully. "Is there anything he might know that is damaging?"

"Every successful businessman has vulnerabilities."

"Do we have anything on him that could stifle his tongue?"

"You've seen all the detectives' reports, plus all the financial records, so you probably know better than I do, Skye. But as for anything personal . . ." Harold shrugged.

"What about Helen?"

"What do you mean? As far as I remember, she has never met Blackwell, let alone had anything to do with him."

Skye took a slow breath, let it out, and then said, "Just out of curiosity, what does Blackwell look like?"

"Why?"

"It seems odd that he keeps his face out of the media."

Harold grimaced. "If you knew him, you wouldn't think it odd at all."

"He's deformed in some way?"

"He's white, dead white, like something that crawled from under a stone. White hair, white eyebrows, pallid skin. If it wasn't for the bright blue eyes, you would think he was albino. But apparently it is some kind of mutation."

"Really?" said Skye. His voice was casual, but he was thinking *My God!*

Twenty-one

Helen Pederson could not read Spanish, but as she passed the little shop on her way down the street the headline stopped her in her tracks. 'PEDERSON STRATEGIC' it blared. When she raced inside there were no English-language papers, but she bought a Mexican one anyway, anxious to take it back to her room and get to work with a dictionary.

But it told her nothing useful. She had never had any talent for languages, and her mind was in too much of a muddle. Then she abruptly remembered that Pierce had sent his vague threat by email. So he must have internet access, she belatedly realized, and grabbed up her tablet and ran along the street to his cottage.

Her heart was bumping. Harold could be in big trouble, because the Department of Justice was investigating Pederson Strategic for money-laundering. Terrible memories beset her, of her American father's suicide after he had been found guilty of embezzlement. She and her mother had been forced to flee to New Zealand, and Helen remembered the shame of the whispered comments overheard in corridors. Surely it was not possible that it could happen twice? That Harold, who might be an entrepreneur and shipping tycoon, but had always been upfront and honest, should be accused of embezzlement?

Pierce had been drinking again. He scowled at her as she rushed in, but she ignored him. The tablet got a signal, thank God, and when she asked for his password he gave it, though reluctantly. Then, as she feverishly scrolled through the pages, she found the *Straits Star.*

It was even worse than she had dreaded. Where with her father it had been hundreds of thousands stolen, with Pederson Strategic the figures quoted were in the many millions. Billions. She winced. But where was this information coming from? It was all so precise, purportedly the result of sorting through hundreds of secretly released accounts.

The by-line was a name she had never seen or heard before. Graham Waters. He was getting inside information from somewhere. Somehow. From someone. Someone who knew the details of the agreement between Saudi Oil and Pederson Strategic from the very beginning. Someone like . . .

She ran out of the cottage, down the street to the road and then to the beach, tapping out Harold's private number as she ran.

He was a long time answering. Then he barked, "At last!"

"Sorry. I did talk to Skye and Jerry. Didn't they tell you?"

Silence. Then she could hear Harold talking to someone – Skye, most probably. She stopped to look around. The sun was plunging to the horizon, and it was getting dark.

Then Harold got back to her. "Are you still there?"

"Yes, I'm here – and I'm still in that nasty little village in Mexico, with Pierce. My ex-husband, Pierce Brooke, the one I divorced after you sent me those photographs." She was gabbling, but couldn't stop. "He's bitter and twisted and the only way I can get a cellphone signal is if I stand on this awful beach!"

"So why aren't you on the way to Manila? I miss you, Helen."

"Thank you." Her voice was gentle, reflecting her smile. "I miss you too, Harold, I miss you a lot, and I am so very worried about you." Then she thought that the ship must be close to some island or other, because there was such a strong cellphone signal. For the umpteenth time, she fervently wished she had a satellite phone. But they were illegal here – because of the drug trade, she'd been told.

Harold said, "You've seen the newspapers?"

"Not really, as this place is so tiny and there is only one store that sells papers and they are all in *Spanish*, but I managed at last to get online, and so I have read the headlines. And Harold, I am so very fearful that you are in big trouble."

"So come back."

"But I want to help, and I think that perhaps I could do that from here. Wasn't Pierce the man who set up your agreement with Saudi Oil? Could he be the man who is now leaking details of Pederson Strategic to the press?"

"No," said Harold, his tone definite. "It can't be Brooke, because he doesn't know enough. He made the initial approach on the behalf of Saudi Oil, and it would be very useful to have his testimony. But there is no way he could be the source of the scandal. The actual mediation was set up by another man."

She sucked in a breath, and then said carefully, "Was it by any chance Adrian Blackwell?"

"Yes." The word was very sharp.

"And the papers also mentioned the name of a Saudi, Zaid Feisal. I seem to remember that Feisal was Blackwell's close friend. Am I right?"

Harold's answer came slowly. "Yes. He was involved in the arrangements, too."

Helen started to speak, but Harold turned away as Skye said something to him. When he came back he sounded distracted. "There's more news. The office of Saudi Oil in Geneva has burned to the ground, along with all the records. It's a high-rise, so must have been a huge blaze. And the editor of the paper that broke the news has been arrested, and their operation closed down. The

Saudi Oil people are busy covering their tracks."

"Paper? What paper?"

"*Straits Star*. Isn't that the one you were reading?"

"So is the writer arrested, too?"

"Graham Waters?"

"Yes, that is the name I saw."

"I don't think he has been arrested, as he is not in Malaysia. As far as we know, he is in Manila – where we are headed right now. To fix damage," Harold grimly added.

"Damage? Oh my dear, are you alright?"

"The ship was requisitioned for a military exercise – which did not go well. I mean, the pirates have been captured, and are now on the way to Brunei, but *Storm Swept* suffered some damage when two terrorists escaped. Which the military had promised would not happen."

Storm Swept. That was the ship, she vaguely remembered, that had been attacked on a previous cruise.

Terrorists? She said nervously, "Harold, dear, do take care. As you know, promises are worth nothing until they are carried out."

"I am fine. Just extremely irritated."

"I'll see you soon, I promise." Then she laughed wryly, remembering that she had just told him that promises were worth nothing until they were carried out. "As soon as I can – except there is a problem."

"Problem?"

"Didn't Skye or Jerry tell you? Oh, I can't remember now who I told and what, but the doctor here – Dr. Dominguez – says that I have to bring Pierce with me. He doesn't have long to live, and the doctor says he is now my responsibility. And yes, I know it sounds crazy. The doctor says he has cancer, but he doesn't seem to in pain, except for his back. Though maybe the medication for his back is calming the cancer pain, too, but . . ."

Harold interrupted, his voice urgent. "Helen, stop blethering, and listen to me, because that changes everything. Tell him he has to testify, as he was involved in the start of Pederson Strategic, and he will be summoned when there is a trial. I could send out a lawyer, or organize a video link, but if he hasn't long to live, it has to be soon."

"I don't think a video conference would work," she objected. "Not here, not where it is so primitive."

"Then bring him with you. It's crucial that he is available to give evidence."

Helen grimaced. "I certainly don't want to be in his company one minute more than necessary. I don't like him, and I don't think I ever liked him, not really, but if you think it is really necessary . . ."

"It is. Hire someone to help."

"Oh Harold, couldn't you come out and take over?"

"Helen, I can't. It would be stupid of me. Flying to somewhere remote would make matters worse, as it would look as if I was running away."

"All right, then." She sighed deeply. "I'll do my best."

Harold rang off. And slowly, with her head down, she trudged back to the cottage.

Twenty-two

As *Storm Swept* was on the last leg to Manila, Jerry took over the theatre for a final lecture. This time only the deckhands and room and table stewards were there, as the engineers, chefs, and design team were not needed. Accordingly, the audience was entirely Filipino.

His audience, having seen action firsthand, was at full alert, ready to give him complete attention, but for a couple of minutes Jerry didn't speak. Instead, he scanned the rows of short, muscular men with bullet heads and intelligent eyes. All men, he thought. Apparently, Harold did not employ women on his discovery ships – unless they were guest lecturers, of course. Jerry wondered why. And one of them, he meditated, was a traitor.

Then he roused himself from inner contemplations, and switched on the projector. The first image was of a map of the world.

He began by flattering them – with nothing but the truth. "Filipinos can be found in all the seas and every ocean," he said, "because they are by far the largest group of seafarers in the world. Most of the hands on container ships and tankers are Filipino. They can be found on fishing trawlers, floating oil rigs, cruise ships, and luxury mega-yachts – adding up to perhaps half a million Filipino sailors at sea at any time. Not one of them is afraid of pirates. Indeed, they consider it part of the job. But it is undeniable that their lives are in constant danger from attack, so it is *my* job to make it safer for you all."

He paused again, looking at them all, row by attentive row. "It was very painful for me to see you put in danger in Borneo. It was entirely due to military mismanagement, and I assure you that I have made my feelings known. It was a disgrace, and the top brass send you their apologies."

There was a murmuring, and a few grins. None of them, he saw, believed for an instant that anyone on the frigate had apologized, but they appreciated his tact.

Then a hand went up. "After what happened, Major, sir, have you changed your mind about issuing us with guns?"

"Absolutely not. We have discussed this already. Would you be allowed to travel in a plane with a gun in your hand luggage? Of course not. It is the same at sea. Not only would it cause complications in many ports, but guns mean stand-offs – if you know what I mean." And he repeated it in Tagalog, together with a comment about American Wild West movies, which made them all laugh.

"The pirates will always be there," he said when the murmurs subsided. "Kill one, and three will leap up in his place. Piracy is a hydra-headed monster. It is profitable for many – and a mission for some. Like Abu Sayyaf, for instance."

Many nods of agreement, but one said, "So what do we do, if we don't have guns?"

"Well, as I told you before, we avoid them, by keeping out of the way. That is the first thing I was hired to teach you – pirate identification."

Images popped up on the big screen as he listed one clue after another. "Good giveaways are extra fuel drums, unusually powerful outboard motors, coiled ropes with grapnels, and, of course, guns. Pirate skiffs are notoriously badly maintained and rusty," he went on. "Other things to look out for are suspiciously large crews, vessels that are in the wrong waters for that kind of craft, crewmen who *look* wrong, being of the wrong nationality for that kind of ship, or that area. If you are on duty – particularly if you are the lookout on the bridge – you must keep alert. Deckhands at work must have a constant eye on the sea. Innocent-looking fishing *prahus* could turn into pirates at a second's notice – fishing spears turn into weapons, and the fishermen will take every chance to board."

The images on the screen changed to the various electronic monitors on the bridge. "An officer on duty has to keep a close eye on the Electronic Chart Display screen, the Automatic Identification Sysem, and the radar. If a vessel fails to register on the AIS, it is likely it's because the transceiver has been turned off, which is a very good clue that something is wrong. In short, if the officer on watch sees anything to raise suspicion, he must send out a message to every vessel in the vicinity, along with notifying the nearest port authority."

A series of images of skiffs attacking a container ship, and the crews of outrigger canoes boarding tankers then passed across the screen. "This can be prevented," Jerry emphasized. "And it is much better that way. Back in the day, a Russian crew dropped armed hand grenades into the skiffs as they came alongside – which seemed a good idea, until one of the pirates scooped up a grenade and threw it back."

The audience laughed, and Jerry laughed too, though he shook his head at the same time.

"We do not want that kind of situation. Once a likely pirate has been detected, the job is to *forestall* the boarding of the ship. And we have already practised ways and means of that. I am sure you will remember well enough to answer the questions on the sheets I will be handing out."

"But our pirates were already on board, sir," someone called out. "The soldiers brought them, and then did not guard them properly. So what should we have done?"

"That is a very good question. Leaving the captives not properly guarded could have been a fatal blunder. There were two factors in our favor, however. Can anyone guess what they were?"

"That only two escaped," a steward suggested from the back.

"Excellent." Jerry nodded approvingly.

The speaker grinned. Evidently he had taken shelter on the same deck as the captives, as he added, "There were seven, altogether, but while the others hammered on their doors and yelled to be let out, the first two took no notice. *I* heard them, but their comrades either did not hear them, or chose not to listen."

"Which was much in our favor," Jerry agreed. "If they had released the other five, we would have been in very big trouble."

A short silence, then another man called out. "Another advantage was that we had been trained to get to our safe places, so the pirates were not able to capture us as hostages. It was good that they couldn't easily find us."

"Yes indeed, but we learned that as a safeguard if the pirates did manage to board us, not as a precaution when attackers were here already."

"Del had a bottle of whisky, which was very good," said another, and everyone laughed again.

Jerry chuckled, too. "He was definitely resourceful, but we can't rely on him being here all the time."

A steward spoke up. "But perhaps we should have some kind of blunt weapon kept handy in our safe places. Not whisky," he hastily added, though with a wide grin. "But something about the same shape and weight."

"A very good idea." Jerry made a note on his clipboard, and then looked up as more suggestions were made. But every time he shook his head.

"So what is it?" several chorused.

"It really goes back to the main thing we have to watch out for when pirates threaten us from the water – the vulnerability of the bridge. All pirates aim to take over the bridge first, as they believe that it is the heart of the ship. Now, we all know that this ship can also be operated from the engine control room, but the terrorists do not. So what else was greatly in our favor was that the two men who escaped were so intent on getting to the bridge that they forgot everything else. Because it was their natural target, they didn't delay to release the other five. They knew that they had to run up a number of stairways to mount to the right deck, and that they were vulnerable to counter attack all of the way, so it's no wonder they were in a hurry."

"So that's why Del was able to kill one," a hand commented from the back.

"Exactly. If the ship had been boarded from the outside, the bridge could have been seized much more quickly. The time it took the escapers to get to the bridge gave me enough time to hurry Mr. Pederson and Mr. Hamilton into the bathroom of the owner's suite. The officers and two deckhands on the bridge were not able to take shelter, but it meant that once Del had put the second pirate out of action, I was able to put the first one out of business."

Everyone was silent as they thought this over. "You had a gun," one said. "The same rifle that the pirate stole from one of the two soldiers they had overcome."

Jerry nodded. Obviously, they had all heard the details of how he had retaken the bridge after Del had knocked the first pirate out of action. "That was a piece of luck," he admitted. "But I would never willingly carry a gun on board a ship."

"Should we have an assigned citadel on the bridge deck?" a steward asked. "It could be useful even if the ship is attacked from outside." He was the same steward who had suggested keeping blunt weapons in the citadels, and Jerry studied him with interest, thinking that he showed a good sharp mind.

"A very good idea." And Jerry made another note on his clipboard, along with the man's name. Anyone who was that perceptive deserved promotion, he thought.

"The trouble with the grilles," an voice interjected, "is instead of keeping the pirates out, they kept the pirates in."

"I don't see what you mean?"

"Well, if the grilles had not been there, the pirates who escaped would simply have jumped into the sea and swum to the freighter, to join their comrades there."

Jerry lifted his brows. "So perhaps it was to our benefit that the grilles kept them in?"

This led to a lively discussion, which Jerry brought to a conclusion by handing out test papers and pencils.

Two hours later Jerry knocked at the door to the owner's suite. He had the pile of marked examination papers under his arm.

Skye opened the door. He looked rumpled and tired. Obviously, he and Pederson had been working hard. Jerry supposed that now they were not confined to the internet and radio calls, they could do more to counter the fallout from the newspaper reports.

Harold turned from his computer, and said, "How did it go?"

"Very good indeed." Jerry sat down under the portrait of Jewel, so that he would not have to look at it. "The test results were flawless, completely one hundred percent, probably because they know firsthand what it is like to be attacked. Unfortunate as the breakout was, it was an excellent learning experience for both me and the crew. One of the stewards also made some excellent suggestions – that some kind of blunt instrument be kept in the citadels, and also that a safe place should be assigned on the bridge deck, as a refuge for the bridge personnel. I'll give you his name, as he shows promise."

Harold nodded. "Do you need more time with them?"

"Not with this lot. They are now well aware that an alert lookout is the best preventive measure, and that it must be kept up at night as well as during the day. I'll check the deck lighting tonight, but expect that it will be good. The spotlight proved an excellent aid during the night departure from the head of the estuary, and it should be on standby all the time we are at sea. There is also the problem of onboard security. The system will have to be changed so that no one gets on board without clearance. And supervision of guests, decks, and the wharf – if we are in port – will have to be around the clock. At sea, onboard survellience every watch."

There was a tap on the door, and Jerry silenced. Ryan came in with coffee and biscuits. He looked as bland and helpful as usual, but when he smiled, ready to go, Jerry said, "Please stay."

Ryan looked puzzled, but waited.

"When we sailed back to the freighter after the raid on the pirate stronghold, someone warned the pirates that we were coming. They were ready for our attack."

Ryan blinked. "Sir?"

"We were within cellular range, so they got a phone call or a text. From someone who knew what we planned."

Ryan said nothing, but his tongue touched his bottom lip.

"Do you have a phone, Ryan?"

"Yes, sir."

"Give it to me, please."

Slowly, with great reluctance, Ryan fished in his pants pocket, and handed it over.

Jerry took it, turned it on, and flicked through the messages. He vividly remembered Ryan coming to the bridge with mugs of hot chocolate while they were discussing the chances of dropping down the estuary to seize back the freighter. Stewards were so often invisible, and Ryan must have been relying on that.

He hadn't even deleted the texts he had sent. Jerry looked up, straight into the steward's innocent eyes.

Deliberately, he stated, "And you also released two of the captives while the soldiers were away from the ship. Then you stood by while they tied up the two men who were on guard, and did nothing when they ran upstairs to take the bridge."

Ryan said nothing. He stood still, his face expressionless.

"Why did you do this?"

"Do I have to tell you, sir?"

"Sorry, but you definitely do."

"It's about my brother."

"He's a hostage with the terrorists?"

"He is an inspector with the government, sir. It is a very dangerous job. He goes on foreign fishing vessels to watch what they catch and make reports back."

"Can you name the last ship he was on?"

"It's Chinese, sir."

"Some Chinese have him captive?"

"He has been murdered, sir. His body was washed up on a

beach."

"I am sorry for your loss, Ryan. But I still don't understand your motive for warning the terrorists and letting out two of our captives."

"Abu Sayyaf are fighting China."

"Who told you that?"

"No one, sir. It was on the internet."

"Have you heard of fake news?"

"Many people believe this, sir."

"People you know?"

"Yes."

"Anyone on board this ship?"

Ryan shook his head. "I do not know. Everyone has secrets."

Jerry gazed at him for a long silent moment. Ryan's eyes dropped. Skye and Harold were very still, watching from their computer chairs. It was so quiet that the cries of circling gulls seemed very loud.

"Ryan."

The steward looked up. "Yes, Major?"

"I want you to write down the links to the websites where you are getting this false information. Bring the list back this afternoon."

"I will need my phone for that, sir."

"No, you don't. Use your excellent memory. I will keep your phone, and give it back to you just before you leave the ship. You do understand that you will have to take all your belongings when you go? And that you will not be given a reference?"

Ryan nodded. He was on the verge of tears. He mumbled, "Sorry, sir," to Harold Pederson, and with that he went.

The door closed slowly and softly behind him.

Twenty-three

Brooke snorted in derision. "You said you would never agree to take me to Manila. You reckoned it was a mad idea – and it is. Insane. Forget it. I'm not going."

Helen snapped, "Meeting up with Harold is a chance for you to get back at me. Tell him how you slammed into the apartment and had sex with me the night before I moved in with him. Then tell him about your accident, and how sorry you feel for yourself."

"Oh, for God's sake, Helen."

"You have to testify – give evidence. Pederson Strategic is being investigated, and you are involved."

"What?"

"Read that." She thrust her tablet at him, the screen set to the newspaper headlines.

For a moment she thought he wouldn't take it, but then his hand reached out, and he turned the tablet so he could see the screen. Silence, as she watched his eyes widen, more silence, and then his mouth stretched into the thin, bitter smile she was getting to know so well.

"So your lover is getting his comeuppance at last."

"I thought you worked for him – not against him."

"Oh, I certainly set up the deal with Saudi Oil, and it looked a very good one, too. And I did not make a single cent out of it."

"That was not Harold's fault. You went away, and weren't available any more. He wouldn't have cheated you, because he isn't like that."

He sneered. "Such loyalty, my dear."

"He is a better man than you would ever believe. And, like it or not, you are involved in this scandal, and you have to give evidence."

"Help Pederson get out of this fix?" He snorted again. "No bloody way."

Helen tilted her head, looking at him intently, studying the lines that years of pain and bitterness had drawn in his face. Trying another tack, she said, "You hate it here, and keep on telling me that. This is a chance to get away."

"To Manila?" He snorted.

"You like studying those pictures of Kate. Don't you want to see the real person?"

Pierce's eyes became unfocused, and she knew he was looking at something in the distant past. His dead mother? Or was he remembering that last night in the Washington apartment? The thought made her wince.

Then he was staring at her again. "And what happens after Manila?"

Helen frowned. Surely Dr. Dominguez had told him what a short time he had left? Or had the doctor told her a lie, simply to get rid of this cantankerous patient?

She shrugged, and said, "We will see what happens. I will make sure you are looked after, never fear."

"Like one of your charities?" Pierce sneered, "Thank you very much, my dear ex-wife, but I do not wish thy charity."

Helen muttered, "Oh, for the good lord's sake," and stormed out into the street. As she hurried down the road, she was thumbing her phone. To her relief, when she got to the beach she found a signal, and Harold answered almost at once.

She said, "Pierce flatly refuses to come."

He was on speakerphone, because she could hear him consulting with Skye. A movement caught her eye as she waited, and then she glimpsed the rowboat that was coming from the factory to the beach. The light glittered on the water, but she could see that there were five men inside it. Two were rowing.

Then Harold's voice became louder. "Well, tell Brooke he is implicated in the scandal, no matter how much he hates the idea. One way or another, he has to testify – now that we know he is alive. He was instrumental in setting up the joint venture agreement, and so he will be involved in the court case. He needs to give evidence, and sooner rather than later, considering his prognosis."

"He says it was Zaid Feisal who set it up."

"Zaid Feisal was there, too. And Blackwell. Feisal has vanished, but Blackwell has not. Instead, he is still talking to the press."

She frowned. "But didn't you tell me that the paper that published Blackwell's gossip has been shut down?"

"It has, but we don't know what happened to the reporter – Waters. He could be anywhere, but wherever it is, he is bound to be with Blackwell."

"Oh God." She sighed, and her shoulders slumped. "Harold, you know I want to help, but getting Pierce to Manila is looking more impossible by the minute. Even if he was being cooperative, it would be hard to get both him and his wheelchair onto the local buses, but the way he is right now, it's in the too-hard basket. I don't speak Spanish, or understand more than a word, so I just can't see myself doing it."

A pause, while Harold consulted with someone – Skye, perhaps. The boat grounded, and the five men jumped out and hauled it up on the sand. Then they waved as they walked towards her. They were the same men she had talked to as they were waiting for the bus, and she supposed they were on the same mission.

Then Harold said briskly, "Is there anywhere in the village where a helicopter can land?"

"What?"

"You heard me. I will hire a helicopter and pilot to get you on the way to Mexico City, and from there flying to Manila should be easy."

She blinked. "Are you sure?" Even after all these years, the casual way Harold could spend significant amounts of money was startling.

"The pilot won't need a helicopter pad, just a clear space. How hard is the sand of the beach?"

Helen gathered her wits. "There's a concrete turn-around spot at the end of the road, where the bus makes a circuit to get back to town."

"Take a photo of the turn-around and send it to me, and then go and tell Brooke to get packed and ready, as he will be flying with you in the morning."

"Are you sure?"

"Of course I am. Call me in a couple of hours, when I can let you know the exact time that the helicopter will be there."

While Pederson was barking instructions to staff in New York to arrange the hire of helicopter and pilot, and book flights for Brooke and Helen from Mexico City to Manila, Skye was checking his computer screen.

"More breaking news," he said with a grimace.

Harold sighed, and turned away from his desk. "Hit me with

it."

"The Saudi government has issued a press release. They say that they have no connection with Saudi Oil, and never did; that they have never been a part of the operation. That any money that was transferred to Pederson Strategic came from a Swiss bank account controlled by Feisal, and had nothing to do with them."

Silence. Then Skye went on, "It's impossible to believe that, of course. They are covering their backs, just like everyone else. You told me that the fact that the Saudi government was willing to be involved in the background of the operation was part of the pitch made by Brooke, Feisal and Blackwell?"

Harold grimly nodded. "Brooke introduced me to Feisal, who definitely touted the link to the Saudi royal family. I already knew he was a prince – a minor one in a very large family, but a prince nevertheless. He intimated that he was just a vehicle, but that his connections had virtual control of vast oil fields in central Asia. It was easy to assume that they were any of the multitude of his royal relatives."

Jerry had been sitting quietly throughout. Now, he looked around, sighted the minibar, and walked over. There was a bottle of single malt, untouched. He opened it, poured three drams, and brought them over. Instead of objecting, as half-expected, Harold nodded, took the glass, and drank the entire contents. Skye looked equally grateful, but just sipped.

"So that is what hooked you into investing in Pederson Strategic," Jerry mused aloud. He sat down again and waited, expecting to be blasted with anger. Instead, Harold nodded again.

"But, my God, it looked so good," he said. His voice was almost too low to hear. "It looked like the key to an amazing venture. Brooke was the the first to suggest the idea, and when

Feisal and Blackwell came to the party they had it all laid out, including detailed lists of potential clients, men who were controlling potential oil fields."

"Potential?"

"Yes, only potential. Potential all the time. But very convincing."

"And your name gave them access to huge amounts of money," said Skye. He looked back at his computer screen. "Here's another release. According to the writer, mind-boggling amounts of money that have been borrowed or given by grateful governments for eco-friendly ventures have vanished into the void. This is backed up with so much data that it reads like a spreadsheet."

Harold said, "Oh damn."

"Yes. It's a big, big story. Blackwell is still talking, and guess who has the by-line again."

"So they've found another paper willing to pay a big fee for the story?"

Skye checked, then turned back. "It's one of the London dailies. Definitely capable of paying big money, and not nearly so likely to be shut down."

Jerry finished his Scotch, his expression wry. "So the paparazzi will be out in force when we get to Manila. It could be an exciting arrival."

Twenty-four

The first person Helen Pederson sighted as she stepped through the arrivals gate at Manila airport was her husband.

"Harold!" she cried, and flew into his arms. "Oh Harold, how I have missed you!"

"So I gather," he said dryly, and held her out so he could look at her properly.

"Oh Harold, Harold." Laughing, she hugged and kissed him again, and then looked around. "Where are Skye and Jerry?"

"Skye is manning the computers and phones, and Jerry is dealing with the crew."

She laughed again. "I'm surprised you are not using the girls as slave labor, too."

Kate and Maggie were standing close together, holding hands and whispering to each other. They were surreptitiously studying Pierce Brooke, who was scowling back at them, a crumpled, miserable heap in his wheelchair. The airline steward who had pushed the chair through customs and immigration was watching them too, but his expression was warmly appreciative.

As soon as they spied Helen looking at them, their faces lit up with radiant smiles. Unclasping hands, they raced over to her and engulfed her in huge hugs, with many kisses.

"You are looking so good," exclaimed Kate.

"She always looks good," said Maggie, standing back with her head on one side. "Helen has style."

"But she must be so jetlagged!"

"I am, I am," said Helen, laughing. "But it is worth it all to see you again. And do stop talking about me as if I wasn't here."

There was a grunt behind the girls, and they turned. The airline steward was looking more appreciative than ever, but Pierce Brooke's expression was dark and brooding. *He's jealous*, thought Helen, as she introduced him. And, she thought, I am not at all surprised. Then she looked at the woman who was standing alongside the wheelchair. She had remarkably heavy eyebrows, and was scowling almost as darkly as its occupant.

"Pierce," Helen said. "Please introduce your carer to Harold and the girls."

Grudgingly, he did so. The carer was Maria, the same Mexican woman who had been Brooke's housekeeper in the village, the same one who had made the complaint to Dr. Dominguez that had triggered all this. A small but bulky person, with gray hair pulled back into a severe bun, she was wearing a shapeless coat, and gripping a carpet bag as if she expected it to be stolen. When the girls addressed her in Italian, they merely got a scowl in return.

"Charming," murmured Harold.

"Indeed."

"Did she have a passport?"

"Amazingly, she did." It would have been very hard to get Pierce here without her, though Maria had been almost as big a burden as Pierce throughout. Nothing about the last thirty hours had pleased either of the miserable souls. And the only words spoken had been in Spanish.

"And you managed to talk Brooke into coming."

"I had help," she said, and smiled reminiscently. It had been the five men from the fish factory, who had been so enchanted with the idea of loading someone onto a helicopter that they had readily agreed.

She told Harold about it, while his bristling brows rose higher and higher. "They kidnapped him for you?" he demanded at the end.

"Virtually – though it was all in Spanish, and I couldn't understand a word. Maria did the packing, and the men pushed Pierce to the helicopter and then loaded him into it."

"Then I owe them."

"I offered the leader – the only one who spoke English – a ride to Mexico City, but he said no, he was happy to wait for the whale-watching season."

Harold was looking more entertained than ever, and Pierce even more foul-tempered. He muttered, but no one could hear what he was saying. Ignoring him, Helen turned back to Harold, and said brightly, "So where are we staying?"

"On the ship. Brooke has one of the handicapped suites, and Maria has the cabin next to him."

"But not on the same deck as us?" she said, and mouthed the extra words, *I hope.*

"You will have the suite right next to the owner's suite, which is currently my office."

"Well," she said demurely. "I do hope you will join me."

"Yes?"

"Yes."

The limousine driver had to nose the car very slowly along the wharf, forging a way through the crowd. Cameras snapped, and microphones were thrust at the windows, while the pack of journalists and cameramen shouted out deafeningly. They were mostly yelling questions at Pederson, all of which he ignored.

"My God," said Helen. She couldn't believe it.

"I warned you," said Maggie.

They all scrambled out the doors nearest to the gangway, and climbed up to the promenade deck while the driver unloaded Brooke and the wheelchair. Two deckhands hurried down to heave up the chair and its grimfaced occupant. The limousine glided away – very slowly, as the reporters were still yelling.

It was a relief to get into the quiet, cool foyer – but then both girls let out a squeal. "Del!" they cried.

An eye-catching sight, this young man they called 'Del' was wearing baggy black trousers caught at the ankles, and a knee-length gold tunic. His ballet flats were gold, and his wide-brimmed black hat had a gold and black feather. Helen, fascinated, thought he looked as if he had wandered off the set of *Pirates of the Caribbean*.

"Why have you come back to the ship?" Kate demanded.

"You wish I'd stayed away?" His English was perfect.

"No, no," said Maggie, and all three laughed and hugged.

"He saved our lives," said Kate to Helen.

"Then I should hug him, too. Who is this spectacular young man?"

"He's Del! Proper name, Carlos del Rosario," said Maggie. "He designed all the wrought iron protection for the ship."

"And he is a brilliant designer," said Kate. "Even if Maggie does not think so."

"Not true!" cried Maggie.

Pierce Brooke interrupted, startling Helen. It was the first words in English she had heard him say in hours, and then she realised he was talking to her.

He sneered, "Those girls want you to sponsor him, Helen. To make him yet another one of your charities."

His mouth was twisted into that familiar thin, bitter smile. Helen glanced quickly at the Filipino designer, and saw that he had flushed hotly. His temper might be as quick as Brooke's, she thought.

Tucking her hand into the crook of Harold's arm, she said lightly, "Well, why not, if Mr. del Rosario is as good as the girls say? And he must be good, if Harold hired him, as my husband has very high standards. I must have a tour of the ship and the wrought ironwork, but not until I have showered and slept off at least a little of my jetlag."

And, smiling sweetly, she allowed herself to be borne away.

Twenty-five

Harold walked into the office and said, "The latest?"

Skye turned from his computer. "Blackwell is releasing emails."

"My name involved yet?"

"No, except for Pederson Strategic – the company, not the person. But this is very interesting. Two of the emails prove that Saudi Oil was in the game from the very beginning. The first is from Brooke – yes, our involuntary guest, who could be very useful indeed. It is dated the same day that he introduced you to Blackwell, and was sent to Feisal, passing on Blackwell's suggestion that he use Saudi Oil as a vehicle for the operation. Moments later, there was a reply from Feisal, saying that he would certainly go along with that idea."

Harold whistled. "We will certainly talk to Brooke about that. Any news of the whereabouts of Blackwell?"

"Not lately, but Maggie has finally remembered the name of the man who looked familiar – the one she glimpsed in the airport on the day she and Kate arrived. Waters. The journalist who is breaking the story. She is sure of it. So, if Waters is here, by logic Blackwell is, too."

"So why aren't the paparazzi baying at his hotel door?"

Skye shrugged. "He and Blackwell would be keeping a very low profile."

"Okay, so what else is new?"

"According to the ongoing story, the writer has been shown spreadsheets that give more away. Two weeks after those emails, three hundred million greenbacks were transferred from the newly formed Pederson Strategic into Saudi Oil's account. But only one hundred million actually got there. The other two were deposited with a shell company in Cyprus called Black Seal. The story makes a guess that the shell company belongs to Feisal, but I think we can take it as read."

"Do we have any better idea where Feisal is now?"

"Still the same. The paper repeats that he is on his yacht *Masha'Allah*, somewhere in the remote western Pacific."

"So he can't be far from here."

"As the crow flies, perhaps. But there are a lot of islands, and many secluded bays."

Jerry walked in, and Harold turned to him and said, "Ryan has left the ship?"

"Yep. Not without a few tears. Being fired without a reference is the worst punishment he can imagine."

"Did he obey orders and give the list of websites to you?"

"Of course. And I gave him back his phone – after I had deleted everything. As for the list of websites, I'll pass them privately to Captain Crawford. He is supposed to be an intelligence officer, even if he doesn't act like one."

"You are keeping in contact with the Brunei station?"

Jerry shrugged. "It could come in useful, some day."

"Maybe Crawford will find Blackwell."

"I can do that myself," said Jerry.

"You sound confident." Skye's eyebrows were arched.

"I am. All I need is Kate and her phone."

Harold barked, "You are not to put Kate in any danger!"

Both men looked at him with quick interest.

"Of course not," said Jerry.

When Harold slipped into bed beside Helen, she was fast asleep. Curtains had been drawn across the big oblong portholes, but enough late afternoon light came in for him to see her. The food he had sent in with Lester, the new chief steward, had been eaten, and the tray placed neatly on a table near the door.

Helen smelled of soap and shampoo, the scent of lemon balm that was so piercingly familiar. Harold thought she would sleep until morning, and though it was late afternoon, he was more than ready for a nap, himself. But just as he was nodding off, she blinked, turned her head on the pillow and smiled. Then she stretched luxuriously, and curled her naked length along and over him.

"You joined me," she said, and kissed his bristly cheek.

"I did," he agreed, waking up most pleasantly. "Just for a siesta before dinner."

"Lovely. But we need to talk."

He smoothed her hair. "Later."

"It's urgent. I have to talk to you before Pierce does."

He stroked her back. "Later."

"But ..." She silenced as he kissed her, and he was vividly aware of her slim form curled around and along his solid body, and knew that she was on the verge of purring like a cat. Many long moments after that, she was arching with pleasure.

"I had forgotten how good you are," she whispered teasingly, at the end.

Harold lay on his back, with her long body sprawled over him. Helen's face was buried in the corner between his shoulder and his ear, and he could feel her soft breath, and the flutter of her eyelashes. They had always been good together, despite the great difference in their ages, and though he was almost seventy, there was still the same marvelous cohesion. It had always been good, he thought, but this was even better, a most enjoyable reunion.

He thought back to the first time. She had arrived at his apartment without warning. He had been alone, eating breakfast, and without a word she had dropped her bags and her coat, and come up to him and kissed him. When he stood up, she clung to him, kissing him all the time.

Helen had been on fire, desperate to be with him in every way possible, and his own body had flared in response. He'd often pictured making love to her, but what had followed had exceeded his wildest expectations. It was like nothing he had ever experienced before, despite two previous wives and several liaisons.

And now she had something to tell him about it, because he knew she was mulling the same memory. As if on cue, Helen lifted her head, and said, "We do need to talk."

"It's not necessary, and I'd rather sleep. With you. Just until dinnertime, which should be about eight. Lots of time for a nap."

"No, it's important."

After she turned on the light, Harold slid up against the pillows, and watched her appreciatively as she walked over to the minibar. Helen was only two years away from her fiftieth birthday, but was still amazing when naked; she looked after her body well, and didn't mind his open appreciation, smiling as he let out a soundless whistle. As she often declared, her body was a temple, and she treated it as such, so worship was perfectly in order.

She handed him a generous dram of single malt, and nestled back beside him with her own drink in her hand. After a quick sip, she put the glass on the bedside table, and said, "We really do need to talk."

He sighed. "Okay."

"Truly, it has been on my conscience since the day we married." She took a deep breath, and then said, "The night before I moved into your apartment, Pierce came home in a rush, in a rage. He always had a hot temper, and something that had happened that day had triggered that rage. And …"

"He raped you?" Rage instantly filled him, and he spat the words out.

She shook her head. "We were still married, and — well, it happened. It was for the very last time. Harold, I have never, ever even *thought* of cheating on you. But the fact that I had slept with both you and Pierce the month my baby was conceived preyed on my mind throughout the pregnancy. And now…"

Harold put a hand on her arm and said, "Stop."

"What?" She blinked.

He stared right into her wide eyes. "I know exactly what you are going to say."

"But…"

"You are going to tell me that Brooke could claim that he is the father of your child."

She paled. "Did Jerry say something?"

"No one needed to say anything. I am not a fool, Helen."

She flushed. "Of course you are not a fool, Harold. You are one of the most intelligent men I have ever met. But…"

"Helen, I've known for a very long time that I was not Jewel's father."

"*What?*"

He paused while he contemplated her paling face over the rim of the glass. After swallowing a bracing mouthful of Scotch, he said, "I have a confession of my own to make." Another pause, another sip of whisky, and then he confessed, "I had Jewel's DNA analyzed."

"You did … *what?*"

"When she was ten, when they told us that her mental illness was incurable, that it would get more severe as she grew older, I took a mouth swab while she was asleep, and sent it to a laboratory."

"Without telling me? How dare you!"

"You were in a state. The diagnosis had affected you badly, too. There was no way we could have had a reasonable discussion. And when the doctors asked me whether there was a history of mental ill-health in my family, it became personal. A matter of pride. I refused to believe that I was responsible, so I checked, to make sure."

Helen took a deep breath. Reaching over to the table, she picked up the glass, and took a shaky gulp. Then she said, "You did that when Jewel was ten? So why did you wait *twelve years* before telling me?"

"I didn't want my marriage to end, but I did want to put it on an impersonal basis. Like a business."

"And so for ten years, before we sailed on the *Odyssey* and everything became changed, I was nothing more than your hostess, right? To be summoned whenever needed, to whatever place necessary. It certainly was a business arrangement, Harold. There was no affection or kindness at all. I did my job, the way you wanted. I coped — I coped, but it was truly awful."

"Please don't be angry. I am fully — totally, utterly — aware that it was the worst thing I ever did."

He put the glass down, and cupped her face in his hands, gazing into her eyes. "I fell crazily in love with you the first time I laid eyes on you, Helen, and our marriage was exactly as I had hoped it would be. Everything was wonderful — perfect. Because I was insulted, hurt, bewildered by the discovery that Jewel was not mine, I did my best to fall out of love with you. But it never happened. This year since our reconciliation on the *Odyssey* has been the best of my life."

Helen stared into his face for a very long moment. Then her expression crumpled. "Oh, Harold, I am so sorry. We should have had this conversation years ago — but it's my fault, as I was so preoccupied, *obsessed* with Jewel."

"There is more," he said.

"There is?"

"Brooke is not Jewel's father, either."

"Harold." She began to weep, tears running down her cheeks as she stared at him. "I swear there was no one else. You and Pierce were the only…"

"Think about it, Helen."

"I know that Jewel did not resemble Pierce, but…"

Again, he interrupted. "The only answer is that Jewel was never your daughter. Her mother and father were another couple. There is no other explanation possible."

"But…"

"Face it, Helen, we claimed the wrong baby."

"But that means…"

He shrugged, and finished his drink. "It does mean that our real daughter is either Kate or Maggie."

"You haven't taken their DNA?"

"Of course not. It's illegal, as well as not very nice. And it makes no difference, anyway."

"Why? What do you mean?"

"It doesn't matter who took which baby, because of the way things turned out — because the girls are both Bacchantes, and nothing we do or say is going to change that. Maggie might be the real Bacchante, or it might be Kate. Who knows? At a very long stretch, it could even be Jewel."

Her expression became stricken. "Would Jewel have had a better childhood with the Bacchantes?"

"Of course not. You did everything humanly possible to help Jewel, and no one could have done better."

But, he thought, his own life and their marriage would have been infinitely better if Helen had claimed either Kate or Maggie when she chose her baby. Then he pushed the thought away, because it solved nothing. What had been done had been done.

Instead he said, "When we took baby Jewel away, the Bacchante family didn't care whether the other two were biological Bacchantes or not; they simply adopted them as their own. And somehow, miraculously, those girls became Bacchantes, so alike that it is easy to confuse one with the other. Oh, I have learned that Maggie is the naughty one, while Kate is the dreamer, but they are both so *Italian*. They look Italian, and they talk like Italians; they wave their arms around like Italians; they are as passionate as Italians. Somehow, the Bacchante magic worked, and they became Bacchantes. Kate told me it was by osmosis."

"You think Maggie is naughty?" Helen pouted.

Suddenly the atmosphere was lighter. He grinned in relief and said, "Ask Del. She steals his designs."

"I must get to know that young man." Then she became more serious. "So what are you going to do when Pierce claims to have fathered my child?"

He shrugged. "Nothing. That you slept with him the night before you came to me is just part of your previous marriage, and no business of mine. And I don't believe he will try."

"Why?"

"If he persists in believing that he fathered Jewel, a glance at her portrait would persuade him that it's impossible."

Helen's breath caught. "That is exactly why I made all those phone calls, and agreed to bring Pierce to Manila."

"Not because he needs to testify about the beginnings of Pederson Strategic?"

"When I knew about that, of course it was a factor. But I have a personal reason, too — one that might stop Blackwell from leaking all that horrid stuff to the press."

He frowned. "Tell me."

"I showed Pierce a little print of Jewel's portrait with the same idea in my head. And Harold, he went crazy. Quite insane. Hysterical. He raved about a time when he had caught Blackwell and Feisal torturing a young prostitute."

"What?" Harold was suddenly objective, sensing that this could be crucial. His mind was running over conversations with Jerry and Skye.

"The two men had captured the poor child in order to do dreadful things to her, and he had the bad luck to see what they were doing. Well, when he saw the picture of Jewel, he jumped to the conclusion that it was a picture of the poor girl they had kidnapped. It reminded him of the awful scene he'd blundered upon— and the effect on him was truly terrible, even after all these years."

"Did he describe this in detail?"

Helen picked up her glass and took another gulp. "Not really. But he did tell me how it happened."

"Keep going."

"After Pierce had made the first arrangement for you to meet Blackwell and Feisal, something urgent about it cropped up.

Maybe you changed the conditions, or something, but whatever it was, he needed to see Blackwell in a hurry, to talk about your latest demand. Blackwell had a penthouse apartment in the Saudi Oil building in Geneva, so Pierce went there."

"Yes, I know the apartment."

"It was Sunday night, to the offices were empty, but Pierce had the codes to get into the building, and to use the elevator. He took the lift to the apartment lobby, and had expected that he would have to knock on the door until Blackwell answered. But the door was open."

Helen swallowed, and Harold slid his arm around her. "When he described what he saw, he said he wouldn't go into the details. But what he did tell me was just horrible. Awful. Ghastly." She gulped more whisky, blinking hard.

"Do you want to wait for a better time to go on?"

"No, I want to get the story finished. Pierce said he heard a girl whining with pain and terror, and so he went in. And there they were in the lounge — on a carpet. Weirdly enough, he remembered that it was a valuable Persian rug."

There were tears pouring down her cheeks. "She looked like Jewel, Harold, like Jewel! And they were — they were …"

She broke off, too torn to go on, and leaned on his chest, clinging to him as she cried. Muffled, she heard him say, "Did Brooke tell you the girl's name?"

"Yes. He knew it, because he grabbed up her bag and clothes when he took her to the hospital. Her passport was in the bag, which meant that he could take her to London when the hospital discharged her. When he got to his apartment he found — he found the divorce papers you had sent him, so — so he gave the keys and a lot of money to the girl, and hired a nurse to look after her. And then he flew to Washington, and — and that was the night he seduced me, the night before I moved into your apartment. He was very, very angry and upset and — *driven* — and I think that was why — why he behaved the way he did. And I threw him out!"

"It was not your fault."

"Oh Harold, I love you so much, and have never for a moment regretted that I moved in with you. But I can't help feeling guilty."

"Don't. I certainly have never regretted that you moved in with me." He held her close, and then said into her hair, "But you still haven't told me the girl's name."

"Oh." Her voice was muffled. "Debbie. Debbie Parkin. The girl who changed her name to Kelly."

Twenty-six

Dinner that night was an odd experience. Neither Skye nor Harold were there, as apparently they were reluctant to leave their computers, so Del and Pierce Brooke had taken their places. As far as Kate was concerned, Del was very welcome indeed, but she felt a lot less happy about Mr. Brooke, who seemed so grim.

And strangely focused on her.

He had been wheeled in by his carer, Maria. After an awkward silence Maggie had greeted Maria by name, trying out some Spanish, but the Mexican woman simply stared at her from under heavy eyebrows, her expression one of deep dislike. Then, with an equally hostile sideways glance at Helen, she had taken off without a word, presumably to have her meal in the crew mess — or maybe to eat alone, in her stateroom.

The table was better by her absence, though the man in the wheelchair was dour enough. He was drinking a lot of wine, but it didn't seem to improve his mood. When he looked at Helen, his expression was as full of dislike as Maria's had been, but most of the time he was staring at Kate, frowning as if he were sizing her up for a job. Though she tried not to meet his eyes, she couldn't help glancing back to find that he was still studying her face, and feeling indefinably threatened.

To distract herself, she tried to keep her attention on Helen, who seemed rested. There was an indefinable glow about her, but she was not her usual talkative company. Then Kate realized that Helen kept on looking at her in the same assessing way as the ex-husband, which made her feel even more uncomfortable. But then she saw that Helen was looking at Maggie, too; was studying them both as if she had forgotten what they looked like in the interval, and needed to refresh her memory.

It was not reassuring. Kate wondered what was going on in both their minds, and felt an inner chill. But when she looked at Maggie to see if she had noticed the strange atmosphere, her foster sister seemed perfectly oblivious. Instead, she was describing the mission that had been given to them by the British frigate.

"Crazy!" she said. "Those soldiers looked so competent, but weren't competent at all! Poor Harold, they nearly lost this ship."

"But the scenery as we sailed up the estuary was just so amazing," said Kate, glad to be diverted. "All those animals! And the growth, such a riot of green and brown, so many brilliant birds. But," she added with a shiver, "there were crocodiles. I didn't like them at all."

"It was later, when the soldiers decided to seize the freighter in the dark that it all turned bad," Maggie agreed. "That's what I meant about their incompetence. They hadn't left enough men to guard the captives who were already on board, and two of them escaped."

"And raced up to the bridge — well, one crashed into the bridge with his rifle, while the other one was searching the suites on that deck. And that's how he found Maggie and me," said Kate. "And held us up with his rifle, and made terrible threats in some foreign language."

"Bahasa," said Jerry, who was listening with a grin.

"Really? I thought it was Arabic, but it sounded really horrible. I was sure he was going to make hostages of us, and then behead us later on. On television," Kate added ghoulishly.

"But Del rescued us," said Maggie, and related the story with relish.

"Oh Del, I could kiss you," Helen exclaimed, and Del blushed and concentrated on the food on his plate.

"What I can't understand," said Helen, "is why Harold agreed to let them use *Storm Swept* for the exercise."

Jerry shrugged. "It looked like a safe deal at the time. There was no way Harold could have known the military would make such a hash of it."

"And inside every man there is a little boy who never quite grew up."

Both girls clapped their hands, enchanted with the idea. "Was that why you were so brave, Del?" Maggie asked. "Because of the little boy inside you?"

Which made poor Del more embarrassed still.

When the meal was over Maggie and Del headed aft for the promenade lounge, evidently to talk over designs, so Kate resigned herself to watching television in the suite.

The local commentators seemed to be discussing the weather, but they were speaking in Tagalog, so she couldn't understand them. Behind their talking heads there were images of a growing blob in the Philippine Sea, to the east, which brought uncomfortable memories, of last year, when they'd become trapped between a thunder belt and a cyclone. The storm had been tremendous, and people had died. Again, there was a chilly presentiment inside her.

But, when Kate switched to one of the international channels, there was no mention of any brewing typhoon, so she put it out of her mind. She turned off the television, deciding to read a book instead, but was interrupted when Maggie came rushing into the cabin.

"Come, come," she cried. "You must come, Kate!"

A jolt of alarm. "Why? What is it?"

"I've found the Bellissimo summer show on YouTube! They posted it online overnight, and I got the text just now. We found it and paused it, so that you can see it too."

"The New York show?"

"No, the Italian one, the one promoting the parent house in Rome, but still …" Maggie rushed out again, with Kate hot on her heels, down the stairway and into the lounge.

Helen was there, talking to Del, obviously finding him interesting. To Kate's surprise, Pierce Brooke was there too, silent as ever, with a glass of something amber in his hand. What an old misery guts, she thought, but at least they could be thankful that his even more miserable carer was absent.

She took a seat and Lester, the new chief steward, came in with a tray of nuts, chocolates and grapes. He was a good-looking young man, with a face that was creased up impishly in a constant wide grin. Obviously, he was delighted with his promotion. Ryan had been nice, though, and Kate wondered why he had left.

They all ordered drinks, and saluted each other with their glasses. Then, with a fanfare — "Tra-la-la!" — Maggie turned on the YouTube show.

Jerry arrived, and sat on the settee beside Kate. He said, "What is it?"

"Bellissimo, the summer show."

"It's in Italian."

"You noticed?" Maggie laughed. "But all the staff in the New York house are bound to be watching."

When Lester came with an enquiring smile, Jerry shook his head at the offer of a drink, but he did take a chocolate. Then he said, "So none of the New York designs will be on display?"

"Of course not."

The show had been filmed at night, but there was plenty of dramatic lighting. Young men with designer stubble were striding back and forth along a terrace, turning and posing to show off variously colored outfits. Tight yellow pants, tight pink pants, brocade vests over tailored shirts with Nehru collars. Blazers, lots of blazers.

Maggie said, "Bad news for you, Del. Baggy pants are out."

The Filipino designer merely smiled. He was wearing purple painter's overalls over a lime green shirt. For once, he was not wearing his hat, revealing a thick mop of unruly black hair.

Jerry said, "I am not sure I would wear any of that stuff."

"You have to look past the glitz!" Maggie protested.

"At what?"

"The length! The snugness! The collars. The shoes, the pockets!"

The men revolved, then walked off screen, their bottoms tight in their close-fitting pants. Supple women took their place, and the camera moved back, to show them leaving the terrace one by one, and mincing confidently down a wide flight of stone steps. It was somewhere in Italy, Kate thought, perhaps Sicily, the ancestral island of both the House of Bellissimo and the *famiglia Bacchante*. With the wider view she could see an old church in mellow stone at the back of the terrace.

Most of the women were wearing long gowns, some with trains, some with bouffant skirts, yet they managed to stare straight ahead as they descended. Then, at the bottom, a pause with one hand on one hip, a smooth turn, and the same kind of walk back up the stairway to the terrace.

"That's quite an art," she said.

"You have no idea," said Helen. When Kate looked round,

Helen smiled, and said, "I used to do that."

"You were a fashion model?" The girls stared, impressed.

"In my youth, yes. What you call a runway model. It takes a lot of training." She stood up to demonstrate, while Maggie paused the show. "Watch how I put one foot in front of the other. Left foot forward, then swing the right foot to keep in the same line. It makes the hips sway, and gives a flip to a longer skirt, or an extra dimension to leggings, tight pants, a mini-skirt, hotpants or whatever. The other trick is to keep the back straight and the shoulders square. Tip the hips forward, just a little. Stare straight ahead, never meet anyone's eye. It helps to listen to music, even if the music is just in your head. At the end of the runway, stop, turn, one hand on hip, one ankle cocked into the other, as a ballet dancer would do. Turn, drop hands back to the sides, and walk away. See how the catwalk flatters the garment?"

She sat down, laughing and flushed, looking a lot younger than her forty-eight years. Maggie smiled, shaking her head in wonder, and restarted the video. More models sashayed down the steps and along the terrace.

"I can see why they call it the catwalk," said Del. He was leaning forward with his elbows on his knees, intent on the television screen. "For that is the way a cat would walk along the top of a narrow wall, or a fence. One paw in front of the other, then pause. Paw, paw, pause."

Jerry and the women laughed. Pierce Brooke snorted, but no one took any notice.

"Florals," said Maggie. Her fingers twitched, as if she wished she were taking notes. "Frills. Gauzy fabrics. *Tiers* of frills. Tight bodices, frilly skirts. Nipped-in waists. I need to change my portfolio!"

Kate protested, "But what about your snowdrop dress? I

thought they loved it in New York."

"They did, they did, but now it is so, so outré. *Fuori moda,* Kate!"

"But why?"

"Look at the waists!" The models now stepping down from the terrace were wearing day dresses with big skirts and square-necked bodices.

"Back to the days of the twist," Helen observed.

"What is the twist?" asked Del.

Helen laughed. "That dates me," she said. "It was a really energetic dance that involved a lot of whirling around, and demanded a big skirt, preferably with lots of frilly petticoats. The skirt was circular at the hem, and tightly crimped in at the waist."

Maggie sighed, "And my snowdrop dress falls straight from right under the bust."

"Oh, the fashion will come back," said Del.

"I don't honestly care, Del." Maggie was intent on the evolving fashion show again. "This is so *inspiring.* Boleros, boxy handbags, lots of blazers in crazy materials, and oh look, paneled skirts in the most wonderful glossy fabrics — and the colors! All the panels different, and yet they blend. And flowers — tropical flowers and ferns."

Then, to Kate's alarm, Maggie let out a shriek. "Oh my God," she cried. "*O Dio, Dio* —my God, my God!"

"What is it?"

"My fabric designs! Remember how inspired I was in French Polynesia? The brilliance of the flowers and the birds, the amazing colors of the sea, how everything happened in curves? I created the designs back then, back last year. The creative directors in New York loved the designs, but I had forgotten! And now, oh Kate, they are using them in Rome! No wonder the junior designers are so jealous of me!"

She lunged out of the settee, hugged Kate and Helen, and kissed Del and Jerry lavishly on the cheeks. "Oh my God," she said again. She was crying with delight.

"Oh my God," snorted Pierce Brooke. It was a disgusted echo.

And without another word he wheeled himself out of the lounge.

Twenty-seven

When Jerry walked into Pierce Brooke's suite without knocking, Brooke looked up from the minibar, and said, "What?"

Jerry sat down on the other side of a coffee table, and looked around. The handicapped suite looked just the same as the verandah suite as he had on the bridge deck, two levels above, except that it was more spacious.

He said, "You left in a hurry. Were you bored by the fashion show?"

Brooke turned around with a filled glass in his hand. "The steward forgot to top up my drink."

"Oh, I am sorry about that." Jerry kept the sarcasm out of his voice, as he did not want to alienate an important witness, but couldn't help adding, "I'll have a word with him."

"Why do you care? Are you in charge of the stewards?"

Jerry laughed. "Not exactly."

"So what the hell are you doing on this boat? There don't seem to be any proper passengers."

"I'm head of security."

A pause, and then Brooke said aggressively, "So you've come to limit my drinking?"

"I have no idea why you thought that. I see you have poured yourself a single malt Scotch. Do you mind pouring me one, too? I can promise you that the bottle will be replaced, when empty."

"You can?"

"Indeed I can."

For the first time, Brooke smiled. It was a wolfish grin. He poured a large portion, and wheeled over with the glass.

Jerry reached over the coffee table, took it, held it up to the light, nodded, and sipped. "Excellent," he said. "Very peaty, the way I like it. Laphroig?"

"How did you guess?"

Brooke wheeled back, and saluted with his own glass. He was relaxing at last. Jerry lounged back, crossed one ankle over the other knee, and sipped.

"A change from tequila?" he remarked.

"Nothing wrong with tequila in its home country," Brooke countered. He sounded defensive, and his eyes slid away from Jerry's face. They were very expressive eyes, dark brown with gold lights and long black lashes, unusually good-looking eyes for a man. Vivid. They reminded Jerry of someone, but he pushed the thought away.

Instead, he said, "No single malt in Mexico, I imagine."

"Depends where you are. Did Helen tell stories about my love affair with tequila?"

"Nope. But she did mention that you had something to discuss with Harold Pederson."

"Oh yes." A flash that looked very like hatred crossed Brooke's face. "I had sex with Helen the night before she moved in with Pederson, and I was going to tell him all about it. In detail."

"You were married to her at the time, so it would hardly be a surprise to him."

"I enjoyed the idea of Pederson having to bring up my child."

Jerry's eyebrows shot up. "That's an interesting notion. What was your logic?"

"Helen fell pregnant the same month she had sex with me."

"How do you know that?"

"The internet, naturally. Dr. Google knows it all, if you know where to hunt. The birth of the Pederson daughter made news at the time, so it was easy to track down."

"So what made you feel certain that you were the father of her child?"

Brooke shrugged.

"You must have a good reason for jumping to that conclusion."

Silence. Brooke merely drank whisky.

"Otherwise it looks a lot like wishful thinking."

Another shrug.

"And so many years have passed. Her baby was born over twenty years ago."

"Until I checked on the internet, I had no idea that she'd had a child. For some reason, I had lost all interest in the woman."

This was definitely sarcastic, but Jerry ignored it. He probed, "This was a recent search?"

"Yes."

"So what triggered it?"

Brooke sighed impatiently. "Oh, for God's sake! If you really want to know, it was because of a woman's magazine — one of those glossy, gossipy rags that they keep in doctors' rooms. I was leafing through it, just to pass the time while I waited for my turn. And I saw a photograph of Helen with a girl — a girl who looked a hell of a lot like my own mother."

"It must have been a striking resemblance."

"See for yourself." Brooke fished about, and produced a wallet. Taking an old photograph out of it, he handed it over to Jerry.

Jerry studied it carefully. Though it was black and white, and stained brown with age at the edges, it was obvious that Brooke's mother been beautiful. She'd had dark hair that was streaked with the sun, and dark eyes, black-fringed. They sparkled as she laughed into the camera. So, he thought, that was where Brooke got his remarkable eyes. Again, the haunting resemblance nudged at his mind.

He put the picture on the coffee table, took out his phone and photographed it. Handing the photo back to Brooke, he said, "I'm sure you don't mind. Your mother was a very lovely woman."

"She died when I was eighteen."

"I am sorry to hear that. But why did you assume that the girl who looked like your mother was Helen's daughter?"

Brooke's tone became defensive. "They looked a pair, very compatible, as if they had been together a long time. In the picture they were holding hands, and laughing. And it helped that I really liked the idea of blackmailing Helen about it. A threat to tell her husband should have repaid some of what she owed me for twenty years of hell."

Jerry paused, then said, "But you were wrong. The girl in the illustration was Kate, the writer Helen was sponsoring."

"It's not the first time I've made an idiot of myself — as Helen has undoubtedly pointed out."

"To err is human, and lots of people look like people they are not related to; there are only just so many physical types in the world, I suppose. But it is still interesting. Did you still see a resemblance to your mother when you met Kate in person?"

Unexpectedly, Brooke barked with laughter. "Maybe in looks, but she has nothing like my mother's refinement. My mother was a Cabot; she came from an old New England family, one that went right back to the seventeenth century. Was on committees for the Daughters of the American Revolution. She moved in the highest social circles, and had strict ideas of deportment, dress and etiquette. Not only would she have greatly disapproved of that girl's free and easy behavior, but she would have let her know about it, too. Quietly and discreetly, but firmly."

Jerry had trouble not shaking his head. Looking at the messy, half-drunk shambles in the wheelchair, it was impossible to imagine Brooke being raised by a Boston-Brahmin snob.

He said mildly, "Kate was only trying to be friendly."

"And her sister is even worse. All that hysteria, just because some fashion house had used her flashy designs!"

"It's the Italian influence. They are Bacchantes, and the Bacchante family is demonstrative like that. The Bacchantes have been in New Zealand for five generations, but still have a strong emotional link to Sicily."

Brooke didn't answer. Instead, he wheeled to the minibar again. Watching him pour another large dram, Jerry ruminated that he had to focus the questioning while his subject was still conscious. At this rate of drinking Brooke was going to pass out.

When Brooke had wheeled round to face him again, Jerry cleared his throat, and said, "Helen told me that you became very agitated when she showed you the photo of her daughter."

"She did?" It was a snarl. "Well, she was right. It was a horrible shock."

"She only intended to demonstrate that her daughter was not at all like your mother, certainly not to distress you in any way. But, as she went on to describe, the picture brought back bad memories of a girl you rescued from some ordeal."

Brooke's eyes narrowed over the rim of his glass. "Helen told you about Debbie Parkin?"

Jerry nodded. "As it happens, I have a personal interest."

"Why?"

"I knew Debbie Parkin well. Only I knew her as Kelly. By the time I met her, she had changed her name. I learned her real name only because she didn't change her passport."

"When was this, exactly?"

Jerry told him, and Brooke's expression became bleak. "She had good reason to change her name, very good reason indeed. I am glad she had the sense to do it."

"Why?"

"I don't want to talk about it. How did you meet her?"

"I'd just got back from Saudi, where I had put out a huge fire — you can check that with Dr. Google too, if you want. As you can imagine, I was keen to have some social life. And I picked Kelly up in a nightclub — a kind of fancy cabaret, where they had a show. She was one of the dancers. I hung around until her shift was over and then asked her to come out with me. She was a great date — we were great together. I liked her so much that I wanted more of her company. I'd always hankered to go to New Zealand and explore the country at leisure, and when I invited her to come along, she jumped at the chance."

Brooke was staring into his glass. "It must have seemed like a godsend. A golden chance to get out of danger."

Jerry's pulse jumped. "She was in danger?"

"In terrible danger. You have no idea. Why do you think she changed her name? And her job?"

Jerry paused, but when Brooke didn't elaborate, he said easily, "We were together for four months. It was a wonderful holiday, one of the best I have had — except for the hurricane, of course."

"Hurricane?"

"That's just a detail. The important thing is that we were still in New Zealand when her baby was born. It was a bit of a panic, because it happened during the height of the storm, and that's how I ended up with Kate. Kelly — Debbie Parkin — disappeared the day after the birth, leaving me with this newborn infant. Well, that took the wind out of my sails, as you can imagine. I've always been a footloose sort of guy. But as it turned out, it was not a problem."

Brooke's eyes widened. "Debbie Parkin was *pregnant* when you met her?"

"Four or five months gone. Not that either of us knew it. Kelly — Debbie, I mean — was as surprised as I was when it was confirmed. She went to a doctor a month or so after we got to New Zealand, because she couldn't think why her stomach was getting so swollen, and after the examination and a few tests he gave her the bad news. I'm sure that if she had known earlier, she would have done something about it."

Brooke's expression became very grim. He drank deeply, half-emptying his glass. "There was so much damage inside that it's not surprising she didn't know," he muttered. "It's unbelievably horrible that a child was conceived at all. No wonder she ran away from the infant."

Ran away? No, she had died. With grief, Jerry remembered finding her gravestone. However, he merely said, "Damage?"

Brooke shut his eyes, then opened them again, his dark stare unfocused. "You couldn't possibly guess what they were doing to her when I walked into that apartment — not outside a horror film."

Jerry let out a silent breath of relief. He had finally got the man talking. "Please tell me about it."

"It's not a pleasant story."

"So I gather." Jerry leaned forward and fiddled with his phone, which was still on the coffee table. "You don't mind if I record this part of the conversation?"

"I certainly do!"

"It might spare you having to testify in court." When Brooke stared, Jerry nodded and said, "It could very easily come to that.

We want to bring this crime to justice."

"The bastards should be hanged!"

Jerry said quietly, "I agree."

"So you already know something? Helen repeated what I told her?"

Jerry nodded.

"I spared her the details, believe me."

"I know." Again, Jerry nodded.

And with that, Pierce Brooke finally launched himself into the retelling. The story burst out of him, his tone fierce and passionate. The details that poured out were even more grueling than Jerry expected. Feisal and Blackwell might have been totally out of their minds with drugs, but the joint brutality was beyond belief.

Jerry had to keep on swallowing. He was a hard man in a hard business, yet it was difficult not to gag. This obscenity had happened to *Kelly* — beautiful, vulnerable Debbie Parkin, who had already suffered so much in her short life. Her mother had been a drunk and an addict, and there had been a series of stepfathers, some more unpleasant than others. There had been a great deal of abuse, all the way from when she was a toddler.

Surely that was enough? No girl, and certainly not poor Kelly, deserved what Brooke was now describing. Jerry had to keep pretending to adjust the phone, so that he could blink moisture away from his eyes.

"The hospital report has it all." Brooke's stare was distant, focused on terrible events in the past. "There were bite marks all over her body; they had to remove objects that had been shoved up inside her — stitches were needed in her private places, and half her scalp had been torn loose. The sick bastards had forced her to take a cocktail of drugs. It's in scientific language, to make it objective for the doctors, I suppose, but I was there — I saw it! I saw what those psychopaths had done! And I have had to live with that nightmare ever since — have been deeply scarred with their evil. So when Helen brought it back to me…"

He silenced, and emerged from a kind of trance. After looking around dazedly, he picked up his glass, and finished off the drink.

"You were quite the hero," said Jerry, finding his voice at last. He leaned forward, and turned off the phone.

"Any decent man would have rescued her. If I hadn't been there…" Brooke broke off and then said grimly, "I am absolutely certain that when they had finished with her they would have killed her — that is, if she hadn't already died. Removed the evidence. She was too badly hurt to be bribed to forget it. She would have had to go to a doctor or a hospital to fix what they had done to her, and during the consultation she would have had to describe what had happened. There was no way they could let her go free. I believe without doubt that I saved her life."

Jerry winced, looking down at his tightly gripped hands. Such evil was beyond belief, and yet it was obvious that Brooke was right. If he hadn't blundered into the apartment, Debbie would have been murdered, and her remains interred in some remote Swiss field. No wonder, he thought, she had changed her name. And her job.

He looked up again. "So what happened after that?"

"After she was discharged from the hospital, I took her to London. The flight was an ordeal, as the poor girl was still dazed and hurting, and it was a huge relief to get her to my apartment. I gave her my bed and hired a nurse to come in daily and tend to her wounds. But then I was distracted."

Brooke's voice had become flat and embittered again.

Jerry prompted, "By what?"

"Legal papers were waiting there. Someone had slipped them under the door. A lazy lawyer's clerk, I suppose. He or she would have been ordered to hand them to me personally, but I was away, of course."

Brooke's breath hissed between his teeth. "Helen was suing for divorce — on the grounds of my infidelities. *She* was suing *me*, when I had seen her behaving like a cat on heat. You know what her job was, when I met her? Yes, of course you do — she was bragging about it in the lounge. Swinging her hips on catwalks, one foot in front of the other, modeling tight dresses with plunging necklines. Believe me, she might boast about her wooden face as she minced along the runway, but her body was super-sexy."

Jerry shrugged. "She was a beautiful woman who had to do something to make a living."

"You think so?" Brooke laughed, a humorless sound. "She certainly knew how to use her looks. After I was fool enough to marry her, she set up business in Washington, teaching the wives of diplomats and politicians how to behave the same way. Even getting me on board that helicopter to come here — when I did not want to come at all! — was assisted by men who had succumbed to her wiles. Five ignorant Mexicans! And she was suing me! Me! After I got those papers my one idea was to have it out with that bitch, so I took the first plane home."

"You flew to Washington to teach Helen a lesson?"

"Believe me, I had no trouble getting her to spread her legs," Brooke spat. "I promise you it wasn't rape."

Jerry paused, and then said calmly, "And when you hunted the internet for the timing of the birth of her daughter, you jumped to the conclusion that Helen's child was conceived the night you returned to Washington?"

Brooke shrugged. "It seemed logical."

"But what about Kelly — Debbie Parkin? The girl who also fell pregnant about that same time. You just left her in your London apartment?"

"I *gave* her the apartment, as it turned out. I left plenty of cash and the keys, and there was food in the pantry, the fridge and the freezer. I did *not* leave her in the lurch. She could have stayed there as long as she liked without owing me a cent. It was freehold, in my name, and all the outstanding bills would have been paid automatically, as set up with my bank. It wasn't meant to be permanent, because I intended to go back, but a divorce and a car crash got in my way."

"But you can swear that you didn't have sex with her?"

"My God, no! Never! I am not a monster, whatever Helen might be saying. You have to look at Blackwell and Feisal to find which one was responsible for her pregnancy. They were the monsters who raped her!"

"Helen has never called you a monster. But do you still think Kate resembles your mother?"

Brooke shrugged. "As I said, it's not so obvious, now that I have met her. There is a physical resemblance, yes, but in nature she is entirely different. Why do you ask?"

"Kate is Kelly's daughter — she was Debbie Parkin's baby. That's why her writer name is Kate Kelly."

"*What?* But—"

"Which means that when you claimed that Kate was your child, the natural conclusion was that you'd had sex with Kelly — with Debbie Parkin."

"Never! Oh my God! Does it really look like that?"

Brooke clutched his forehead, his expression fraught. "That terrible night was the first time I had ever seen Debbie! I swear that I would *never* have forced myself on that poor girl — and forcing is what it would have needed. She was torn down there, and hurting like hell!"

"I believe you," Jerry said quietly.

They were rudely interrupted. Maria marched in without knocking, and looked around aggressively, and Jerry realized that Brooke had been shouting.

Without another word, he picked up his phone and left, feeling very shaken indeed.

Twenty-eight

"Where the hell is Jerry?"

"You have to ask Kate," said Skye. His tone was absent, as he was reading the latest headlines in the London tabloid.

Harold looked impatient. "He's not answering his phone."

"Perhaps he's asleep. He was up and about really late."

"No, he's not on the ship."

"So he is asleep at Rosita's place."

"Then he'd better wake up real soon."

Harold walked over to Skye's computer, and hunkered down to see the update. "What's the latest?"

"More emails have been released. You remember the two hundred million that vanished in a transfer from Pederson Strategic to Saudi Oil, just over five years ago? According to this, it was deposited into the Black Seal account in Cyprus, and then disappeared again. The claim is that the account belongs to Zaid Feisal, who diverted the money to somewhere else. All to make it hard to trace, of course, but the emails reveal that the Cyprus bank checked back with Saudi Oil to make sure it was legit, got an affirmative right away, and moments later Feisal emailed Blackwell with the message that the money should be cleared soon. And Saudi Oil has issued another disclaimer, saying that whatever money was unaccounted for must have been for brokering services."

"That's a hell of a lot of money for brokering services. Do they expect anyone to believe it?"

"They had to say something, I suppose."

"So we will have to issue a legal notice that we are suing them for two millions' worth of misappropriated money."

"It's the logical step," agreed Skye."

Harold said gloomily, "Wherever the money is now."

Skye shrugged. "In a wallet somewhere in the cloud, stuffed with cryptocurrency?"

Harold winced.

"It would certainly be easier if we could prove it had been splashed out on consumer goods — property, paintings, that kind of stuff." Skye thought briefly about Brooke's London apartment, wondering whether it had been bought with dirty money, but as a lead it went nowhere, so he discarded it.

He then remembered Harold's original query. "So why the urgency about Jerry? Does it matter if he isn't on board?"

"There's a storm on the way and Captain Calamari is starting to panic."

"What's new?" The comment was dry, but Skye got up and went through the door to the bridge.

When he arrived, Captain Calamari turned away from the screen he had been intently watching. He certainly looked panicky; his hair was wild, and his eyes darted back and forth.

"*Tempesta!*" he exclaimed when he focused on Skye. "*Enorme tempesta, in arrivo!*"

Skye didn't bother to remind him that English was the language of the ship. He left that to Harold, who was following close behind. Instead, he bent down to look at the screen himself. There was an area of low pressure south of Guam that looked as if it might be ominous, but as far as he could tell, it was not evolving into a typhoon.

He straightened, and said in English, "What is the problem?"

"That!" The captain pointed at the blob.

"So I see. Where does that image come from?"

"PAGASA."

Skye blinked. *"Who?"* When he looked at Harold, the ship's owner shook his head.

"The Philippine Atmospheric, Geophysical and Astronomical Services Administration." Calamari recited the words slowly and portentously, like a mantra.

"Oh," said Skye. "Their weather bureau."

The captain's expressive face lengthened into disapproving lines. "It is a most important agency. The Philippines suffer the greatest number of annual typhoons of any country in the world, so PAGASA is of importance most critical. They have posted a tropical cyclone warning signal," he said, then added, "Category four."

"And what does that mean?"

"We can expect 100-mile gusts, perhaps stronger. All the schools and colleges and offices buildings are closed. If it is upgraded to category five, all public transport will shut down."

"But it is only June."

"That is the beginning of the typhoon season, which reaches its peak in November."

Skye looked at the screen again. "But the blob isn't starting to spin. Surely they are overreacting?"

"Soon it will be replaced by an image more recent. While the storm is developing at sea, the warning is issued every twelve hours. Soon, it will be every three hours, once it starts to spin. And," Calamari went on, more portentously than ever, "it has been given a name. Polly."

"Oh damn," said Skye. He knew exactly the dire significance

of giving a storm a name. Obviously, it was going to get chaotic downtown. So where the hell was Jerry?

"Just six years ago, a storm like this one killed over six thousand Filipino people."

Skye frowned, thinking that Calamari was so obsessed with global warming that he had turned himself into some kind of expert on weather disasters. Then he looked out the bridge windows. The sky was filled with gray clouds that scudded fast, and flags were standing out stiffly. As he watched, ships were loosing their moorings, ready to go to sea.

"Why are they sailing?"

"In a storm like this one some ships broke free in this very harbor, and a Taiwanese freighter was severely damaged."

Harold shifted. "So what does that mean for us?"

"So, sir, we need to promptly sail south. Though the storm will pursue us, it will moderate when it reaches the South China Sea. The colder waters will weaken it."

"Fair enough. We have to get to Singapore anyway, to pick up a party, and it's no problem if we get there earlier than expected."

Skye interrupted, "But we have to wait for Jerry."

"Where do you think he might be?"

"I don't know. He questioned Brooke at length last night, and then had a private talk with Kate."

"What about?"

"All I know is that he needed her phone."

Harold said briskly, "So we had better go and ask Kate what it was about."

They left the bridge through the door that led back into the suite they were using as an office, and then hurried across the corridor to the girls' verandah suite. The door wasn't shut, and was swinging back and forth with the increased motion of the ship.

Kate was at her computer. She turned around as they came in and said, "Is Jerry back?"

"No, and we have to sail soon, as a big storm is on the way."

"*Sail?* But aren't we safer in port?"

"Apparently not."

Harold said, "What did Jerry want with your phone?"

Kate grimaced. "He wanted me to phone that horrid Waters, and make an appointment to meet up."

"The journalist?"

"That's the one. I didn't want to do it at all, but the number of his last call was on my phone, so it was easy enough to ring back."

"But why him?"

She paused, and then said very reluctantly, "Waters has this weird idea that the *Honourable* Adrian Blackwell is my biological father. That he was the man who impregnated Kelly — my mother. And, of course, there is a story in it, the sort of story that sells sensational magazines."

"But it's simply not true!" Harold exclaimed.

Skye looked at him sharply, but then shook his head. "Of course not."

"So what was the point?" Harold asked Kate. "Did Jerry tell you?"

"Waters wanted to meet up with me for an interview, so Jerry told me to accept. He's keeping the appointment for me, of course, and headed off a couple of hours ago. And I think he was really hoping to meet up with Blackwell himself."

"Blackwell is in Manila?" Pederson's question was quick.

"They both are."

"Dear God." Harold sounded shaken. "Blackwell is bound to

have a bodyguard."

"Jerry can take care of himself," said Skye. His tone was confident, but inside he was feeling very uneasy indeed.

He tried Jerry's phone, with the same lack of success as Harold, then dialed Rosita's number, but just got an out of service message. The storm, he realized, was having an impact already.

He said to Harold, "I'll go to Rosita's, make sure she is okay. Jerry might be there."

"It will have to be fast, or we will sail without either of you."

When Skye looked out Kate's window, more ships were leaving port, their funnels trailing ragged skeins of smoke. As he ran down the gangway, a gust flicked hard, tugging at his hair and slapping at the legs of his jeans. On the other side of the pier, a flag snapped above a new arrival, and when he looked it was a frigate, flying the British ensign under the Philippine flag.

Why had it come into port when all the other ships were leaving? For quick refueling before dashing away from the cyclone? Or to render aid? Skye supposed that it might be the same frigate that had requisitioned *Storm Swept* off northern Borneo, but could not be sure. To him, one modern frigate looked like another; the shape was the same, along with the gray camouflage coloring. There were a few seamen on the deck, but no other sign of activity.

It seemed a long dash through the port area before getting to the gates, but then he was able to hail a *tuktuk*. The boy on the motorbike that powered the taxi was as cheerful as if nothing out of the way was about to happen, lifting a thumb as Skye clambered into the cab. There was the usual debate over the tiny cost of the ride, and then they were off.

The sidewalks were full of hurrying people, and the

motorways were packed with cars, all part of the rush to get to home and shelter, or so Skye supposed. As the *tuktuk* negotiated the thick traffic, he saw that the shops were all closed, with grilles and screens locked tight over doors and windows.

It took a lot of hammering on Rosita's door before she answered it. She looked as cheerful as ever, even in the face of possible disaster, but Skye had learned long since that that was the spirit of the Philippine people.

She did look concerned when he asked after Jerry, though. Was he not on the ship? Skye reassured her that Jerry was fine, and then asked if he had let her know where he was going. But no, she hadn't seen her ex since the day before, and not heard from him, either, so had no idea where he might be. Skye wished her luck, and left.

Luckily, the *tuktuk* driver had waited, his expression optimistic, and was happy to rush him back to the port gates. Skye paid him double what they had agreed, and the lad chugged off happily. Then Skye started to run. It was starting to rain. In the distance, he could see a couple of deckhands on the promenade deck of *Storm Swept*, standing at the ready to unlash the gangway. Stevedores were waiting by the bollards, set to release the hawsers when hailed from the bridge.

The frigate, he saw, was also readying to leave. The ship might have been only partly refueled — if indeed that was why it had come here — but there was a definite air of urgency. There must have been another update from PAGASA, which meant that the typhoon was touching land earlier than expected.

Then, to his astonishment, Jerry materialized from behind a container stack, also running for *Storm Swept*. Three men came out just behind him.

Skye yelled Jerry's name, and when Jerry stopped and turned, he shouted, "We have to get on board!"

To his relief, the deckhands at the top of the gangway had also seen him. Skye grabbed Jerry's arm as he arrived alongside, then saw to his surprise that the three men had also stopped and waited.

He said, "What's going on?"

He recognized one of the men as the face next to the byline in the newspaper stories. Waters — Graham Waters. The writer behind the Pederson Strategic revelations. The other two were strangers. One was entirely clad in black, with a black hat crammed over his head, tied down with a black scarf that was also wrapped about his neck and chin despite the humid heat. The fellow with him was a heavyset Chinese, and so like the bodyguard of a thriller movie that it was almost funny. Despite the gale and rain, the fellow was even wearing black wraparound glasses.

Jerry's name was being yelled — from the other side of the wharf. Skye turned to see a man in uniform running towards them from the frigate. Captain Crawford, wearing the same intelligence corps outfit that he had worn when he first visited *Storm Swept*. Miraculously, the green beret was still neatly tucked on his head; it was as if it had been glued into place.

He rushed up, panting, and said to Jerry, "I got your message. You have something for me?"

Jerry said, "Yep," and fished around in a pocket. He came up with a page covered with neat, small writing, and said, "I tackled the member of the crew who forewarned the terrorists that there was a plan to retake the freighter."

"You worked out his identity?"

"Yep. And he also got word to the pirate lair up the river. That's the reason there were so few left in the camp, just those seven to guard the hostages."

"The Abu Sayyaf had something on him?"

"Nope. He was just an idiot who had fallen for crazy conspiracy theories. Internet, of course. This is the list of websites he wrote out before he left."

"Great." Crawford looked at the paper, holding it hard as it flapped in the wind. "Terrific. You are still at the top of your game, Major."

"Hardly. And I doubt that the websites are still there. Mists in the dark, Captain, mists in the dark. And we have to get going."

Men were yelling from the decks of both the frigate and *Storm Swept*. To his amusement, Skye saw that the heavyset Chinese had quietly left. Crawford's military uniform was the trigger, no doubt. Another yell from *Storm Swept*. Skye put his head down and ran for the gangway, with Jerry close behind.

The wind was gusting hard as they ran up to the promenade deck. Waters and the other man followed. Neither, as far as Skye knew, had said a word. They were right behind when he shoved open the heavy door to the foyer. Then they were all safely inside and the door slammed shut against the wind.

He turned, lifted one eyebrow, and said, "The *Honourable* Adrian Blackwell, I presume."

"Bright as ever, Skye," Jerry said, and introduced them.

Skye merely nodded at Waters, disregarding him as a sensation-hunting hack, but studied Blackwell with interest. The man had the most intensely blue eyes he had ever seen, as focused and unblinking as the beam from a laser gun. They reminded him of… A shiver ran down the back of his neck as he tore his own eyes away.

He looked at Jerry, and said, "I don't like this, not one little bit. Are you sure it's a good idea?"

"I think so, definitely," said Jerry.

Blackwell said nothing, but unwound his scarf and removed his hat. It was weird to watch, like a vampire rising from a coffin, because his skin was so dead white. His pallid head was shaved, and his eyebrows were so pale he looked as if he had none. If it had not been for the intensely blue eyes, it would be easy to assume that the man was albino.

As it was, he just looked creepy. Skye mused that it was no wonder that Blackwell kept his image off the internet. Or that he had to hire escorts for female company. The man reminded Skye of nothing so much as Gollum in *The Lord of the Rings*.

Waters said nervously, "What the hell is happening?"

Under their feet, the deck trembled as the engines roared. *Storm Swept* was edging away from the wharf.

Jerry said, "We are rescuing you from the typhoon."

"What typhoon?"

"And you call yourself a journalist? Are you blind, deaf, and dumb? A big storm is on the way, the first major typhoon of the season. The city is shut down. There is no way you can get back to your hotel. I assume that you have your passport with you?"

"Of course! A journalist has to be stupid not to keep it with him all the time."

"Excellent. That means there should not be a problem."

Blackwell spoke at last. He had a crystalline upper-class English accent. "I came here to see Debbie Parkin and her daughter. Waters promised they would be here."

"Office first," Jerry said briskly, and led the way up the stairs. "There are a couple of men I want you to meet."

The office was empty. Skye, who had followed, went to his computer, sat down to have a quick look at the screen, and then turned the chair round so he faced the room.

Blackwell was staring at the portrait of Jewel so raptly that Skye looked properly at the painting for the first time in what seemed ages. It was as compelling as ever, the blue eyes magnetic with laughter, the skirt and hair flying, the subject young and radiant.

Blackwell smiled, very slowly, in a mirthless grin that promised great evil. "Where is she?"

Jerry said, "Not here."

"Then why the hell am I on board this boat?"

But before Jerry could answer the door to the corridor opened. Pierce Brooke wheeled in, sober for once. Maria must have shaved him, Skye thought, and dressed him in clean clothes. He looked surprisingly awake, as well as more respectable — and had no trouble recognizing Blackwell, either.

He roared, "You sadistic bastard!"

"What?" Blackwell whirled round from the portrait, stared rigidly, and said, "Oh my God, you're supposed to be dead."

He then swung on Waters, who was enthusiastically photographing the portrait, and snapped, "Stop!"

"What?" the journalist's mouth hung open.

"And do not record this, either."

"We can make that easy," said Skye, and stood up, stepped up, and reached for the phone.

Waters was so shocked that he gave it up limply. Then he gathered his wits. "That is theft, sir! My private property."

Blackwell shouted, "Shut up!" Then he said to Jerry, "I suppose this maniac has told you a wild story."

"If you mean Brooke, he did," Jerry allowed. "And I have it recorded."

"He's insane, of course. And now that I know the bastard is alive, I am going to have him charged with grievous assault. He broke my right arm and dislocated the shoulder — I thought he was going to pull my arm right off — you have no idea how much it hurt! And he punched and kicked me in the stomach when I tried to fight him off! My pancreas was so damaged that some of it had to be removed, so I'm on insulin for the rest of my life. And he broke all of Feisal's front teeth."

"I did all that?" said Brooke. He had been gazing at the portrait, looking puzzled. Now, having heard all this, he looked surprised. Then he slowly grinned.

Brooke had a firecracker temper, or so Skye remembered Helen saying, though it didn't look as if Brooke remembered beating up the two sadists now. Then his thoughts were interrupted as the door to the bridge opened.

Harold came in, drawn, no doubt, by the shouting. His bristling brows snapped down as he took in the scene, but then his craggy face became businesslike. "So you came," he said to Blackwell. "Giacomo said he could draw you out, but I was not sure that I believed him."

"My God, is this a trap?" Blackwell's eyes blazed, and there were red patches on the cheeks of his dead-white face. "My lawyers will hear about this!"

The ship suddenly surged and plunged. Everyone had to grab for a handhold, and Brooke's wheelchair ground back and forth. Obviously, *Storm Swept* had left the shelter of the port.

Blackwell kept his balance easily, however, straddling his feet as he hauled out his phone. "I'm calling my lawyers right now."

"Good," Harold said. "You've been robbing me for years, and have blackened the name of Pederson Strategic — and I can prove it. My forensic accountant and my lawyers in Washington, Geneva, and Singapore have accumulated enough evidence to advance our case at a moment's notice. And Brooke is going to testify, if necessary. However," he added, sounding regretful, "just in case you haven't noticed, we are sailing out of Manila, so all that has to wait."

"Then you can bloody well sail back. And when we get there, I am formally charging Brooke with assault and battery."

"I wouldn't do that, if I were you," said Brooke. His tone was remarkably mild, though Skye noticed that his hands were clenched on the arms of his wheelchair.

"And why not?"

"Because I still have the hospital report."

"What report?"

"The report the hospital in Geneva gave me when Debbie Parkin was discharged."

In the utter silence that followed, there was a tap on the door to the corridor, and Lester came in. The new chief steward's eyes were very inquisitive as he looked from one face to another, but his smile was as obliging as ever.

He said to Harold, "You called for me, sir?"

"Yes, thank you, Lester. Please arrange for these two gentlemen to be taken to cabins on two separate decks, a good distance away from each other. Then, when they are settled, tell them to batten down, as the sea is going to be very rough."

Blackwell scowled, and obviously thought about arguing. Then as the ship lurched again he shrugged, and followed the steward.

Waters, however, hung back, looking as alert as a ferret. He nodded at the portrait and said to Jerry, "That's not the girl I interviewed for *Balustrade Magazine*."

"You are right," Jerry said amiably.

"But just now Blackwell thought that she *was* the girl I interviewed."

"I am sure you are right about that, too."

"So who is she?"

"All you need to know is that she isn't Kate Kelly, the author."

"So where is Kate Kelly, the author?"

"You will see her when the time comes."

Waters opened his mouth, intent on another question, but was forestalled by the arrival of a second steward.

Reluctantly, looking back at the portrait, he left the room.

Twenty-nine

As Jerry arrived at Pierce Brooke's door, he could hear Maria vomiting somewhere along the corridor. Grimacing, he turned the knob, and went in. To his amazement, both Kate and Maggie were there, along with the designer, Carlos del Rosario.

All three were sitting on the floor with their heels planted on the edges of a portfolio, bracing themselves with a hand on the carpet. Brooke was sitting in his wheelchair with the brakes on to keep it as immobile as possible, and watching the trio. His expression was more interested than usual. Predictably, he had a glass of amber liquid in his hand.

When Jerry lifted a querying eyebrow at Kate, she said, "We thought we would find a cabin lower down in the ship. It is really, really rocky up on the bridge deck, and we met up with Del on the way. And then, because he speaks Spanish, we tried to see Maria."

"He speaks Spanish?" Jerry looked at Del, feeling curious. For the first time, he realized that the designer did not look altogether Filipino. His nose was hooked, and his face was long, with prominent cheekbones. He was also taller than most.

"His father was Spanish," explained Maggie. She dimpled, and said, "The descendant of conquistadors."

Del merely smiled, as content as ever to let the girls do the talking for him. Today he was wearing patterned leggings in a variety of reds and yellows, and a white blouse that was belted in at the waist and had tight bands at the cuffs. Give him a sword, a flashy bolero, and a crimson cape, thought Jerry, and he could take on any number of fighting bulls.

"But when we found Maria she was horribly seasick."

"I noticed," said Jerry.

"I don't think she has ever been to sea before. But she didn't want help or sympathy. Instead Del told us that she yelled at him to go away and leave her alone to die."

It was hard not to laugh. As soberly as he could, Jerry said, "So?"

"So we thought Mr. Brooke might need help," explained Kate. "Because his carer was out of action, so to speak."

How typical of Kate. Jerry often thought that her altruistic nature should have doomed her to be a nurse or a doctor or the head of an aid organization like Helen, instead of a struggling novelist.

"And?" he said. He looked at Brooke, who merely shrugged.

"He only wanted us to pour him a drink," said Maggie. "Then he absolutely insisted that we stay here. He said it would be safer. And so we are discussing my portfolio."

Jerry stared at Brooke, feeling curious about his motives, but the man's expression was noncommittal. Then the ship gave a mighty lurch to port, soared up an unseen breaker and plunged down again. Jerry fell into an armchair and hung on as another wave was breasted.

He, with Skye and the girls, had endured a really big storm last year, but that had been in the motor yacht, which had skipped like a flat stone across the crests, kicking huge bow waves over the bridge and superstructure. That had been perilous enough, but this was even rougher going. Because of the windage, he supposed; *Storm Swept* exposed a much bigger vertical surface to the gale than the yacht. And, because Calamari was racing the storm, the ship was battling gusts that blew off the bottom edge of the depression.

Feeling breathless, he said, "I think I'll have a drink, too."

Maggie rose to her feet with the enviable litheness of youth. When she lifted the whisky bottle Jerry nodded, so she poured a glass, and stepped over draft pages to hand it to him. After she returned to the minibar she lifted the bottle inquiringly at Brooke, and he nodded, so she topped up his glass before putting it back. Then she perched cross-legged on the carpet again, and the trio resumed their lively chatter.

Evidently Maggie's portfolio was being revised, in view of the show they had seen the night before. To Jerry's surprise, though, the girls were talking about ballet. His smile became indulgent. When Maggie and Kate were little they were determined to be world-famous ballerinas, and when Skye and he were home, they took turns to drive them to and from their lessons. He remembered how they would come darting out of the studio on tiptoe, their hair tied up in buns, their skinny little legs in tights, their faces radiant. He was filled with remembered affection.

"Did you really expect to get onto the world stage?" Brooke asked. His expression was cynical, but at least he was showing some interest.

Kate laughed. "Well, you have to understand that we were raised in a very small town. Our horizons were huge, but our environment was limited."

"I thought you were raised on a vineyard."

"Well, of course we were — a very big vineyard, out in the countryside. It's wonderful there. The original house and the press house are made of great stones, in the old European style. You can find similar places in the Napa Valley, in California, if you look. But, while it is wonderful, it is a long ways from town — and the town is small. The Bacchantes dominate the population."

"I could have guessed that." Brooke sipped from his glass, then said, "Do you know what the first thing ballerinas and runway models do when they give up their careers?"

"No." Kate stared at him, and Jerry was watching, too, wondering if Brooke was about to pour cold water on the happy scene.

"They cut their hair."

"Oh." Kate and Maggie looked at each other, and Maggie fingered her glossy dark-brown ponytail. Today, Kate's long black hair was loose. "Well, we didn't," said Kate gamely. But Helen did, Jerry thought; Helen's hair was a smooth silver and blonde cap. Reflectively, he lifted the whisky he had neglected until now.

The ship rose and plunged, and the entire contents of the glass shot down the front of his shirt. Jerry swore, and stood up during the next reasonably calm moment.

"I'd better head off and check the ship," he said, and staggered out of the room.

Maria was still vomiting, or so he noticed. The ship rose and plunged again, and he grabbed the handrail and ran unevenly along the passage, then down the stairs.

Jerry headed first to the engine control room, where the images from the security cameras from all around the ship were displayed as a mosaic on one of the screens. The two engineers were standing at the various controls, looking phlegmatic, and the engines were rumbling hard, because of the pace they were being set. Then they roared as another huge gust was encountered and the propellors were briefly lifted out of the water, so it was impossible to hear, even in the secluded control room.

The images from the security cameras were even more disturbing. Up on the promenade deck, restaurant tables were sliding from one side to the other, and in the lounge, settees had fallen onto their sides. Worst of all was the lowest deck, where the boats, provisions and bosun's workshop were sited. One of the two forklifts, normally used to shift great cartons of foodstuffs and passengers' luggage, was running loose, crashing about the mostly empty hold.

Jerry said, "What the hell?"

"I would not go down there, if I were you," one of the engineers said. He grinned and then added, "Even with good whisky inside you."

Jerry only heard him because there was a lull, and protested, "That Scotch was spilled, not imbibed, unfortunately, and I certainly won't send anyone down to the hold — yet." He thought of old stories about the sailing navy, where cannons that lost their lashings rushed back and forth on the decks, killing and maiming seamen as they went. Still, people talked of a *loose cannon* as something or someone running out of control.

"But in future the forklifts should be safely secured after use," he said.

The engineer who had spoken shrugged. "Tell the bosun. His job."

"I will," Jerry promised grimly, and headed up to the bridge deck.

As he passed through the promenade deck he could see stewards moving about, securing furniture and lashing door and cupboard handles. In the office, Skye was sitting in his computer chair with a foot braced against the top edge of the desk. The monitor seemed to be on some kind of gimbal, because it rocked back and forth without falling. Perhaps the base had been glued to the desktop somehow, or so Jerry thought.

He said, "Anything new?"

"Oh, yes indeed. I've downloaded the contents of Waters' phone."

"Wasn't there a password?"

"Yes." Skye shook his head and laughed. "It was no trouble finding it. I even managed to get at the stuff he filed in the cloud. You'd be amazed what people use for passwords. A quick check of Facebook or LinkedIn or wherever they have posted a profile yields plenty of clues."

He sniffed, and said, "Have you been drinking?"

"Not a drop."

Harold came in from the bridge, and said, "New developments?"

The ship lurched, and Harold grabbed the edge of the desk. Jerry braced himself at the other end, and said, "I'm worried about the hold."

"What about it?"

"I checked the security cameras, and one of the forklifts has broken loose."

"Is that bad?"

"It could be, particularly if it hammers one part of the hull too many times. But there is no way I can send anyone down there. Far too dangerous. It'll be the first job when the weather moderates."

"It's not going to moderate very soon," said Harold.

Jerry grimaced, and when the ship steadied a little, he went through the door to the bridge.

The captain, the first officer, the second officer, the helmsman, and two lookouts were all there, so it was unusually crowded. Captain Calamari was peering at the latest image from PAGASA and looking more gloomy than ever. Jerry bent and had a look for himself, then straightened, feeling not at all relieved. The storm had touched the outskirts of Manila, and the center was blazing red and orange. He wondered how Rosita and the family were getting on, and hoped they were fine.

The tail curled menacingly. It was like a dragon, he thought. They were running through the dragon's tail, battling to get out of its grip. He said to Calamari, "What is our heading?"

"Southwest. We will make port at Kota Kinabalu, God willing."

"Not Singapore?"

"No, we have a medical emergency."

"Someone had a bad fall?" The way the ship was plunging and rolling, it was certainly on the cards.

"The Englishman, Mr. Blackwell, he needs insulin soon."

Jerry frowned. "But there must be some in the first aid kit. And the idiot should carry a supply."

"He is making a large fuss, so I have informed the authorities in Kota Kinabalu. They know he is coming, and have ordered a nurse."

"Dear God," said Jerry, and went back into the office.

"I don't care if the bastard dies," said Skye, after being told about it. "We have so much of the background to the scam that we don't need him around any more."

"Background?"

"Yup. All in the records that Waters kept on his phone and in the cloud — ready for more well-paid revelations, I suppose. The most interesting is a set of emails dating back more than twenty years, in which Feisal winds Blackwell deep into the Saudi Oil web. First, he offers him a director's position, which Blackwell declines."

"Any idea why?"

"He was busy. And anyway, Saudi Oil looked like a wild venture at the time. Then, as Saudi Oil begins to boom, Feisal's offers become financially tempting, with nice gifts attached, including the penthouse apartment in Geneva. It begins to look a very good idea to make the suggestion to Pederson industries that Saudi Oil might be willing to take a large part in a proposed eco-friendly operation. Finally, Blackwell succumbs and accepts a directorship, at a very, very nice rate of payment, plus promises of millions in bonuses."

"I did not have a clue of all this," Harold said moodily. "And at the time it seemed so plausible that an oil business would want to branch into something green."

Jerry said, "So all the while that he is managing director of Pederson Strategic, Blackwell is also a director on the board of Saudi Oil? Has his snout in both troughs?"

"Exactly." Skye nodded. "He is a very, very rich man. Worth about four billion, according to the internet."

"Dear God." Jerry shook his head. "One can only wonder why he is spilling all this to the press."

"My guess is a simple one — that the friends have fallen out."

"Over what?"

"Probably nothing whatsoever to do with Pederson Strategic."

Skye said, "Where are the girls?

"In Brooke's suite. He insisted that they stay there."

"Any idea why?"

"He said it was safer."

"Dear God," Skye murmured, almost to himself. His mouth was turned down, and the pale gray eyes were very narrow under deeply curled black brows. He scrolled through the newspaper he had on the screen, and pointed to a small item.

"Look at this," he said.

"What?"

He didn't answer. Both Jerry and Harold hunkered down to look. The Swiss police had made a gruesome discovery, after an anonymous tip. The remains of three girls had been uncovered in the grounds of a country house near Geneva.

Silence. Then Jerry said, "Any idea of the exact location of the house? Or the name of the owner?"

"I'm looking it up."

Jerry gripped the back of a chair as the ship plunged and soared again, the interview with Brooke running through his mind. When Brooke described his rescue of Kelly — though without mentioning his attack on the two men who were torturing the poor girl — he had been positive that if he hadn't blundered onto the scene, Kelly would have been murdered. She knew too much, had too sensational a story to tell, so had to be put out of the way.

Murdered. And now that Brooke knew that Kate was supposed to be Kelly's daughter, he had told the girls to stay in his suite. As it was safer.

Safer. And Debbie had changed her name to Kelly for a reason that Brooke reckoned was obvious. When Jerry had invited her to come along with him to New Zealand, she had grabbed the chance to get far, far away.

And Kate was supposed to be Debbie's baby — conceived during that brutal attack. The short hairs on the nape of Jerry's neck were bristling. When the motion settled, he asked for the number of Blackwell's cabin. Harold had to radio Lester to find out, but within moments Jerry was heading back down the stairs.

Thirty

Jerry tried Blackwell's door before knocking, a trick he had learned in the army when approaching a suspect. It was unlocked, so he walked in without warning.

Blackwell was sitting at the desk with a laptop in front of him and his phone in his hand. At the sound of the door opening he whipped around, so that Jerry was abruptly impaled by that strange blue stare. He had to quell yet another shiver, for Blackwell looked so like a creature that had crawled out of some crypt. Did he always wear dead black, as a contrast to his dead white skin? The image of vulnerable and beautiful young Kelly being raped and tortured by this weird thug was sickening.

Despite his thoughts, Jerry managed to relax into the nearest armchair, crossing one ankle over the other knee after snuggling his bottom securely. Then he studied Blackwell dispassionately, while Blackwell stared back with flat aggression.

Jerry waited until the ship settled a little, then said, "I'm not sure if you were told that I am the head of security for the Pederson cruise line. You reported a medical problem?"

"You heard what I told Brooke," Blackwell snapped.

"Yes?"

Turning back to his laptop, Blackwell said over his shoulder, "That bastard Brooke dislocated my shoulder and broke my arm. But worst of all was the punching and kicking in my stomach that damaged my pancreas. I now need insulin."

Jerry paused as the ship swerved and plunged and glass crashed somewhere down the corridor. Then he said, "We are headed for the nearest big port, and have arranged for a nurse with insulin to meet us. Though I am very surprised that you do not carry a supply of insulin with you."

"And," Blackwell continued, just as if Jerry hadn't spoken, "I am informing my lawyers that Brooke is alive and on board this boat, so that he can be served a warrant for his arrest."

"He said that he held a hospital report that might mitigate his actions."

"A report of what?" Blackwell spat.

"Of how badly Debbie Parkin had been hurt."

"That whore was well paid for her services, believe me — though it was Feisal who hired her, so you will have to get the financial details from him. I had nothing to do with it. I simply invited Feisal for the weekend, and he brought her along with him. But I am fully persuaded that she was just a very expensive harlot who needed no persuading to come to Geneva and take part in our games. If she was damaged when Brooke went ballistic, that was her bad luck."

Games? Jerry paused, fighting down the urge to hit Blackwell himself. Then he said, "You might change your mind when you hear this."

He took out his phone, turned up the volume, and played back Brooke's testimony. The slightly mechanical voice was even more disturbing than the original recital. When it came to a stop, silence descended. Despite the creaking of the ship, the crash of the sea and the howl of the gale, the silence felt all-encompassing. Yet Blackwell hadn't bothered to turn around.

Finally he drawled, "You've been drinking."

"I have not."

"You stink of whisky."

"It was a spill."

"I still think you must be drunk. Do you really reckon people will believe that cripple's raving?"

"I reckon that Waters and his newspaper will be very interested indeed. It would certainly stop them from publishing any more of the stuff you are leaking. They may even ask for their money back."

"So this is blackmail."

"If you want to put it that way, yes."

Blackwell heaved a dramatic sigh, and said, "How much?"

"*What?*"

"Well, I do assume you want money."

Jerry again had to fight down the urge to thump this man. He said evenly, "We want your phone and that laptop, for a start, and then we want you to make a statement to the Department of Justice."

"*We* meaning you and Pederson?"

"Of course."

"And Department of Justice meaning the department in the United States?"

"Yes indeed. But many governments will also be interested, as they have lost a great deal of money through your activities, too. Malaysia being the latest."

At last Blackwell turned and faced him. He pursed his lips in a silent whistle, and observed, "You really do mean blackmail."

"If you want to call it that, yes."

"What about Feisal? You haven't considered that you might be barking up the wrong tree?"

"What do you mean?"

"He was the prime instigator of the operation. He is the ultimate culprit. Why focus on me, and not Feisal?"

"Because you are the one leaking cherry-picked information."

Another long silence. Again, Blackwell pursed his lips. He was either thinking deeply or pretending to think, but it was hard to tell which. Jerry felt uneasy. The strange man was too calm and confident. It was almost as if the interrogation were being turned against him, something that was new to him and very unpleasant.

Then Blackwell said, "That portrait in Pederson's office, upstairs."

"Yes?"

"The girl looked just like that whore, Debbie Parkin. I assume she was the daughter Waters was going on about?"

"The subject is Jewel, Harold Pederson's daughter."

Blackwell did not betray surprise. Instead, he lifted a brow, smiled, and said, "So he hired Parkin for escort services before I did? And then kept the child?"

Jerry snapped, "That is a ridiculous suggestion."

"Is it?" Blackwell lapsed into deep thought again.

Jerry wished he could get a glimpse into the strange man's mind. Obviously, Waters had promised him that he would meet the girl he had fathered, which, for Waters, would be a sensational story. But what was in it for Blackwell? Why he had consented to the meeting?

Then Blackwell suddenly lifted a hand, and said, "Take them."

"What?"

"The phone and the laptop. If you track Feisal's movements, you will find the emails and spreadsheets quite riveting. But I must have both back."

Jerry shrugged, trying to hide his surprise. "Of course, once we have downloaded what we need."

"And I have flash drives, of course — just in case you delete everything by accident. But you will need a warrant to search for those."

The ship gave a greater lurch than ever before, as a breaker smacked *Storm Swept* amidships. Blackwell had to grab the desk to save his chair from falling over, and Jerry's armchair lifted on one side and then slammed down again. There was a mighty crash from below, and Jerry thought, *My God, the forklift.*

Without another word, he grabbed Blackwell's laptop and phone, and ran.

Thirty-one

Storm Swept was plunging heavily in the teeth of the gale, but still running at a full fourteen knots, racing the typhoon to northern Borneo. Maggie volunteered to go up to the bridge to see what was happening, and Del went with her.

"They seem fond of each other," Pierce Brooke observed when they were gone.

"Like minds, I think," said Kate. "And he is very nice."

"An odd combination, though."

Kate laughed. "We all think that, but are happy to see how it turns out, Mr. Brooke. As you heard, he saved our lives by hitting that pirate over the head with a bottle of whisky, but if Jerry had told him that he had killed the terrorist, he would have thrown up, or fainted. Del is an artist, and very sensitive, so naturally he and Maggie are kindred souls."

Brooke paused, almost as if he were quelling a laugh, then said, "Call me Pierce."

"Thank you. And you must call me Kate." Though he was already doing that, she thought. She added rather shyly, "Pierce is an unusual name, I think."

"Nowadays, maybe. It is a very old name, once spelled P-I-E-R-S."

"Oh. How is your name spelled?"

He told her, and she nodded.

"You and Maggie are very alike."

She smiled. "We were raised as twins. Maggie's mother — Rachel — was widowed the same day we were both born. I was … orphaned, I guess … and she took me in as well as Maggie, and mothered both of us. It was a reaction to her loss, I suppose, as she still misses her husband badly. And the entire Bacchante family helped. I suspect we were spoiled. We were treated the same by everyone — the entire extended Bacchante family — and so we became Bacchantes, too."

"You were very lucky."

She nodded, but then grinned. "I have probably made it sound more romantic than it really was. Rachel was a down-to-earth mother, very firm with discipline. And Maggie got us both into big trouble with her mischief at school. The nuns could be fearfully strict and disapproving, particularly when they discovered the caricatures she had drawn of them."

Brooke was watching her intently, his dark eyes glinting between thick lashes. She waited, but he said nothing, so she smiled and continued, "And of course we had to work on the vineyard, like all the Bacchantes. Quite hard, in the season. There was a terrific lot of weeding and raking to do. But I loved working the ground between the vines. We had a Clydesdale horse, such a gentle giant, with enormous hooves, and he pulled a sort of plow."

"A horse — isn't that kind of old-fashioned?"

"I suppose so. But Skye had been to France on business, and had toured some of the vineyards there, so came back with all sorts of revolutionary ideas, such as the horse instead of a tractor. It is much, much kinder to the soil, and I am sure the grapes do better for it. And Maggie and I loved old Clyde so much that he was more like a pet than a worker. He died, which made us cry, but they have replaced him with another."

Still, he said nothing, seeming more fascinated than ever.

"And once we were teenagers, we had to help usher the tourists who came on the Sunday tours, and tell them stories about how the vineyard began — not that that was a trial, not at all. Rachel — my mother — runs a little shop with artwork and fruit preserves as well as wine for sale, so we helped her with that. But it was not all work. For school and village dances, we had lots of partners, right there in the family. Maggie's cousin Paulo was the town heartbreaker, and all of our schoolfriends were terribly jealous. So, withal, I was very fortunate indeed."

Pierce was smiling. After a pause, he said, "I got Maria to read a magazine article about you."

"But why?" She was puzzled.

"It was in Spanish, and I don't read Spanish, so she read it aloud."

"Spanish?" she said wonderingly. "About me?"

"Yes. There was a story about you being born during a storm. You had described it in detail to the writer."

"That's strange. The only journalist who has asked me about that was Graham Waters, the man with *Balustrade Magazine*."

"It must have been translated from the original."

She frowned. "Do you think that's why *Men Who Play With Fire* is being translated into Spanish?"

"It is?"

"Yes. My agent has only just informed me."

"Then congratulations are in order. You are a very clever girl."

"Just lucky. In the right place at the right time with the right story."

"Quite apart from your amazingly good luck, it was an amazing coincidence that two babies were born in the same place, and in the same storm."

"But there were more than two," she exclaimed.

"Really?"

"Yes! Helen's baby was born the same day. In the same clinic and in the same storm. Yes, I know it was an amazing coincidence, but there were three of us! And the third was her baby, Jewel."

"Ah," he said, and nodded. "The girl in the painting."

His voice was quiet, as if he were talking to himself, and for the first time she realized that the sounds of the sea and the gale were diminishing. But before she could comment, Maggie and Del stumbled their way back into the cabin.

"Captain Calamari says we are almost out of the worst of it," Maggie announced, and landed in a chair with a thump. "He is very pleased with himself, though I think the updates from the weather bureau in Manila helped a lot."

Del said, "I think he called it PAGASA."

"And the captain was very insistent about that, too," said Maggie, giving Del a radiant smile, which she then turned on Brooke, who blinked. "He is quite the pedant, in that way."

Pierce Brooke said, "Kate was telling me what a terror you were at school."

She looked at Kate reproachfully, and said, "You didn't tell him about the caricatures of the nuns, did you?"

Del said, "What are caricatures?" He said the word slowly — excellent as his English was, it was obviously new to him.

"Cartoons," said Brooke.

"*Cartoons*? Of the *nuns*?" Del looked scandalized.

"Well, they deserved it," said Maggie. "And I drew a cartoon of the headmistress, too. She was a terrible old bird with one wooden leg. She was usually easy to hear coming down the corridor, because every second step was a thump, but it was amazing how she could sneak up when you weren't watching.

Then she would draw a circle on the floor with chalk — a *small* circle — and make me stand inside it for what seemed like hours. But luckily she didn't find the drawing."

Kate, who hadn't been listening, said, "Have you seen Skye and Jerry?"

"Skye is running the printer red-hot. Jerry gave him something that he found very interesting. And Jerry is on the lowest deck, at the big door to the hold. He is instructing some seamen who are throwing chains and other stuff at a forklift that is running out of control. When we left, they had managed to slow it down, so Jerry is pleased with himself, too."

"What about Helen? I haven't seen her at all."

"Harold said she is asleep. She gets seasick, so she took a pill, and the jetlag is still catching up with her."

Skye walked in and said, "He was wrong, and you are wrong, too."

He was holding a folder of print-outs. The girls looked at him, and Maggie said, "We are?"

"Yep. Helen is awake and up and wants you three to keep her company for drinks before dinner. In the promenade lounge."

Kate blinked and said, "Are you sure?"

"She is looking forward to it."

So the girls stood up, still looking at him questioningly, but when he merely smiled, not saying anything more, they went. And Del went with them, leaving Skye and Brooke alone.

Thirty-two

When the door had shut Skye said briskly to Brooke, "I printed these off for you. It's only fair and honest. They are early emails sent from Blackwell to Feisal and back again, and they are all about you."

Brooke put his drink aside to read the print-outs carefully, one by one, while Skye watched. When he had finished he looked up. "I hardly remember any of this, but thank you."

"It certainly helps us with our case against Blackwell and Feisal."

Brooke nodded. "If you look, the dates of the emails match the weekend I went to the office building with Pederson's latest objection — not that I can remember what that objection might have been. And that was the last I had to do with them, along with the Pederson Strategic proposal that turned out to be so disastrous."

"Helen told me you have a laptop."

Brooke frowned, looking annoyed. "Why would she tell you that?"

"Well, it wasn't direct information, but part of a conversation. She was telling me that for some days she thought that your village did not have internet access, but then she saw your laptop, and remembered an email you had sent, so she knew that you could go online. Did you bring it with you?"

"I did." Brooke nodded at the desk, and Skye found it in a drawer.

It was newer than he had expected, about ten years old. When he looked round enquiringly, Brooke smirked.

"Amazon does deliver — to even the remotest villages of Mexico, you know."

"Good lord." Skye sat down at the desk, plugged in the laptop, and said, "May I?"

"Do you really need my permission?"

Skye didn't bother to answer. Instead, he said, "I'd be interested to see your side of the email conversation that's on those printouts, but I suppose you didn't transfer the data from your old computer to this one?"

Brooke looked at him for a long time, very consideringly. Then he said, "It's on a disk. When the new laptop arrived, I belatedly realized I had forgotten to make sure that it had a DVD drive."

When Skye looked, sure enough, the laptop did not have a disk drive. "You wouldn't have the disk with you, would you?"

"As a matter of fact, I do. I also have the hard drive of the old computer."

Skye kept silent, merely lifting an eyebrow. At length Brooke nodded, and said, almost to himself, "It could be for the benefit of us all." Then he rolled over to the closet, and rummaged in the lid of his bag.

"Thank you," Skye said as both were handed to him.

Brooke, he thought, was turning out to be a much more amenable person than he had expected. After that, the cabin was silent, save for the rustle of paper as Brooke went through the print-outs again, and the occasional tap of the laptop keyboard as Skye copied files onto a flash drive.

Brooke had used the laptop for searches, it seemed, as there was very little email, just updates from his doctor — which, surprisingly, were in English — and a few notifications from his bank. It was easy to find the email he had sent to Helen, the one that had brought her to his village. Skye read it several times, and then leaned back, frowning.

It seemed very vague, and should have been easily ignored. Evidently it had triggered a doubt and a worry that were already there in Helen's mind. She had already confessed that she had slept with both Harold and Pierce Brooke the month she fell pregnant, but when Jewel's portrait was considered, it was highly unlikely that Brooke could be the girl's father. This meant that Helen held quiet, secret doubts about whether she was really Jewel's mother . . .

Skye looked up at Brooke, who had finished reading, and was frowning into space. There was no way to tell what was going on in his mind, but Skye ventured, "How do you find the girls?"

Brooke looked at him, and blinked. "What do you mean?"

"I believe that you found them rather flamboyant. Now you have spent time with them, do you still think the same?"

"They are so bloody *young*."

Skye was only forty-one and kept himself very fit, but had no trouble agreeing. He grinned and said, "I often wish there was a battery that could store all that excess energy."

He paused, remembering Brooke's reason for jumping to the conclusion that Kate was his daughter, and then said, "Does either of them remind you of anyone?"

Brooke stared at him, and then laughed wryly. "Helen probably told you about it. Or Jerry, because he knows the story, too."

"Story?"

"When I saw Kate's picture in that magazine, I thought there was a strong resemblance to my mother, but since then I have changed my mind."

"Yes?"

"The girls look a hell of a lot like each other — and a hell of a lot like you. Are you sure you aren't their father?"

"Oh my God." Skye's laugh was one of utter astonishment. "I was only nineteen when they were born, for heaven's sake!"

Brooke shrugged. "So?"

"I had been at university for three years, so I would have had to be busy in the holidays."

"University?"

"Yep. Auckland. I had just passed my final exams, and had won a scholarship to Melbourne for a graduate degree, but Andreas — the founder and patriarch of Bacchante wines — decreed that I would have to spend a gap year working for the vineyard."

"What about the scholarship?"

"I forfeited it, but Andreas simply said that the family would pay for the Melbourne study — once I had filled in the gap year with work for the business."

"And you went along with it?"

"I owed the family everything. They had taken me in when I was not quite five, and hadn't even been to school. Like Kate, I was raised as a Bacchante, so I became a Bacchante by what she calls osmosis. You should get her to lend you a copy of her latest book, as it is based on the story of my father."

"So what did you do during that so-called gap year? Prune vines, tread the grapes?"

"Harder work than that. Stefano Bacchante had been sent a hundred miles south to break in land for a satellite vineyard, and they decided he needed help. Which he most certainly did."

"What kind of crime had *he* committed?"

"Marrying a girl who was not good Bacchante material. Too

modest, too shy, too quiet. After a year of marriage, she still didn't fit in with the extended family, so Andreas and Eva — his wife, the matriarch — decided that the couple should be sent away, but still, of course, work for the firm. I was driving to join them despite the storm — well, you know how thoughtlessly brave teenagers can be — and found Rachel trudging through the mud. She was trying to get to the hospital, as Stefano had had a terrible accident back on the farm, and their car had been trapped by a fallen tree. It wasn't until I got her into my old wagon that I found that she was in labor. Then my old wagon broke its axle, and so I delivered her baby."

"Maggie?"

"Yep. It was the most wonderful moment of my life." Skye shook his head, knowing he had a silly sentimental smile on his face, but unable to wipe it off. "She came out all pale and waxy, and then went bright red as she screamed."

"I bet she was a handful, even then."

"She kicked so hard I thought she was going to break my arm."

"And Stefano died?"

"He did. He was rescued, but not in time."

"And Rachel?"

"She and the two babies went to live with the family."

"So what happened to the satellite vineyard?"

Skye's eyebrows lifted. "Oh, all that changed. A couple of Stefano's brothers took over the job, and Andreas changed his mind, so I went to Melbourne, after all."

"Rachel must have been very unhappy to be back at the vineyard."

"Well, she was desolate at the loss of Stefano, of course. We all were; he was a great favorite, terrific fun. But with two babies to look after, she had too much to do to waste time pining away.

And of course the Bacchantes wanted to help, so it was much easier for her to fit in with the family."

"They spoiled the girls shockingly."

"You think so?" Skye considered. "Yes, I guess you are right. I had that year in Melbourne, and then a scholarship to Harvard for yet another graduate degree, so I didn't see all that much of them, but from what I remember of the holidays, yes, they were pampered." He thought again, and smiled lopsidedly. "And every time Jerry or I came home we spoiled them, definitely. We were doting godfathers."

"They were cute?"

"You have no idea."

Brooke was silent a moment, but then wheeled over to the minibar. "Drink?"

"We should really go to the lounge and join the others. The sea has settled down a lot."

The motion was indeed a great deal easier, and the scream of the wind had gone. "We've outrun the storm," Brooke agreed. But then, instead of moving, he said, "Did you happen to meet Jerry's girlfriend — Debbie Parkin, the girl who is supposed to be Kate's mother?"

Skye noted the *supposed to be*, but didn't comment. Instead, he shook his head.

"Well, I did, in most unpleasant circumstances. I still have nightmares about it. She had been beaten badly, was covered with bites and bruises, and there was a lot of blood. But after the hospital cleaned her up, she looked a hell of lot like the girl in the portrait in the shipboard office — the girl who is supposed to be Helen's daughter."

Again, Skye disregarded the *supposed to be*. Instead of commenting, he said, "I noticed that Blackwell took a lot of interest in that portrait, and demanded to know where the subject was now. I wondered if he jumped to the conclusion that it was a painting of Kelly — of Debbie Parkin."

Brooke laughed. "Why would Pederson have a painting of an escort on display? Even if he used her services, he has a perfectly beautiful blonde wife — one that he did a lot of conniving and spent a lot of money to snare."

"You sound bitter."

"Well, she was my wife first. But the point I am making is that Blackwell is hardly likely to jump to the conclusion that this was Debbie Parkin. He is far too bright for that. He is much more likely to have played with the notion that this was a picture of Debbie Parkin's daughter."

Skye was finding it hard to breathe evenly. He said, "And how do you come to that conclusion?"

"Easily. Jerry told me that Debbie was four or five months gone when he met her — which means the pregnancy dated from when Debbie was tortured and raped, so who is likely to be the father of her baby? Not Jerry, and certainly not me. So it is likely that either Feisal or Blackwell was the father — and Blackwell is the one with the pale, pale skin."

Skye contemplated him very thoughtfully, thinking that there was still a sharp brain behind the dissolute exterior. "I think we should go to the lounge," he said at last. "I have to drop the hard drive and disk off at the office, but will join you there."

Then, at the door, he turned on a sudden thought. He said, "I don't suppose you remember the name of the magazine where you saw the pictures of Kate."

"Sorry. It was Spanish, and I don't read Spanish."

"Never mind," said Skye, and left.

Thirty-three

When Jerry walked from the passageway into the bridge, he was feeling rather pleased with himself. The forklift had been harnessed before it did any major damage, and he had delivered a lecture to the bosun in both English and Tagalog that he was sure he'd driven home. But when he found Harold and the captain, the mood abruptly changed. They were consulting the screens, and talking in low voices, looking serious.

He said, "What's wrong?"

Calamari waved eloquent hands. "Nothing is wrong with our ship, praise God. We have successfully outrun the storm. It is there on our tail, wishing much to attack us again, but once we reach the coast of Borneo we should be out of its reach."

Harold shifted heavy shoulders. "The problem is that we have had a radio call from the frigate."

"*What?*"

"Yes, again. And it sounds as if they want the same favor."

"After what happened last time?" Jerry's tone was incredulous. "Didn't you tell them that we have a medical emergency on board?"

"I certainly did tell them, and they offered a doctor and an operating theater."

"Good lord." Jerry could picture several surgical operations he would like Adrian Blackwell to go through, particularly on board a pitching ship. "And?"

"So they offered us a supply of insulin pens."

Captain Calamari said, "We are making a rendezvous, and that same man will come on board."

"Oh God. Don't tell me it's Crawford."

"Why not tell you?" Calamari was puzzled. "For yes, it is Captain Crawford who will bring the insulin. He says he has had some special information."

"It would have to be bloody special." Then they were silenced by a noise in the owner's cabin. Jerry frowned, and looked at Harold. "Are you expecting anyone?"

"Only Skye."

"Well, then." But Jerry opened the door into the office, just to make sure — and there was Waters, snooping around.

He said, "What the hell?" — and the journalist spun around, obviously shocked that there was another entry to the suite.

Jerry shut the door, and turned intimidatingly. Waters put up his hands as if threatened with a gun, and delivered a gummy smile. "Mr. Giacomo," he said. It was as if they had happened to run into each other at a cocktail party.

"So you know who I am, and have written a great deal about me that was not authorized," Jerry said. "And I am well aware of who you are, so why not explain what the devil you are doing in here?"

Obviously, the journalist had been poking through the papers on the desks, hoping for some kind of scoop. But he said defiantly, "I have come for my phone. Mr. Hamilton took it without my permission, and I want it back."

"Well, as you may have noticed during your rummaging, he isn't here, and neither is your phone."

Waters nodded, and said meaninglessly, "Yes."

But he was looking at the painting. He pointed. "She's not the girl I interviewed."

"You have already said that. And I have no idea why you should be interested in the portrait."

"At that interview, Kate spun a long and fanciful story about being born during a storm and abandoned into your care. I wasn't sure whether to believe it or not."

Jerry shifted from one foot to the other, thinking that the reporter was at his old trick of making people angry and indiscreet. He said, "As I remember, you were not very interested in anything Kate had to say."

"That's unfair," the journalist protested.

"But your article in *Balustrade* hardly mentioned Kate. Rather embarrassingly, it was mostly about me."

"Doubly unfair! I wrote another story, which evidently you have missed."

"For *Balustrade*?"

"Initially. It was very popular, and was reprinted by a New York magazine, with photographs."

"One that was translated into Spanish?"

Waters shrugged. "Once it is sold, I know no more."

Jerry was silent, thinking that if the magazine was the same one that Brooke had picked up, the ramifications had been significant. Then Waters delivered another grin that showed off his pink gums, and said, "But the English version did lead to some interesting correspondence."

"So?"

"People will send in tips — expecting money, of course. Money," he repeated, and snapped his fingers.

Jerry frowned. Surely the man wasn't expecting to be paid for more information? But it seemed that he was. The gummy smile widened, and Waters actually put out his hand.

"You're a fool," Jerry snapped. "You are in deep enough trouble with your sly stories of financial misdoings, many misdirected to focus on Pederson Strategic. Skye could slap a *subpoena* on you when we get into port."

"And I could charge you for kidnap on the high seas, intimidation, and theft of my phone."

Jerry turned and opened the door to the bridge, saying over his shoulder, "Get out before I send in security."

Waters crumbled. He said, "I'll tell you more."

Jerry shut the door again. "Go on."

"A retired nurse got in touch with me, via the magazine, offering a story. For money, of course."

Jerry planted his thumbs in his belt, shifted his stance, and waited.

"It was interesting. Well worth what they paid her."

Still, Jerry waited.

"Okay." Waters heaved a deep, artificial sigh. "She was with Debbie Parkin when she died. Not from the storm, but something else. Preeclampsia, she said, whatever that is."

Jerry already knew that. "So?"

"Parkin talked to this nurse about the man who had fathered the baby she had just given birth to, said that when she got back to London she would tackle the bastard — and I quote — because he was bloody rich and she would make sure that she and the baby were rich too. In a word, Debbie Parkin was going to blackmail him. But she died, instead."

"And did she name the man?"

"Oh yes." Waters paused as if he still hoped for payment, then shrugged. "Adrian Blackwell."

Jerry was forcing himself to breathe slowly and evenly, though his mind was racing. "So you got in touch with him?"

"Of course. Where there is big money, there is often a big story. He was interested, and we exchanged a lot of emails and phone calls. At the time, of course, I thought the baby involved was Kate."

"But when you finally clapped eyes on Blackwell, you knew it wasn't."

Waters shrugged. His expression changed to one of distaste, and he lowered his voice. "What is the condition that makes him so white and weird, do you reckon?"

"I don't have a notion. But I am sure that didn't stop you from probing further."

"Well, I mentioned that I had information about a daughter he had fathered on Debbie Parkin."

"Without mentioning that Debbie Parkin was dead."

"Of course not. But I did say I could arrange a meeting."

No wonder Waters had phoned Kate. What a snake, Jerry thought with disgust, but the threads were weaving together in his mind.

He said slowly, "Then a most unexpected plum fell in your lap. You could not have timed it better, as Blackwell was a prospective whistle-blower. All he needed was a journalist with plenty of contacts in the newspaper business, and there you were."

The journalist pouted. "It did work out rather well."

"It didn't worry you that the details he was leaking were all very one-sided, and detrimental to Pederson Strategic — which was founded with the best of ecological intentions?"

"Of course not. When copies of sensational correspondence and financial operations are handed over, one does not ask what correspondence or whatever might be missing."

"And it didn't worry you that you might be putting Kate into danger?"

"What?" Waters looked startled.

"As the retired nurse said, he is very bloody rich," Jerry grimly pointed out. "And the very rich can be very possessive of their riches."

"But surely not — why would he hurt her? Anyway, Kate is brunette and couldn't possibly be his — I mean…" Waters broke off, looking confused. Then he pointed at the portrait of Jewel Pederson. "The eyes," he said. "Look at the eyes."

Jerry usually avoided looking at the painting. Though he had been very fond of Kelly — Debbie Parkin — and the painting did indeed resemble her, it was a portrait of Jewel Pederson, who had been a dangerous fellow passenger on the *Odyssey*.

But, now that he was focused, he realized that the eyes were different from his memories of Kelly. The dancer's eyes had been a darker blue, almost purple, fringed with long black lashes. He had sometimes sentimentally likened them to pansies. But Jewel's eyes were a lighter, brighter blue … the same blazing blue as Adrian Blackwell's.

His thoughts stopped. He remembered what Blackwell had done to Debbie Parkin, and said grimly to Waters, "Never, ever underestimate Adrian Blackwell. He is a very dangerous man."

And for God's sake convince him that Kate could not possibly be his daughter. But he didn't speak the thought aloud.

There was a shout from the bridge, and the ship perceptibly slowed. "Time to go," Jerry said. He opened the door to the passageway, and the journalist reluctantly left.

Thirty-four

When Crawford looked up from the boat and saw Jerry peering down from the promenade deck rail, he grinned happily. "I've got some fascinating info'," he shouted, and clambered on board as bright-eyed and bushy-tailed as if he had never blundered so badly on this ship. Jerry thought he looked a lot like a Welsh terrier, but even more innocent.

Harold stalked up to him, hedge-like brows bristling. "I suppose you've come for dinner."

The sarcasm didn't register. Crawford smiled as he handed a small medical case to the steward who was waiting to collect the insulin, and said, "That's very civil of you, sir." Then he sent the boat back to the frigate without bothering to consult either Harold or Jerry. Did it worry him that he had stranded himself on a ship where he was not at all welcome? Apparently not. He was still smiling and making small talk as they walked into the promenade lounge.

Helen Pederson, the perfect hostess, stood up when they arrived. "I know you have met some of our company before," she said to the soldier, but proceeded to introduce the rest without waiting for an answer. Crawford's grin widened when he saw Kate, only slipping when Graham Waters stepped up to greet him effusively, first shaking his hand, and then thrusting a business card at him.

"Perhaps you have seen my story about Major Jerry Giacomo in *Balustrade*," he said.

"Yes, but..."

"I would love to interview you about your reaction to it."

"Yes, I mean no. You must understand that..."

"And I am sure you have some interesting anecdotes about army life in the tropics. My readers loved my story about Major Giacomo's adventurous life, and it sold very well."

"I don't think so — I mean, there is a press officer..."

"Oh dear me, I think we could do better than a press release. I want — my readers *crave* — the intimate stories, not the bureaucratic handouts."

"I would have to ask permission, and anyway, I wouldn't want to give an opinion."

Crawford looked at Jerry with open desperation, to receive nothing better than a knowing smile. Then, to Jerry's private regret, Blackwell and Brooke arrived, one after the other but carefully apart, and they all filed into the promenade restaurant.

The tables seated only four or six. Harold steered Jerry to one that held four, and said in a low voice, "What the hell does the fellow want?"

Jerry sat down. "He reckons he has some exciting information."

"It would have to be world-beating."

"I can't argue with that."

Helen and Skye joined them. Crawford was at another table, talking animatedly with Kate, Maggie and Del. Waters joined Blackwell, who had taken a table on the far side of the room. They were eating little, but conferring instead, their heads close together. Jerry wished he could overhear the conversation, and wondered what Skye was making of everything he had downloaded from the phones and laptop.

Pierce Brooke wheeled in, looked around, and went straight to the girls' table, which held six, and came to a stop at the end, next to Kate. When food was placed in front of him he nodded, but was not interested in eating, instead watching the young ones, who were laughing. Crawford was doing his utmost to charm Kate, who was smiling but evasive.

Jerry thought Brooke looked amused. His wine glass was in his hand, but he was drinking very little.

Helen was watching, too. She said, "Pierce looks so much better."

Jerry shrugged. "He's over his jetlag."

"It's more than that. I wonder if Dr. Dominguez was fibbing."

"Why?"

"He told me that Pierce doesn't have long to live, that he has incurable liver cancer. That was his excuse for demanding that I take responsibility."

"Well, he doesn't look ill."

"I'm totally with you on that. I think the doctor simply wanted to get rid of him. Apart from Maria, who is quite besotted, I don't think the village liked him much — because of his drinking, which really was excessive. You have no idea. And he was so determined to be miserable that the doctor probably found him a nuisance."

"Where is Maria, anyway?" said Skye.

Jerry shrugged. "In the crew mess?" He didn't care.

Crawford, he noticed, was pushing down good food at a great rate, while at the same time trying to hold a flirtatious conversation. As a demonstration in multi-tasking it was quite a sight. Jerry wondered if Crawford had completely forgotten his reason for boarding *Storm Swept*. As the meal came to a close, however, the soldier stood up, looked around, and came over to their table.

"May I join you for coffee?" he said.

Harold said, "The office."

Without waiting for an answer, he led the way up the stairs and into the owner's suite. Then he sat down at one of the desks, glowered intimidatingly, and said, "What?"

Crawford was gazing at the portrait of Jewel. He started, pulled his thoughts together, and said, "My commanding officers would very much appreciate your assistance."

"For another mission?"

"Well … yes."

"On the same basis as the last one?"

"It would involve taking a force up to the head of the estuary, yes. But just twelve men this time, plus myself and an American observer."

"You must be joking!"

Crawford's tone became anxious. "But we have learned something new. An informant has come forward, and I am certain that when you hear what he had to say, you will be persuaded."

Skye sat at his computer, swung the chair round to face Crawford, and said, "What is it?"

"What?"

"The name of your informant."

"I think that might be privileged…"

"You are asking a mighty lot of us, sir," Harold snapped.

Crawford hesitated, and then said in a low voice, "You know him as Ryan."

"The steward I fired?" Jerry was incredulous.

"He came to us in Manila, asked for me, was very anxious. And his information has been confirmed."

"By what?"

"By our drones. I can show you the pictures." Crawford

hauled out his phone and flicked through a file. Then he gave it to Harold, who studied the image and then handed the phone to Skye without comment.

Skye expanded the image and squinted at it, swung round to his computer, and tapped quickly. Then he swung back, and said, "It's real. My God."

"What?" said Jerry.

"It's Feisal's yacht."

"*Masha'Allah*?"

"Yep. Right at the head of the estuary."

"Where the seized freighter was anchored?"

"Further up the estuary than that. About exactly where we were when we released the boats. I can see the end of the little concrete jetty."

Crawford was looking bright-eyed with enthusiasm again. "And the heat-seeking drones confirm it," he said. "The terrorists have re-established that lair. It's hidden from above by trees, but the heat patterns are there."

Jerry said slowly, "That's very quick — which means Abu Sayyaf — which also means that the information could have been fed to Ryan. On that mission the pirates looked like amateurs, but if the professionals have taken over, attacking that lair is going to be a much harder proposition."

Harold was concentrating, his eyes narrowed. "Does that lair have to be attacked? I would consent to help with the seizure of that yacht, and could get legal backing for claiming the value of it, once it is in British hands, but I don't see why I should assist in an assault on an Abu Sayyaf hideout."

"There is a suggestion of a drone strike," Crawford admitted.

"All very well, but not until after we have captured that yacht," Harold said sharply. "By rights, it belongs to Pederson Strategic, as property obtained by theft from the company. And Pederson Strategic does not want it destroyed."

"Or even damaged," said Skye.

"I'm sure that it could be discussed in detail. On board the frigate."

"Nope." Harold shook his head. "I need a proposal in writing."

"But I don't have the authority."

"So radio the frigate and get it."

Crawford said rather desperately, "It would be better if we talked it over on board first."

"Then go back to the frigate, and we will see you in the morning."

"But the yacht — if you want it captured…"

"It's not going anywhere," Jerry pointed out. "Not while a frigate is lurking around."

Skye said, "And I do want to do some research, international commercial law being such a dark area to me. So why don't the frigate and *Storm Swept* creep closer to the mouth of the estuary overnight? Unless you want the operation to happen in the dark?"

"Daylight would be better," Crawford allowed. "It would be easier to capture the yacht. And sailing closer to the coast makes sense."

"Right," said Harold. He opened the door to the bridge, and issued instructions to proceed slowly to the coast — once the British Intelligence officer was off the ship.

"But the storm! Which has changed the predicted direction!" Captain Calamari protested. "Instead of west, it is heading south, as PAGASA is informing us. All the time growing and coming near to us."

"The frigate will be with our ship."

"But what difference makes that to the storm, Mr. Pederson sir?"

Jerry couldn't see what difference the company of the frigate would make, either, but naturally Pederson prevailed. Just moments after the tender had returned from delivering Crawford to the frigate, the engines grumbled, and *Storm Swept* eased away in the dark.

Thirty-five

Helen Pederson said nervously, "What's happening?"

Kate said, "Nothing much. We're waiting for something, I suppose." They were out on the promenade deck, and it was only just dawn. She said, "You're up early."

"I couldn't sleep after the engines went so quiet. I was glad to get up, to tell the truth."

It was certainly very quiet. Both ships were sitting on their reflections on a perfectly calm sea. The frigate lay just five hundred yards away, dartlike, gray, beautiful, and lethal. The silhouette of north Borneo was closer, but no less enigmatic. Fog oozed and billowed from unseen forests.

"Was it like this the last time you were here?"

Kate smiled. "It was an adventure — a lovely adventure, with a beautiful blue sky. It was all so serene, even though we had been requisitioned for a military exercise. It was after dark that the weather stormed down, and the exercise went haywire."

It could happen again, she feared. There was another storm in the offing, and Captain Calamari was agitating. Where the heavens had been limitlessly blue before, now the sky was thickening with clouds, white overhead, but gray and roiling on the horizon. The hurricane had been weakened by its progress over the South China Sea, so was now just a storm, but it was a storm, nevertheless. And according to the panicky captain, it had turned south, and was coming their way.

Then Kate was distracted. Like a huge wasp, a drone flew

overhead. Was it scanning the ship? She took Helen's arm, and drew them both under the overhang of the deck above. Then it flew away, over to the coast, so high over the jungle that it was soon invisible. What was it seeking? It had been quite small, but perhaps it could emit killer rays.

She shook herself into sanity as Helen patted her arm and went inside. Science fantasy thinking. Skye came out and joined her on the deck, and she said, "Did you see that?"

"What?"

"The drone? I think it was a drone." She had never seen one in reality before, only in films.

"Oh, that. It's carrying a camera, so the operators on the frigate can see the terrain below."

"Making it safer for us to sail inland to the river?"

"Exactly," he said, and smiled, and she was reassured.

Often, she thought, Skye felt more like a father than Jerry did, even though Jerry was the one who had adopted her. Her earliest memories were of both Skye and Jerry arriving at holiday times with presents and hugs and lots of attention, but let's face it, she thought, Skye always felt like a real Bacchante, because he had been raised that way, while Jerry was a belated member of the family. Hugely welcome when he got back, but a mystery when he wasn't there. What Jerry did when he went away was unimaginable, even though they all knew he was fighting fires, and were awed by it. Perhaps no one really expected him to survive long enough to come back again.

So, she guessed, in the depths of her heart Skye was more reliable, because he did not put his life on the line.

She said to Skye, "What is the plan?"

"You remember *Odyssey*?"

She laughed, and then sobered. "How could I forget? Beautiful yacht, dangerous seas, wonderful landfalls, terrible storm, followed by an even more horrible hurricane that was so nearly the end of us. But why?"

"Because we are sailing up the estuary to capture a luxury yacht that is rather like *Odyssey* — except that it is a couple of years older, and zillions of dollars more valuable."

"Wow, how can we get away with that?"

"We could put up a case that Saudi Oil — meaning Zaid Feisal — bought it with money that was stolen from Pederson Strategic."

"Meaning that Harold is the legal owner?"

Skye hesitated. "I'm not sure of the legal standing," he confessed. "And the timing of Saudi Oil's purchase doesn't fit. But was certainly bought with purloined money, so we are working outward from that."

"And after we seize it?"

He laughed — at her blind confidence, she realized. "It still won't belong to Pederson Strategic, but once it is in the hands of the British Navy, we can mount a claim to prove that it should be Pederson Strategic property. Or the value of it," he added. "Depending on the courts."

"So," Kate said, "getting the yacht captured is just the start of getting Harold's money back?"

"Exactly."

"Then let's go for it!"

There were boats being launched from the frigate, just as she remembered. And, though it was early in the morning, the graying light reminded her of the last venture up the estuary, which had been at dusk. The storm was definitely on the way, but in this moment of ebullience, it didn't worry her.

"Is Jerry in charge of the assault again?"

"Nope." Skye shook his head. "It could complicate the court

case."

"But why?" She was puzzled, even though she didn't want Jerry to risk his life, just for a fancy yacht. "Jerry is not part of Pederson Strategic."

"But he is part of Bacchante Wines. One of the partners."

This was news to her — but then, she was aware that Jerry earned big checks from his fire-fighting ventures, so he would have had money to invest. And what was more logical than to invest in Bacchante Wines? When he was home, he had always worked hard, whatever the job, whether it be weeding or pruning, or even planting roses and calendula at the end of each row of vines.

"But what has Bacchante to do with Pederson Strategic?"

"Aha," said Skye. "I have let on too much."

This was a real puzzle, but Kate was distracted. Soldiers were clambering on board, just twelve of them this time, but looking more serious than the last lot. The sun was fading fast as clouds came closer. Thunder rumbled in the distance as the boats returned to the frigate, and the engines grumbled like an echo. *Storm Swept* began to move to the estuary and the bar at the entrance.

Instead of going below for a briefing, as Kate expected, the military stayed on deck, and this time the frigate did not zoom away, but waited off the estuary. The soldiers, or marines, or whatever they were, were clustered further forward, so Kate couldn't hear what they were saying, but she thought that this time the exercise seemed a lot more efficient.

Was it because Captain Crawford wasn't here? But then she saw him conferring with Harold and Jerry in the promenade lounge, on the other side of the window. There was a fourth man with them, who seemed to be doing most of the talking. They were like shadows behind the whorls and lines of the decorative grilles, and she couldn't hear what they were saying.

There was the remembered bump as *Storm Swept* crested the entrance bar, and then mud, river, and jungle closed in on them, just as before. It was just like the last time, except that the ship was going much faster. Helen came back, followed by a steward with trays of coffee, and then Maggie and Del joined Kate at the rail. They had been busy with drafting and squabbling the last time the ship had come up the estuary, so this was new and strange to them, perhaps.

Then, to Kate's surprise, Pierce Brooke arrived, with a squeak of rubber wheels. He didn't say anything, but just stared at the slowly evolving riverbank, and she wondered if he had ever been in this part of the world before. Helen stood alongside her, but Kate thought it was probably not very tactful to ask her about her first husband's past travels.

Then Maggie emitted a muted shriek. "*O Dio!*" An enormous crocodile had propelled itself down a mud slide and into the brown water.

"They walk on the bottom," said Skye, just as before.

Kate could see the reptilian snout and the bubble eyes progressing along the water, coming towards the ship. Was the estuary really that shallow? On and on they drifted, past patches that had been cleared from the jungle, where the water in the padi fields glistened like mirrors, dotted with green, and other patches that had been planted with dull rows of oil palms, unnaturally regimented in this chaotically varied scene.

Then, just jungle, with clumps of elephant grass at the edge of the river, dense and all shades of green, trees rearing up in their fight for the sun. It looked utterly impenetrable. A distant roaring — tigers? Monkeys leapt invisibly in the high branches, setting them swaying as they chittered and screamed. Birds flew in flashes of color.

Then, more padi fields, the only sign of human habitation to be seen. There were wee thatched huts — for the workers, Kate supposed, and wondered where the people lived. Were there villages in the forest? She thought of the longhouses she had seen in television documentaries.

No one had moved away; they were all riveted by the unfolding panorama. No wonder, she thought, that Harold's discovery fleet was so successful. Monkeys, tigers, crocodiles, exotic birds, all present and camera-ready. And snakes, according to Skye.

She said, "Skye told me they keep the grass short because of snakes."

"Only a guess," said Skye.

"Oh, but it is true," Del assured them. "And I am certain you keep the grass very short in your famous vineyard."

Both girls stared at him. "Because of snakes?"

"Yes, but of course." The bright feather in his hat bobbed as he nodded.

"But we have no snakes in New Zealand!"

This, for him, was amazing. His expression was astounded. "You speak the truth?"

"Yes," said Maggie.

"Absolutely," said Kate. "And we have clover, not grass. Except that the grape pickers trample it down."

"Well," he said, "It is very different in the Philippines. There, the harvesters have to wear special boots."

"You have snakes?"

"Many, many snakes. Vipers, cobras, sea snakes, tree snakes, snakes in a lake, the biggest python in the world."

Maggie's eyes were huge. "But only in the jungle, surely."

"Not true." He smiled placidly. "There is a very poisonous snake that likes the light, and he will come into your yard or your garden and your house if he can, and there is another one — a *very* poisonous sea snake — who likes to rest in the water intake of a motor boat."

"*What?*"

"The cobras are the most fearsome. There are two kinds that rear up, spread their hoods, and spit in your eyes."

"Spit? You must be teasing."

"No, no. And there is the king cobra, a king indeed, as he can raise himself three feet high, and stare at you right in the eye when he spreads his hood."

"How can you *live* with creatures like that?"

Del laughed, and shook his head, "I must come to New Zealand to see this land where you say you have no snakes, for honestly I do not believe that that is possible."

"Yes, yes, you must come," said Kate. She was thinking of the many hours she had spent weeding and planting roses, while the boys trod down aromatic clover between the lines of vines as they pruned. What would it have been like if they'd had to watch out for venomous snakes at the same time? And what about their lovely horse, Clyde? Could he have been bitten? It was just too dreadful to contemplate.

"We are so incredibly lucky," she said, and thought to herself that she had said that a lot, of late.

The others weren't listening. Monkeys had come out of the trees and scrub, and were hunkered along the bank, chattering to each other as they watched the ship go by. Everyone else was exclaiming about this, and taking pictures with their phones, but then Kate felt an arm slide through hers, and when she turned, it was Helen.

Helen, however, was not looking at her — or at the monkeys. Instead, she was watching Pierce Brooke, who was gazing at them both, his expression very thoughtful, and Kate could feel her nervousness.

Why? Was she scared of her first husband? Or was it the primitive surroundings? The smell of wet foliage, rotting fruit, and abundantly sweet flowers was suddenly overwhelming, along with the damp heat — and then the drones flew overhead.

Most were small, like the drone Kate had seen earlier, but one was large, and had a bulbous nose. It was hard to believe there was no human inside — that it, like the others, was controlled by computers on the frigate. They made a lot of noise, and were very threatening, and at that moment she thought she knew how the women in war zones like Afghanistan felt.

She turned to Helen and exclaimed, "I shouldn't be wasting any talent I have by writing novels about the men in my life. I should be writing about conflict, and terror, to bring the world's attention to be sins and troubles of this world."

Helen studied her very soberly. "Oh Kate," she said. "A war correspondent? It's very dangerous — so many war correspondents are murdered."

"But I suddenly feel so — so *guilty*."

"Don't." Helen shook her head emphatically. "I've been in war zones — in countries where the rich and powerful oppress the rest."

"You have?"

"Of course. I don't just raise money for my charities, you know. I do valuable work at the conference tables, but I have also been known to put on my boots and wade out to the villages. And Harold — well, a lot of his business is done in countries where the rich and powerful are in total charge, so I have seen it from both sides of the spectrum."

"Oh Helen, I didn't know."

Helen took off her sunglasses as she smiled, and for the first time Kate saw that she had wrinkles at the corners of her eyes, a testament to sun and dust. Then she nodded in the direction of the doors to the promenade lounge, and said quietly, "You would want to be an investigative journalist — like that man?"

She was indicating Graham Waters, who was standing in the open doorway talking to that creepy Adrian Blackwell, and they were both staring at her.

Kate shivered. "Not like that," she whispered. "Never like that."

They were interrupted. Captain Crawford pushed out the doorway, past the two men, and said urgently, "Inside, please. You can watch from behind the grilles, but you must not come out on deck."

They were approaching the yacht. Though it could not be seen from the ship, the camera drones were sending back images of what lay about the next bend. Kate had expected that the military would assemble down in the foyer to be briefed, as before, but instead six of them lined up along the rail, while the other six went round the stern to line up at the rail on the other side.

They were all wearing body armor, and were carrying weapons, and looked formidable. This time, obviously, they were to present an intimidating appearance, instead of going in undercover like before. It was an echo of Jerry's lectures to the crew — and where was Jerry, anyway?

Storm Swept slowed, slowed, wallowed, and inched forward. The engines quietened and then growled, bringing the ship around a wide bend. For a while it was impossible to see anything but brown water, mud banks, and rioting jungle, but then the backs of the soldiers by the rail stiffened, and between their silhouettes Kate could see the low shape of the yacht. And was shocked.

Had *Odyssey* been that small? According to Skye, this one was even bigger, and yet it looked so tiny. She remembered how spacious — luxurious — *Odyssey* had been inside. Three accommodation decks, with a roomy bridge, a wonderful VIP suite with guest lavatory, a lounge, and informal dining on the outer deck, aft, and an amazing main deck lounge, and dining for ten, along with a two-level suite with mezzanine, and then, on the lower deck, four guest suites, the galley, laundry room, and crew quarters.

She knew it all, as she and Maggie had helped out on all levels during storms and other emergencies. She remembered Maggie saying that the *Odyssey* was like the Tardis, bigger on the inside than it was on the outside. So, she supposed, the yacht they were approaching — *Masha'Allah* — had a secretly huge interior, too. But from here it didn't look possible.

There were four open decks at the stern, but all were empty of people. There was a long ripple in the water at the bow, and she thought it might be a crocodile, before realizing that it was the anchor chain — that the yacht was lying at anchor. Otherwise, the only movement was from the restless drones, circling like gulls. They were all small drones. The big one had headed upriver, over the jungle — to the terrorists' lair, she supposed.

It was hard to see what was happening. Because of the soldiers at the rail, the scene came in glimpses. Like an old film rather than reality. The engines of *Storm Swept* grumbled, and were now keeping them in position ahead of the yacht. The silhouettes of the soldiers along the rail straightened, looked braced for action.

Then figures came out on the uppermost stern deck, with their arms held up, surrendering without a fight. They were wearing whites, and had epaulettes, so were evidently crew. Beyond them, Kate glimpsed men diving over the furthest rails of the three lower open decks. She gasped, remembering the crocodiles.

"What's happening?" she demanded — of thin air, except that Pierce Brooke was there at her right shoulder. He seemed to shadow her, she thought, and wondered why.

"The pirates who seized the yacht are making a quick escape," he said.

"But what about the snakes?" And the tigers, she thought. She was sure there were tigers in Borneo, not only because of the roaring, but because she contributed money to save them.

"I doubt they are worried about snakes."

"So taking the yacht is as easy as that?" It felt like an anti-climax. Graham Waters, she saw then, had got back his phone, because he was up against a window, snapping pictures.

"Yes, thank God," said Skye. He was standing behind Pierce's wheelchair.

In the distance, in the jungle, there was an explosion. Kate heard the thump and saw the flare. It was so big that she felt the ship rock in response.

She said nervously, "What was that?"

Jerry was there. "A drone strike on the terrorists' lair."

"So the mission is accomplished?"

"Apparently so," said Jerry. "But we will find out for sure when a party boards *Masha'Allah.*"

Thirty-six

The storm had arrived. Outside it was dark, the black sky shot through with lightning. The yacht, anchored just a few hundred yards away, was invisible in the murk. Monkeys screamed in the tossing treetops as the rain poured down.

"So where is Feisal?" Blackwell hissed at Crawford. "He was supposed to be on that yacht."

They were in Harold's office. Jerry had shut the door firmly in Waters' face, despite the journalist's loud protests. Even now, he was knocking hopefully.

Crawford said, "Feisal disembarked from the yacht in Kota Kinabalu."

It was out of his hands. All the military under his command were now on board *Masha'Allah* and the only support he had left was the man from the United States Justice Department. Plus his orders, of course.

Blackwell snapped, "Then I want to go to Kota Kinabalu."

He turned his glare on Harold, who shrugged. "You have your wish. *Storm Swept* is going there anyway. We ordered insulin and a nurse when you reported the emergency, and forgot to cancel the order after getting the delivery from the frigate's medical center. Unless, of course, you want to shift to the frigate?"

Crawford said hastily, "I don't know if that would be possible." When Blackwell walked away without bothering to answer, he looked relieved.

"More importantly," said Harold, "I want access to the data that was seized from the yacht."

Crawford turned to the fellow from the Justice Department, leaving him to do the answering. This was a man in late middle-age, with bristling gray hair in an old-fashioned crewcut, his eyes veiled behind the heavy frames of his eyeglasses. He was wearing jeans and a plain dark green sweatshirt — no graphic, no logo, certainly no lanyard, no hint of what his job might really be. But he was definitely a professional. Crawford had indicated that he was a forensic accountant, and a lawyer, too, but Jerry wondered if he was more than that. Then he wondered if the American was carrying, and thought it was probable despite the rule of not bearing arms, because his sweatshirt was so loose.

After a long pause the agent pursed his lips, and said, "Perhaps we can share the data, though with limitation."

"Even with limitation, it would work," Skye said, and Harold nodded.

"In that case," said the man from the Justice Department, "I need to sail with you to Kota Kinabalu."

"Then let's do it," said Harold.

"But," said the American, "that means we have to sail tonight, to get to Kotu Kinabalu before Feisal disappears again."

"Right now?"

The man from the Justice Department smiled. "Of course."

"Despite the weather?" It was as black as a witch's pocket out there, and rain was pelting down.

"Of course."

So why, thought Skye, did he feel that they had been manipulated? Because getting there on *Storm Swept* — if the ship survived — would make a more discreet entry to Kota Kinabalu? It was a complication, too, that Crawford would be on board. But there was no point in objecting, because it looked as if they had won all points possible in this very strange agreement.

He followed Harold through the door to the bridge, arriving just as a bolt of lightning blazed up the black sky, rendering the bridge lighting useless for a second. Then he listened, as Harold conveyed the agent's request.

Predictably, Captain Calamari did not like it. This time, his arguments about leaving the mooring and heading out to sea were even more passionate. As he made eminently plain, he was very unwilling to be doomed to yet another ordeal. But orders were orders, particularly if they came from the United States Department of Justice, and so he was also doomed to be overridden.

Luckily Call-me-Carlo, by contrast, was as keen as ever at the prospect of being the man to con the ship through another big challenge, and Calamari, after checking with Harold, agreed to let him take charge. And so the order to draw away from the yacht was issued, and the engines rumbled in response.

The wind gusted and the rain lashed down. Below, the engines' grumble became louder. The lights on the bridge had been turned low, so that as much as possible of the estuary could be seen. Skye squinted out the side windows when the spotlight popped into action, focused on the lowest deck of Feisal's yacht.

Storm Swept began to wallow sideways, then started to move ahead. Skye kept watching, pinned to the spot by a grim sort of fascination. As *Storm Swept* was swinging to port, the spotlight shone on the yacht's bow. Skye could see the anchor cable stretching ahead — right across their way.

My God, he thought. He was holding his breath with suspense. The engine pulsed, *Storm Swept* came around, and they cleared the chain by mere yards. Captain Calamari let out a half-strangled cry, and even Call-me-Carlo looked shaken.

Then they were past, the yacht's briefly glimpsed riding lights lost in a vicious squall of rain. They had left the boarding force behind. Undoubtedly the yacht would be sailed under the command of whoever was in charge of the military when the weather cleared, in the morning. Skye supposed that once the yacht met up with the frigate, it would be taken to a holding — in Borneo, Malaysia, the Philippines, wherever — while the lawyers took over the matter of ownership.

Marani called for the spotlight to be moved round, and a clump of palms loomed to starboard, forcing another correction. Involuntarily, while avoiding the yacht's anchor cable, he had brought the ship clear across the channel. The spotlight swung further, and Skye could see waves breaking on a nearby shoal. A quick change of course — which would have worked, if it hadn't been for the sudden giant eddy that caught them, driving them right at the breakers. The palm trees were now on the starboard beam, the opposite to where they were supposed to be.

Marani shouted, "Hard a-port!" Tense seconds, as the engines throbbed impotently. Her headway was still sending her onto the shoal — but then the bow touched mud, and *Storm Swept* jinked away as if she were alive.

A shudder as the propellor dragged, but then the incoming tide took her, and after washing back she was headed downstream again. An eddy swirled hard, threatening to send her over to the lefthand bank, but Marani straightened her up, and called for more speed. A moment later, and the palms were lost to sight.

Skye shook his head. The Italian first officer was quite mad, he thought. Two close scrapes within five minutes! If they had hit the anchor chain, *Storm Swept* would have been slammed back and about, with awful damage to follow. If the tide had been going out instead of coming in, they would have stuck on the shoal, and the ebb would have broken the cruise ship's back.

But now, by the grace of God, *Storm Swept* was clear, and the murk had eased just enough to see the leading lights that marked the way to the next long reach. A sudden slash of rain blotted out those lights, but then the weather eased again.

Two hours later the rain was definitely thinner, and the wind was moderating. Skye took a last glance out the bridge window before heading for bed — and his heart stopped. The bank was dead ahead. He heard the Filipino helmsman swear. Marani yelled, the ship swerved, and then they were clear. The spotlight flickered over flat padi fields.

The chart of the estuary was plain in Skye's mind. Only one more turn to make, and then the last hazard was ahead — the bar on which they had briefly grounded on the way in. To the east, the horizon was paling. There was a sense of general relaxation on the bridge, as if everyone was letting out a long breath. Then, as Skye thought about heading off to his cabin, an immense crack of thunder shook the whole ship, followed by a blue flash of lightning. And the skies opened.

He turned back, but it was impossible to see anything. The mouth of the estuary was dead ahead, along with the bar, and Marani was negotiating by instruments alone.

More thunder, and grilles rattled all over the ship with the following gusts. Water streamed down the windows in cataracts, so it was impossible to see even the bow. The spotlight merely scattered the light back at them, blinding them further. The ship was veering back and forth, driven by the wind and rain, fighting the helm. Dimly, Skye heard Captain Calamari demanding to know what course they should be steering.

Marani merely shook his head, and called for full astern. They should have been heading west-nor'-west, but she was swinging to the south, driven by the gusts and the inflowing tide, threatening to come broadside to the bar. There was a roar from below as the engines responded, and then a moment of utter suspense.

Skye caught a glimpse of the lefthand bank as the spotlight flickered through the downpour, and shouted, "She's coming back, Carlo!"

And, thank God, he was right. Carlo called for full ahead. The ship swung, got back on course, and with a bump that was scarcely felt they were over the bar.

"Ease the helm," said Marani. The rain had ceased as swiftly as it started. They were clear, and they were safe. Three hours later, it was dawn. The open ocean lay ahead, and the frigate sat on the pale horizon.

Thirty-seven

When *Storm Swept* glided into Kota Kinabalu the sun was close to a black horizon, and the low profile of the land was capped with a thick mass of cloud. The sun glinted above the clouds, so that the sea was sepia and yellow, flat and unwelcoming. The ships laying there were just inky silhouettes. The closer they sailed, the higher the land profile, and the bigger the silhouettes, but the effect was still like an old black and brown photograph.

Maggie said softly, "Oh my God."

Kate, beside her at the promenade deck rail, said, "What?" She could see the outline of the city now. It looked modern enough, with a few tall buildings, one with a dome on top, like a mosque, and there was a crane, as if more were in the offing, but she could see nothing alarming.

"Look at the water."

Kate looked down, and saw the garbage that was floating around the ship. Plastic wrappers, pizza boxes, discarded diapers, many bits of paper, and — *oh my God* — the carcass of a cat.

Maggie whispered, "And they invested in an eco-friendly venture?"

"What do you mean?"

"I overheard them — Skye and Jerry and Harold, talking about what Graham Waters revealed in his columns — that hundreds of millions of dollars which were supposed to fund a solar energy research project in Malaysia had been diverted to a bank in Cyprus. Hundreds of millions that had come from Pederson

Strategic. They are blaming Harold for *that* — and yet the Malaysian government allows this kind of pollution?"

Kate said uneasily, "In every government there are bureaucrats and lobbyists pushing one agenda or another."

"Corrupted," Maggie said very seriously. "Politicians and bureaucrats must have been bought by industrial interests. The money must have gone from Cyprus to them."

"Money always rules." This was Skye, who had come out of the promenade lounge. He looked exhausted — drained. "It's been a busy few hours," he said wryly. He and Harold had been working all day at the computers, sorting through what the man in the green sweatshirt had brought on board from the yacht.

"Find anything useful?" This was Jerry, who had followed him out onto the deck, and looked a lot fresher. While *Storm Swept* had sailed west along the northern coast of Borneo, he had grabbed a few hours sleep.

Skye shook his head. "Most has been deleted, and the rest is encrypted. There must be shadows of what there was before, but it is up to the geeks at the Department of Justice to find what is hidden. James" —James being the man from the Justice Department — "seemed quite confident, but whether they will share what they find is debatable, in my honest opinion."

Maggie said nervously, "Is it important?"

Both men looked at each other. Jerry said, "To Harold, definitely. And to a number of governments. A few banks, too."

Skye was looking out at the port spreading out before them. It was full dark of a sudden, and the tall buildings were series of bright dots, rows of windows lit up. The ships at anchor were bright with festoons of lights, and all the portholes were brightly lit so that it was possible to count how many decks were on each one. It was like a static fireworks display.

Maggie said, "I suppose it is an Asian thing, to have so many lights? The ships look as if they belong in Disney."

Jerry laughed. "True, young Maggie. But it also makes sure that they won't be run into by incoming shipping."

And it was a blessing that it was now impossible to see the pollution in the harbor, she thought. *Storm Swept* was still moving, edging towards a pier, the side thrusters churning. She could imagine the pieces of paper and plastic and pizza boxes swishing between the side of the ship and the wharf, and the corpse of the cat — but no, she didn't want to picture it. And had it been a cat? Perhaps it was an endangered animal, an orangutan, perhaps. That was an even worse prospect.

The ship touched the wharf with a thump, and there was yelling down below as it was lashed to bollards by stevedores. Then Adrian Blackwell materialized on the deck beside them, as creepy as ever. He was wearing a long black coat, and had his wide black hat swathed about his head with a black scarf despite the tropical heat.

He shot a sharp, dismissive glance at Kate, and then looked at Skye and said, "Goodbye."

They all stared at him. He had a satchel slung over his shoulder, and looked just as he had when he had come on board in Manila.

Skye said, "You are leaving so fast?"

"I have everything I need, thank you. And I have urgent business on shore." With this, he smiled, not a pleasant sight, and for a second Skye wondered what Feisal had done to make such a coldly vicious enemy of his one-time crony.

Then they were all interrupted as Graham Waters came rushing out, saying, "You can't go yet!"

"You can find me at the Marriot."

"But the yacht..."

"I don't know what you mean. I have obtained all the information necessary. Now, all I need is to find Feisal."

The last word was spat like a curse. Waters looked confused, then said, "But we need to..."

"I've already told you," Blackwell said impatiently. "If you need to talk, you can find me at the Marriot." The gangway was being run out, but before he moved, he said, "With my lawyers."

Waters visibly flinched. It was like a threat. He stuttered again, "But..."

"And tell the whore's daughter that if she even thinks of blackmailing me, she will regret it for the rest of her days."

And Blackwell was gone, leaving the sound of shocked gasps behind him.

Then again, they were all distracted. As Blackwell arrived at the bottom of the gangway police cars arrived in a screech of brakes, and policemen piled out and grabbed him.

As the Bacchantes watched in stunned silence, the Honourable Adrian Blackwell was taken away in handcuffs.

Thirty-eight

"So Waters got his story," said Jerry.

"In spades," said Skye.

"But no Feisal."

"He has vanished again."

Storm Swept was on the way to Singapore. The man from the Justice Department had left the ship in Kota Kinabalu, last seen talking on his phone all the way down the gangway, seeking instructions about dealing with the Malaysian police. The journalist had hurried after him, his cries unheeded.

Now, Jerry and Skye were in the office, and Skye was reading out the latest story from Waters, this one a stunning revelation that Blackwell had been arrested on a charge of blackmail — of blackmailing Saudi Oil!

"It's blown up in his face," Jerry observed.

"Again, in spades."

"He must regret this vendetta."

"He had very good reasons, according to this."

Jerry sat down. "Tell me."

"Money, money, money."

"Isn't it always? I do assume the grimy details are now revealed."

"You remember the early emails, where Feisal was luring Blackwell into the Saudi Oil operation with lavish promises? The apartment in Geneva, the gifts, the huge bonuses? Those promises were hollow. The salary turned out to be about half what had been mentioned, and payments were late, to start with, and then as the years went on, they didn't arrive at all. The bonuses petered out, and then became non-existent. But I think what finally turned Blackwell into a whistle-blower was the discovery that he was being charged rent for that apartment in Geneva."

"Just that?"

"Well, the properties bought in his name in Manhattan and the West End of London turned out to have big mortgages, also in his name."

Jerry whistled. "So he was loaded down with debt — and the obvious way to have revenge was to sell the story."

"For lots and lots of money. Everything that he reckoned they owed him. All he needed was a contact in the newspaper business."

"Graham Waters."

"Exactly. When Waters approached Blackwell with that story of the nurse who gossiped that Blackwell had fathered a child, Blackwell found the journalist he needed — for a different story altogether."

"And Waters found a paper that would pay big money for the Saudi Oil story?"

"*Straits Star*, to start with. The owner is a Chinese media tycoon, a seriously rich man. He was given a few fragments of the story, and immediately recognized it as a potential goldmine. Payment was negotiated over a meeting in Kuala Lumpur, along with a contract for further instalments. It was a huge scoop. As we know, the managing editor was arrested, and the paper closed down, but the owner made a very nice profit — profit that did not stop there, as he is also the owner of the London daily that carried on with the story."

Jerry shook his head in wonder. "I would never have believed there was so much money to be made out of journalism."

"Once the internet is counted, it's huge."

Skye silenced then, reading more on the computer. Outside, the sea was calm, and *Storm Swept* was sailing sweetly on her path across the South China Sea. Beyond the big oblong portholes other shipping could be seen on the same route. As always, the South China Sea was busy.

From behind him, Jerry said, "Anything more on the bodies in Switzerland?"

"It is beginning to look as if the property belonged to — wait for it — Saudi Oil."

"So the anonymous tip came from Blackwell?"

"So it seems. There's no end to his vicious need for revenge."

Shivers were running down Jerry's back. *Tell the whore's daughter that if she even thinks of blackmailing me, she will regret it for the rest of her days*, the monster had hissed. He had been talking about the girl in the portrait, of course, but Jerry remembered the protective way Brooke had behaved, always hovering at Kate's shoulder. He had told her to stay in his suite during the storm, as she would be *safer*.

Shaking himself out of grim thoughts, he said, "Where is Harold?"

Skye gestured at the door to the bridge. "With the captain. There's a business conference arranged in Singapore, so I suppose he is making sure we will be there on time." Then he added, "Talking of conferences, it has been announced that there will be a press conference in Kota Kinabalu the day after tomorrow, before Blackwell is flown under guard to prison in Kuala Lumpur."

"Arranged by Waters?"

"Undoubtedly."

"What on earth would Blackwell have to say?"

"He is complaining about his treatment, citing human rights. His lawyers have already filed a report that their client was handcuffed so tightly that his wrists bled."

Jerry shook his head in wonder. "I'm amazed Blackwell had any blood in him."

"His weird coloring is due to a mutation, or so the Justice Department man said."

"Why was the Justice Department man here, anyway?"

"The Department has been investigating Blackwell and Feisal as well as Pederson Strategic, and when the *Straits Star* started publishing Waters' stuff, they became particularly interested in Saudi Oil. Though we didn't realize it at the time, the publicity was taking the heat off Harold."

"It's all so bloody complicated that I am surprised as well as delighted that something is working out." There was a long pause, and then Jerry said, "I am still curious about something."

"What?"

"According to what Waters told me, Kelly —Debbie Parkin — told her nurse that her baby's father was Blackwell. But, if she was raped by both Blackwell and Feisal, how did she know that it was Blackwell who got her pregnant?"

"Presumably she had seen her baby before she was taken to the nurse's house for intensive care. Had hopefully even held the poor mite."

"And her baby was blue-eyed and fair."

"Yes."

"Which means that her baby was definitely Jewel, and not —"

"Yes."

Silence. Then Skye lowered his voice, saying, "It's lucky Harold and Helen didn't hear Blackwell's parting shot."

They both looked at the portrait of Jewel, silently remembering. *And tell the whore's daughter that if she even thinks of blackmailing me, she will regret it for the rest of her days…*

"Though it must be plain to them now that Helen claimed the wrong baby, and that…"

Skye's voice drifted off.

"Say it," said Jerry roughly.

"Quite apart from what Waters told you, now that everyone has seen Blackwell, it's obvious that he was Jewel's father. The eyes." Skye gestured at the portrait. "Jewel inherited his eyes."

"And his psychotic condition, which the doctors thought was genetic."

"But it also means that Kate is either Helen's child, or really a Bacchante. And the same applies to Maggie."

"Does it?" Jerry asked dryly.

"Not really, because I am absolutely sure Maggie was the baby I delivered when Rachel gave birth in my old sedan."

"Leading to another question. Was Harold the father of Helen's baby? And, if not, who was it?"

Skye rubbed his tired eyes and said, "Oh God. Is Brooke persisting with his clumsy attempt at blackmail?"

Jerry laughed. "Of course not. He might have started off with the belief that Kate resembles his mother, but he changed his mind about that when he met her. Kate is not nearly patrician enough to be related to his Brahmin-Boston parent."

"His mother was a snob?"

"And so is her son, though he might look a total wreck to the uneducated eye. More importantly, though, Brooke now realizes that both girls are Bacchantes. Just the way *you* look, act, and think like a Bacchante. What does Kate call it? Osmosis?"

Skye grinned. "You have taken on a lot of the Bacchante style yourself, you know."

"Good lord, have I?" Jerry pulled at his ponytail, his brows very high.

"Another question. Do you think the nurse's story about Debbie Parkin's threat to blackmail Blackwell was forgotten in the excitement of getting revenge on Feisal? That Blackwell didn't remember it until he saw the portrait?"

Jerry shook his head. "Going to the press was the primary issue, definitely, but he saw Kelly and her daughter as a problem that had to be neutralized."

"With murder?"

"Undoubtedly. If Kelly had been here — or Jewel..."

Skye paused, and then said, "Did you give the recording of Brooke's testimony to the agent?"

"God, no."

"Well, don't lose it. The discovery of the bodies on the Swiss estate is now headline news, as the pathology reports involved torture, so you might be forced to release the recording."

Jerry swallowed to calm his voice. "Torture?"

"The bones of the hands and feet had been drilled with some kind of powered instrument. The more sensational journalists speculate that the girls were crucified. If Interpol heard Brooke's testimony, and connected the two, it could be important evidence."

Jerry winced. If it were not for Brooke, beautiful, vulnerable Kelly could so easily have been one of those girls. "Is it definite that Saudi Oil is the owner of the place where they dug up the remains?"

"The company named on the property papers is definitely

Saudi Oil. It's where they held private conferences, and hosted special clients."

"But Feisal isn't named?"

"No, though Feisal and Blackwell both used the lodge quite often, at times when it was empty, with no conference scheduled. But it looks very much as if the anonymous tip came from Blackwell, which would mean that Feisal could be named very soon. God knows how it is going to develop, especially if Blackwell is released on bail. The next few months should be very interesting indeed."

Harold came into the room. He was rubbing his hands together, and looking pleased with himself. To their astonishment, he walked straight up to the portrait of Jewel and took it down.

"We don't need to see that any more," he said, and propped it on the floor with its face to the wall. "I'll have it professionally packed and stored tomorrow."

Skye, like Jerry, was startled into silence, but Harold didn't appear to notice, saying briskly, "Any interesting developments?"

Skye turned his chair and looked at the computer screen, where the front page of the digital newspaper had been slowly evolving. "It's all about Blackwell's arrest, and the blackmail charge against him, plus a lot of the background that we already know."

He shook his head, and laughed. "It looks very much as if you are off the hook. Pederson Strategic is now regarded as just another victim of the Saudi Oil scam."

"So the United States Justice Department agent knew facts when he saw them."

"So it seems."

"But they haven't found Feisal?"

"Nope."

Harold paused, his frown heavy, and then he lifted his brows and shrugged. "Then let's get to work," he said, and Jerry escaped.

Next morning, when *Storm Swept* docked in Singapore, there were red police vans parked all along the wharf. Skye and Jerry stood at the rain of the promenade deck, watching the action.

"Trouble?" said Jerry.

Skye shook his head. "Important visitors."

A stream of limousines arrived, and stopped between the police vans and the ship. Jerry said, "Visitors with *bodyguards*?"

"Yep," Skye agreed. "If you can call the police presence that."

The visitors were three middle-aged, prosperous-looking Chinese men in expensive business suits, who progressed up the gangway trailing a retinue of secretaries, accountants, and lawyers. Harold welcomed them at the top, and introduced Skye as his personal accountant. Hands were shaken, names pronounced, and then they all went inside.

The promenade restaurant had been closed off for the conference, and the tables arranged to suit. Carafes of water were set out, with pens and pads, and copies of the proposal that had been beaten out online. Lawyers from the local firm that worked for Pederson were already there, waiting and ready. The scene was so like the boardroom of some major Singaporean company that it was hard for Skye to believe they were afloat.

Lester, showing remarkable efficiency for someone so new to the job of Chief Steward, even had name tags by each place. Humming with satisfaction, the three visitors settled down. Their retinue took up their pads, pens, and tablets, and the business began.

The conference lasted several hours. Trays of tea, coffee, and finger food were taken in by stewards, but the discussion never faltered. Catalogues and other promotional literature were passed around. But at last Lester and the bar manager ushered in trays of celebratory champagne.

It was perfect timing, as the final papers had just been signed. Hands were shaken all around, warm smiles exchanged, and then the visitors and their retinue departed.

As Skye watched from the open deck at the top of the gangway, the limousines drew up along the wharf, and were loaded with their important passengers. They drove away one after another, followed by the red police vans.

Epilogue

The promenade deck was open again. When Jerry joined the girls, they were sitting together on one of the plush settees, drinking wine and nibbling at olives. The bar steward arrived, and he gratefully took a cool glass. It had been hot and humid outside, just as it always was in Singapore.

He said, "So what did you do all day?"

"We took Mr. Brooke to the hospital," said Kate.

"What? Why?"

"Helen and Maggie came too, and that awful Maria."

"But why? Did he fall ill?"

"No, no, nothing like that. Helen arranged it, as his doctor in Mexico told her he has liver cancer, but she wants it to be confirmed. To tell the truth, I don't think she believes it. They are keeping him in for tests, and he'll be back in a day or two." Kate giggled, and added, "Maria is there in the hospital, too. She refused to leave him, and just shouted at the staff in Spanish no matter what they said, so they eventually gave in."

"And after that we went to the old Chinese quarter," said Maggie.

"Did you like it?" Jerry remembered Change Alley in the old days, and the excitement of colonial Singapore. The changes since then had been too drastic, in his opinion.

"Exotic," said Maggie. "There was a very inspirational temple."

"But we got lost," said Kate. "We were rescued by a tourist bus.

Everyone on board was American, and they were returning to their cruise ship, so we begged a ride."

"They were terribly nice," said Maggie. "They told us about their grandchildren back home, and offered candy all around. And once we spied *Storm Swept*, it wasn't too long a walk to get on board."

"But very hot," said Kate. "And humid. Have you been here before?" she asked Jerry.

"Yes," he said.

"So what did you do today?"

"Today? I went up the river." To his disgust, the crowded river with its godowns and sampans had metamorphosed into a quiet reservoir, rimmed by tall buildings. There was a similar bridge, but it wasn't the same.

But the man he had gone to see still remembered him, and was sitting behind the same desk, with the same ledgers on his shelves. Singapore had been a frequent stopover during Jerry's time in the army and afterwards, too. It was a good place to invest money, and the man he had gone to see — now a very old man — had served him well. He had a nice little nest-egg here in Singapore, if ever the world went crazy.

"But where is Del?" demanded Kate. "We wanted him to come with us to the hospital, but we couldn't find him anywhere."

As if he had heard his name, Del arrived. To everyone's bemusement, he was wearing black dress trousers and a shirt that was pinstriped in black and white. With a tie, as Maggie noted with disgust. He didn't even have his hat with a feather. His shoes were polished, and his hair was tamed. Instead of looking like a flamboyant designer, he looked like an up-and-coming young businessman. Not nearly as interesting, and almost unrecognizable.

"Where were you?" Maggie exclaimed. "We got *lost.*"

"Working," he said, and smiled smugly.

"You look very pleased with yourself," observed Kate.

"I did some very good business for my studio today."

"With Harold? Mr. Pederson?"

"With the new owners, during the conference," he said, still smiling. "I made an excellent presentation of our studio work, and they loved the wrought iron in the conference room. Now, I am to design for the whole of their fleet, and perhaps more after that. I have an excellent contract, all signed, all legal. Good for me, and good for our studio, and good for Manila, too. Tomorrow, when I fly back home, there will be many, many congratulations. A big, big celebration."

"New *owners*?" Kate exclaimed, disregarding the rest.

"Didn't you know?" He looked around, obviously wondering if he had been indiscreet. "Mr. Pederson sold his ships to the men who came today."

Dead silence. They all stared, while his smile became more and more uncertain. Then Harold came in with Helen on his arm, followed by Skye.

Kate said tremulously, "You've sold your ships?"

Harold blinked, startled. "Just the five discovery ships."

Skye said, "They are perfect for Singapore, and the local cruise company had the sense to recognize that."

"Then that's wonderful," said Maggie, and both girls propelled themselves out of the settee to hug and kiss both Harold and Helen, and then Del, too, as he also deserved congratulations. Then they stood back, holding hands with fingers linked the way they always did, still laughing.

Helen was smiling, her eyes misty as she studied them. Then she whispered in Harold's ear, and his own eyes glistened as he nodded. "Our beautiful girls," she repeated, still almost in a whisper. When Jerry looked at Skye, he found an eyebrow tilted at him. They were both, he thought, remembering that Harold had taken down the portrait of Jewel.

"So, what next?" said Kate gaily.

"A celebration," said Harold. "*Odyssey* is at long last coming out of her refit, so we are flying to Auckland to take her back to sea. And there is business to be done there, as I am also now a major shareholder with Bacchante wines."

"Wow," said one girl.

"Terrific," said the other. But both looked rather baffled by the rapid turn of events.

More was to come. Helen's phone rang. She listened, and then said in a strangely hollow voice, "That is wonderful news. We will collect him in the morning."

The call finished, she took a deep breath. "That was the hospital," she said. "Pierce is fine. No cancer. A false alarm, they said."

Then Helen, who never swore, took another deep breath, and exclaimed, "What the *hell* do we do with him now?"

The End

Also by Joan Druett

Daughters of the Storm
Abigail (A Love of Adventure)
A Promise of Gold
Finale
The Money Ship

WIKI COFFIN MYSTERIES
A Watery Grave
Shark Island
Run Afoul
Deadly Shoals
The Beckoning Ice

NON FICTION
The Discovery of Tahiti
The Notorious Captain Hayes
Eleanor's Odyssey
Lady Castaways
The Elephant Voyage
Tupaia, Captain Cook's Polynesian Navigator
Island of the Lost
In the Wake of Madness
She Captains
Rough Medicine
Hen Frigates
The Sailing Circle
She Was a Sister Sailor
Petticoat Whalers
Fulbright in New Zealand
Exotic Intruders

Rick Spilman is the founder and manager of Old Salt Press, an independent publishing company that provides the umbrella for a number of my books. As well as keeping up a hugely popular blog, "Old Salt Blog", Rick has published three very successful nautical books — *Hell Around the Horn*, *The Shantyman*, and *Evening Gray, Morning Red*, plus a novella that I have read at least ten times, *Bloody Rain*. *The Shantyman* won a Kirkus Reviews Indie Book of the Year award, and deservedly so. All four are absolutely firstclass reading.

Alaric Bond, an English Old Salt Press author, is the producer of the hugely popular Fighting Sail series, the latest page-turner being *Seeds of War*. He tells me that he is working on the fifteenth book in the series, which makes me very happy. He has also produced three stand-alone books, *The Guinea Boat*, *Turn a Blind Eye*, and *Hellfire Corner*.

Another very successful English Old Salt Press author (and

blogger) is Antoine Vanner. His Dawlish books — all with 'Britannia' in the title — are compelling yarns about the Royal Navy in the early steamboat years, which feature a complex hero as well as high adventure. When I read *Britannia's Wolf*, I was so impressed with his expertise that I wrote a rave review, calling him 'The Tom Clancy of Maritime Fiction.'

I first came across Linda Collison when I read *Star-Crossed*, and was so intrigued that I got in touch with her. Linda has also published a number of other works independently, including biting satires under the 'Knife and Gun Club' banner, and *Redfeather*, which was a finalist in Foreword's Book of the Year Award. *Water Ghosts*, a haunting tale that was a number one Amazon bestseller in the Young Adult category, is with Old Salt Press, and I look forward to more.

A Canadian author who has joined us relatively recently is Seymour Hamilton, the creator of The Astreya Trilogy. I thoroughly enjoyed *Angel's Share*, which was beautifully illustrated by Shirley MacKenzie. His work, though maritime, is reminiscent of Tolkein's carefully wrought fantasy worlds. I look forward to his further contributions to the Old Salt Press list.

The list also features V. E. Ulett, the nom-de-plume of a very successful Californian writer who normally specializes in steampunk adventures. Her three maritime novels, all proudly presented under the Old Salt Press colophon, are *Captain Blackwell's Prize*, *Blackwell's Paradise*, and *Blackwell's Homecoming*.

Joan Druett

Joan Druett became a maritime historian by accident. In 1984, while exploring the tropical island of Rarotonga, she slipped into the hole left by the roots of a large uprooted tree, and at the bottom discovered the grave of an American whaling wife, who had died in January 1850 at the age of twenty-four. It was a life-changing experience, leading to much travel and much research. Because of this, Joan became a noted expert in the history of women at sea.

Storm Swept is her eleventh novel, and is the sequel to *Daughters of the Storm*. Previous stand-alone novels *Abigail* (republished as *A Love of Adventure*), *A Promise of Gold*, *Finale* and *The Money Ship* were all very warmly reviewed. And then there was the very popular Wiki Coffin mystery series, featuring a Polynesian sleuth on board the United States Exploring Expedition. Wiki has been featured multiple times in *The Alfred Hitchcock Mystery Magazine*.

Joan has also published many award-winning nonfiction books, including the bestselling *Island of the Lost*, which is now a classic in the castaway genre, and a popular true crime story, *In the Wake of Madness*.

Daughters of the Storm

If you enjoyed *Storm Swept*, look for the prequel.

When Helen Pederson enters the room at her estranged husband's California estate, she expects to learn what hostess duties he needs her to perform this time. Instead, she is confronted by six individuals who together stir up a two-decades-old nightmare. Two she knows well. Her husband, Harold Pederson, runs the wealthy family empire that his grandfather founded. Once he makes a decision, it's impossible to change his mind. The second is their daughter, Jewel, who suffers from a congenital mental illness that manifests itself in angry tantrums that have become more violent as she ages…

Twenty years ago, in the midst of a hurricane, three babies were born: Jewel, Kate, and Maggie. Three little girls. Three identical cribs. Amid the chaos, no labels identified who was who or which baby belonged to which mother. Now, Harold wants to know which is truly his daughter. He has a plan to learn the truth – sail to the Pacific island where the hurricane hit – and he has the money to insure that no one refuses to accompany him on the cruise.

Druett steps away from her traditional historical fiction to craft a modern-day mystery… A shady sailing boat, a kidnapping, unexpected deaths, odd financial manipulations, a peculiar assistant, Jewel's tantrums, and a brewing hurricane add further spice to the suspense. Stirring up the past is never a good idea and doing so often results in unintended consequences as *Daughters of the Storm* clearly demonstrates in a fashion similar to Agatha Christie's *The Mousetrap*. Readers who enjoy this first offering in the Bacchante series will eagerly await the next book, *Storm Swept*.

  —Cindy Vallar, *Pirates and Privateers*

www.ingramcontent.com/pod-product-compliance
Lightning Source LLC
Chambersburg PA
CBHW031938110726
47902CB00001B/214